THE
WANDERERS

Center Point
Large Print

Also by Tim Pears and available from
Center Point Large Print:

The Horseman

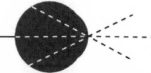

**This Large Print Book carries the
Seal of Approval of N.A.V.H.**

THE WEST COUNTY TRILOGY

THE
WANDERERS

TIM PEARS

CENTER POINT LARGE PRINT
THORNDIKE, MAINE

The text of this Large Print edition is unabridged.
In other aspects, this book may vary
from the original edition.
Printed in the United States of America
on permanent paper.
Set in 16-point Times New Roman type.

ISBN: 978-1-68324-821-7

Library of Congress Cataloging-in-Publication Data

Names: Pears, Tim, 1956- author.
Title: The wanderers / Tim Pears.
Description: Center Point Large Print edition. | Thorndike, Maine :
    Center Point Large Print, 2018.
Identifiers: LCCN 2018010559 | ISBN 9781683248217
    (hardcover : alk. paper)
Subjects: LCSH: Large type books.
Classification: LCC PR6066.E1675 W36 2018 | DDC 823/.914—dc23
LC record available at https://lccn.loc.gov/2018010559

For Alexandra, and Victoria

The Lord said, 'When you till the ground, it shall no longer yield to you its strength; you shall be a fugitive and a wanderer on the earth.' Cain said to the Lord, 'My punishment is greater than I can bear. Behold, thou hast driven me this day away from the ground; and from thy face I shall be hidden; and I shall be a fugitive and a wanderer on the earth, and whoever finds me will slay me.'

Genesis, 4: 12–14

PRINCIPAL CHARACTERS

Leopold (Leo) Sercombe

Arthur, Lord Prideaux, owner of the estate
Charlotte (Lottie) Prideaux, Arthur's only
    child
Lady Prideaux, Arthur's grandmother

Duncan, Lord Grenvil, Arthur Prideaux's friend
Maud, Lady Grenvil, Duncan's wife
Alice Grenvil, Duncan and Maud's daughter

Adam Score, Lord Prideaux's valet
Gladys Sercombe, cousin of Leo, Lottie's maid
    at the big house
Herb Shattock, Lord Prideaux's Head Groom
Sidney Sercombe, Leo's brother, under keeper
    on the estate
Ingrid Goettner, Lottie's German governess
Alf Satterley, gardener at the big house
Patrick Jago, veterinary surgeon
William Carew, Lord Prideaux's estate manager

Gentle George Orchard, gypsy boxer, and his
    wife **Rhoda**
Samson and Kinity Orchard, George's parents

Gully Orchard, gypsy horseman, Samson's
   brother
Edwin and Belcher Orchard, George's brothers
Henery Orchard, Edwin's son
Levi Hicks, gypsy horse dealer

Arnold and Ernest Mann, mine owners

Cyrus Pepperell, mean farmer, and his wife
   Juliana
Vance Brewer, shepherd
Wilf Cann, stockboy

Rufus, hermit tramp

Florence Wombwell, duck breeder on the estate

THE
WANDERERS

PART ONE
FLOWERS

Lottie, June 1912

The girl walked down the wide staircase, through the house all the way to the cellars. She marched along the dank gloomy corridor then climbed up the steps into the bright glare of the glasshouse. The sun was high in the sky. Lottie walked out into the kitchen garden.

What is anger?

It is a fire, smouldering. Memories are pinches of gunpowder thrown into the flames, they ignite and explode. A person's mind, bellows breathing, seething in and out.

The girl strode across the terraced lawns and on through the jungle. She hoisted her long skirt and clambered over the fence and marched across the field. Her passage disturbed bullocks there. It made the beasts frisky. Perhaps it was the dark red of Lottie's skirt. Or perhaps they detected her preference for horses, and affected the spry skittishness of colts. She fancied that they cantered here and there for her approval, clumsily kicking their heels, but they were awkward lumpen creatures, and their ambulation held no beauty. Clouds billowed in the sky and blocked the sun.

Or . . .

Anger is ice, at the centre of a snowbound waste. The frozen core of a heart and nothing will melt it, ever.

Lottie walked through the wood until she came to an area of coppiced hazel. There she slowed and scanned the ground. Soon she found what she was looking for: the wild flowers that resembled nettles at a lazy glance but did not sting. Yellow archangel. A dead-nettle with primrose-yellow flowers, it was easy to pass it by unremarked. You had to look closer to appreciate that each flower was shaped like an angel, its hood curved like a pair of wings.

Lottie picked half a dozen. She possessed little knowledge of flora, but had inherited a notebook in which her mother had pressed certain flowers, and added her drawings and observations, and these wild flowers the girl had committed to memory. The year inscribed in the front of the book was 1894. Lottie calculated that her mother had been two years older at that date than she herself was now. It stated in the notes that archangel was edible. 'Mixes nicely on the tongue with tomatoes and cheese,' according to the young Beatrice Pollard. Lottie sniffed the plant. Both flowers and leaves gave off an acrid smell. She walked on out of the wood.

Anger is pain. It is like some miserable affliction, a headache or gripe of the stomach, except a cure for it is something to be resisted. Rather, the pain should be nurtured.

'Thou didst march through the land in indignation. Thou didst trample down the nations in wrath.'

The girl strode on beside the stream. On a grassy slope rising from the opposite bank she saw a purple rash in the green grass. A patch of bugle. Another dead-nettle, its flowers a paler mauve than the leaves and stems. In the gloomy afternoon she stood and watched a bumblebee working the patch, floating from flower to flower, buzzing in close like some hovering inspector. In search of nectar. But then drops of rain appeared on the water. If you watched closely each drop seemed not to fall from above but to rise up from beneath the surface. Lottie stepped over the stream and plucked six stems, and walked on.

In the meadow, she found to her surprise some last surviving fritillaries. Their purple chequered bells or heads hung on the tall slender drooping stems, like lanterns. She picked a few. She knew they would not last long once snapped from their roots or pulled from the soil, but they did not need to.

At the side of the lane into the village she spotted meadow cranesbill. Most of the flowers on each plant were still enclosed but some had opened, the five petals forming a shape like a saucer or plate. They were violet-blue, and marked with pale veins radiating from the centre, like paths, to draw the bees in.

In the yard Lottie did not seek a jar but laid the flowers directly upon the earth and kneeled down before the stone.

The vicar came out of the door to the church and stood in the porch looking out at the rain mizzling in the graveyard. He did not see the girl at first. He had been given an umbrella by his brother, but on the rare occasions he remembered to take it with him the rain inevitably held off. Usually he did not think of it, and the rain caught him out.

Then he saw the girl, kneeling at her mother's grave. He stepped out of the porch and walked over.

'Miss Charlotte,' he said.

The girl looked up. The Reverend Mr Doddridge loomed over her. He was an unnaturally tall man, lean and bony but broad shouldered. He had white hair and whiskers, and craggy features. He issued grim warnings from the pulpit, scolding his congregation, and when the readings were of Old Testament prophets Lottie pictured them as being much like him. She suspected that he had spent years wrestling with temptation in some desert place before coming to this hidden parish in the West Country. The rain did not appear to bother him.

'I was speaking to my mama,' Lottie said.

The vicar pondered the girl's statement. 'I am sure she hears you,' he said.

Lottie nodded. 'I told her that I do not believe she would have allowed it to happen.'

The vicar said he did not doubt it. He said that the rain was falling more heavily, Miss Charlotte was welcome to come to the vicarage. Mrs Dagworthy would give her hot chocolate and cake. A boy could be sent to the Manor for her father's gig to fetch her. Lottie said that she was grateful but would prefer to stay a moment longer here alone, then make her own way home.

'Mama may be able to hear me, Mr Doddridge,' she said. 'But can she help me?'

The vicar opened his arms, hands outstretched with palms up, as if to catch the rain. He looked at a loss. 'Only the Lord can help us,' he said. 'If we trust in Him.'

The girl thanked the priest. He nodded and walked away through the graveyard.

Lottie did not stay much longer. She put her hands to the ground and pushed herself up. She turned and walked away, as if to collect her thoughts from somewhere she had dropped them. Then she came back. She looked down at the flowers. Already they were wet and wilting, their pale colours fading. She should not stay.

'You know I have a governess, Mama,' she said. 'Ingrid. I have told you of her before. Oh, she is not so bad. I might have exaggerated her defects. But do you know what she told me? Something that she had read. "If we lose those we love, where shall we seek them? Where shall we find them? In heaven, or on earth?" '

Lottie sighed, and nodded to herself. Then she turned and walked out of the yard, through the lychgate and into the lane, and back towards her father's estate.

PART TWO
A SLAVE

1

Leo, June 1912–May 1913

The boy stumbled in the night over dark earth. The land was silver. His steps were heavy. At first light in the waters of a stream he cleaned the charred red mud off his boots, and limped on in a kind of crouch that seemed best to allay the pain that racked many parts of his body. He saw where the sun rose and headed in the opposite direction, hunched over like someone with secrets from the light. He opened gates and closed them quietly behind him. He skulked close to hedgerows though on occasion he crossed pasture from one corner to its opposite. A herd of Ruby Reds chewed the cud and watched him. Where beasts were, so were men, and he wished to pass unseen. In the undergrowth of a copse he made himself a den in which he curled up and slept.

When night fell Leo Sercombe rose and trudged toward the smudge of light left on the western horizon. He struggled up onto and across the moor, every step another into the unknown as he went beyond the limits of the world he knew. Exmoor was less peopled than the farmland and he was glad to reach it, but there was less cover. When he was thirsty he lay beside the moorland streams and lapped the cool water like a dog and filled his belly.

In the evening of the third day he picked bil-berries and gorged himself on them, his fingers stained purple and doubtless his lips likewise, still swollen from the beating he'd taken.

In the night he saw flickering phosphorescent lights. They seemed to beckon or entice him. He knew they were not real but could not help himself and began to follow them. These were will-o'-the-wisps, that lead men into swamps. He turned from the sight and hurried away.

Some time during the night of the fourth day the boy came down off the moor. In the village of Hawkridge nothing stirred as he passed through it but dogs watched him. He plodded through a stand of dead trees, bark-stripped, branches snapped, trunks like bleached white bones.

In a field a flock of pale grey sheep parted for him, bleating. At dawn he crawled into a hedge and slept.

Passing by elder trees, Leo scoured the lanterns of berries and stuffed them into his mouth. He could scarce eat enough to quell his hunger, yet in due course his belly griped and doubled him over. Soon enough he had to squat repeatedly, then wipe his arse with leaves. He needed substance, fodder, but there was none.

In a conifer plantation he came across ant-hills. These he excavated with his hands, fingers pressed together to form two trowels, and ate the eggs. Ants bit him relentlessly. He ate them too, crunching and swallowing, trusting that survivors of his teeth would drown before they bit his guts. The furious insects scurried up his trousers, along sleeves, under his shirt. When the boy lumbered away his bruised skin throbbed in a hundred places. A vagabond upon the face of the earth. In showers of rain he trudged through the darkness, unsure of his direction.

In the day he dreamed of bread and heard others pleading for it, and woke to hear buzzards crying above him, young ones abandoned by their parents to fend for themselves. *'As a bird that strays from her nest so is a man that strays from his home.'* On occasion on his voyage he spotted human figures and averted his eyes, so that for him they did not exist. Once he heard someone yell, 'Hey! Boy!' He altered his course and stumped along.

In a wood early one morning Leo came across a circle of feathers of some nameless bird. What had killed it? A sparrowhawk? His brother Sid would know. He picked up a single feather. The quill was made of material akin to a human fingernail. He stroked and stretched the delicate blade. It was not possible to comprehend or even to glimpse inside the mind of He who had created such a feather, for the wing of a bird that had flown in the sky. Then been destroyed by another.

The boy chewed the stems of dandelion and grass but they gave him little sustenance. He grew more famished. When before dawn he woke and the darkness became less dense he could not understand what was happening. What was light for? What was its purpose? He rose and drifted into the morning. He picked a blackberry and paused to study it. The berry was composed of a cluster of sacs. Inside each one was the seed for a new plant, swimming in a purple seminal fluid. The berry held unfathomable mysteries. Unable to reach them, in the end he ate it.

How the boy knew that the trees watched him and wished to speak with him he was not sure, it just became self-evident. He felt a kinship to a smooth-trunked young beech and stood before it, stroking it as he would the shoulder of a horse. He told the tree it was a fine specimen, and he would like to linger, to climb in its branches, but he had to press on for his destination was a town called Penzance.

One morning the dew revealed spiders' webs strung between branches, tall grasses, across hedgerows. They were like nets cast by fishermen, not of water but of air. Some were such perfect wheels of silk they might have been woven by the designer of the world Himself. Most were not. They had holes, gaps, panels of differing lengths or shapes. Bodge-jobs. Like people, some spiders were more competent than others. As he tramped, the boy pondered this truth with startled wonder.

On the night of the seventh or eighth day he was traipsing through a wood when a sound stopped his heart. He stood stock-still. Someone not far away from him was suddenly wailing. A grief-stricken howl. In the darkness he imagined what beast it might be and stood trembling. Then he realised. A dog fox was calling to his mate, for she answered with her own otherworldly shriek.

Leo's hunger abated intermittently and he forgot it. Then it returned. At dawn he entered a field of cows, their udders heavy. Even if a cow would allow him to milk her, he had no receptacle. But he had to try. He crept under their bellies, between their hooves. Any one of them might kick him, as such a beast had done to the stockman Isaac Wooland. Through malice or fright or unknowingly. He came up beneath the swaying udders of a red cow and took one of her teats in his mouth, and began to suck. She did not kick or buck him off, but walked slowly away. Leo hung on, waddling on his haunches. The cow stopped and he resumed, but he could not make milk come. There was merely a tantalising taste of it on his tongue. He grasped the teat and squeezed and pulled at it, and some drops of milk fell upon the grass. He put his mouth open below the teat and the cow walked on. He held on for a few steps but she continued and he let go and lay head down on the grass, until the herd had ambled around him and away. Then he clambered to his feet and limped on. The morning air was straggled with mist, as if odourless fires had been lit in the night. The sun rose and poured orange through the smoky light.

The landscape was open and rolling, with larger fields than he was used to, and he kept close to the thick long hedges of blackthorn and holly.

He slept in the day and walked at night. His head throbbed. He trudged a short distance then found himself sitting down, and waited until the coloured spots dancing on the inside of his eyelids had ceased, then staggered to his feet and stumbled on a little further. The boy licked dew from wet grass. He knew not where he was, only that he was a vagrant, destitute.

In the afternoon he sat under the hedge of a cornfield ripe for harvesting and watched swallows skim the surface. Gliding and dipping in their flight. They did not touch the corn nor did they rise higher than a few feet above but soared through this narrow layer of air. A realm shared with the insects they hunted. Leo did not know what day it was. He decided it was Sunday. He watched the swallows for as long as he would have been in church, this his open air Evensong.

The boy rose and walked on but took only a few paces. He felt his head fill with a light wind. The hedge and the cornfield attempted to take to the air as birds did and wheeled about him, and the earth embraced him with a thumping hug.

• • •

'Look, he's took a hammerin.'

'He's a scrap of a lad.'

'Aye, leave him.'

'I'll not leave him,' said a quiet voice.

Waking, Leo kept his eyes closed. There were three of them, at least.

'There's nothin to him.'

'No, he's worth nothin.'

'No,' said the woman. 'He's not worth it. Leave him, George.' She walked away.

'He's a scrap of a lad,' said the quiet man. 'I'll not leave him.'

Leo waited for them to go away and let him be.

'He's near dead as dammit,' said the older man. He walked away, following after the woman. 'Leave him, George,' he called back.

'I'll not.'

The boy felt huge hands sidle beneath him and lift his bony form. He was carried, and fell asleep again in this giant's arms. When he woke he was being put in some cart or waggon. He rolled into deep sleep. Then he woke and was given warm milk by a woman, and boiled carrot mushed like the sop for a baby. He was aware of many eyes watching him.

On the days following Leo was fed by children. They plaited his hair as he lay there, and scrawled tattoos upon his skin. Little by little his strength returned.

29

2

The gypsies travelled with five waggons they called vardos, and two trolley carts. Leo recuperated in the vardo of George and his wife Rhoda and their many children. He looked out of the open front of the waggon. He had seen nothing like them. They were not travelling homes but rather cupboards on wheels, containing the gypsies' possessions, and items for sale. Some had cages filled with songbirds hanging off them. The gypsies walked beside the vardos. Dogs accompanied them, mongrels and curs of all kinds but each one spry, with its own ideas, a pack of opinionated hounds.

The men wore long waistcoats and trousers high up the back, wide at the waist, narrowing to the ankle. The older men's were lined with swan's down. One man wore Luton boots of black and brown leather but all the others had hobnailed boots. They wore white shirts and red calico scarves, and hats of different kinds. The women wore brightly coloured clothes and wide, flat-brimmed hats like plates. Each woman had her own smell, a pungent mixture of sweat and woodsmoke and some musky perfume made from personal ingredients. Children seemed to call all the women Ma, though perhaps there was something defective about Leo's hearing. He thought also that all called the man with black and brown boots Grandpa. One other older man they called Uncle.

Keziah, the eldest daughter of George and Rhoda, brought Leo food and sat beside him. As the waggon rolled along she told him who was who in their travelling band of the Orchard family. 'That vardo belongs to our father's father Samson Orchard and our father's mother Kinity. The one there's our father's uncle Gully, and his wife Caraline.'

The girl told Leo of her family as if reciting less from memory than liturgy, an incantation of her lineage. 'The fourth vardo belongs to our father's brother Edwin and his wife and children. The last one there belongs to our father's other brother, our uncle Belcher and his brood.'

Keziah told Leo that he had the dark eyes of a gadjo. It was a pity that his hair was brown and not black. Perhaps he was half-gentile, half-gadjo. His skin was too pale but a season or two on the road with them would improve it.

They meandered south for some days, along lanes bordered by full-leaved, thick high hedges, like winding tunnels. At gateways they would pause and stare as if surprised to see corn growing or

31

beasts grazing in the hidden fields. The lanes undulated up and down and around the irregular landscape. The gypsies appeared to be in no hurry and journeyed at an easy pace. At night they did not sleep in their vardos but in temporarily erected bivouacs.

As soon as he was able, Leo rose from his bed and walked beside the waggons as the gypsies did. Each vardo was pulled by a single draught or dray horse, smaller than a Shire. There were many ponies too. At times the children rode these, bare-backed, but when they came to a hill the ponies were hooked up to the sides of the vardos as trace horses and helped pull them. On such inclines George walked behind his vardo, carrying chocks of wood. If the horses faltered, he dropped these chocks beneath the wheels to prevent them rolling backwards. Then he threw his own substantial weight behind the waggon. As it moved forward, Leo picked up the wood and followed after.

None spoke to the boy, nor much to each other. The weather grew warmer. Flies bothered the horses. They passed a field of rich grass in which a herd of cows had sat down, every one, and were chewing the cud in the morning sunshine. The beasts looked as if some bovine branch of the Agricultural Labourers' Union had persuaded them to go on strike. The gypsies did no work. They stopped at nightfall and heated up a vegetable stew that had some faint trace of meat in its gravy, ate and slept, then without great enthusiasm moved on in the morning. Leo was bemused. It seemed to the boy an inexplicable life. They passed through tiny villages whose scruffy inhabitants stood and watched them pass like some suspicious summer mirage. The pace slowed and Leo thought that the draught horses might simply come to a halt, and the people too, in immobile stupor, only the dogs still sniffing around the grass verges and hedgerows.

One morning he heard a cuckoo, calling from somewhere in the distance. It called again. It felt like the distance not only of space but also time, as if the bird were calling from the past. He thought of Lottie and imagined her riding her elegant pony, the one she had tried to give to him. He wondered what his mother was doing. He wondered when he would see his home again. The estate was his home no longer. He knew this but could not accept it.

One afternoon Samson Orchard brought them to a halt on a wide verge beside a road.

'Hear me, you all,' he said. 'We'll stop here and we'll stay us a while.'

They unharnessed the horses and drove stakes into the ground, to which the beasts were tethered. Uncle Gully tended to the horses but all the other men and older boys disappeared with their dogs. The women gathered wood and lit fires and put up semi-permanent tents. These were benders, made from bent hazel or chestnut poles covered with canvas painted with the smelly tar used on roads, or sometimes with old coats. With the horses unharnessed, wooden steps were placed between the shafts of each vardo, leading up to the door or open front. A woman Leo had not noticed until now climbed down out of Belcher's waggon, in which she must have lain on the journey while others walked, and made her way into one of the benders, holding her greatly swollen belly before her.

Leo asked George's wife Rhoda what he should do. 'Wood and water,' she said. 'Water and wood. See in the trees up yonder's plenty a scrap. That stream there's good for washin. And in the wood's a spring for drinkin water. We've stopped here before, see.'

Uncle Gully meanwhile led the draught horses one by one to the stream and let them drink, and then the ponies. Some were thirsty, and whinnied to let the old man know this, but he made them wait their turn. Gully wore a three-piece suit that looked to have been tailored for his frame, but many years ago. It was faded at the knees and elbows, frayed at the hems, yet it conferred upon him a certain elegance nonetheless. His felt fedora was less impressive, for the brim had long since lost whatever firmness it might once have had and fell down around his head, covering his eyes. It made him look furtive. Perhaps he was. He smelled of horses and of something else, some aromatic oil that Leo recognised, but from where he did not know. Then it came to him that he had detected it on another man, the old horseman Moses Pincombe.

Gully did not speak but whistled to the horses. Between carrying buckets of water for the women, the boy watched him and listened. With his whistling he ordered one horse to be patient, he told another it would be his turn next, he informed a third he would take her to the water soon. All this by whistling. Leo had not known there could be such variety in the sound. He stood near to Gully. Up close to the animals, he spoke to them by clicking his teeth. Perhaps he was a mute.

The first of the men came back carrying pheasants. These they passed to the women, with the pride of hunters. One of the lads, Henery, son of Edwin, was surrounded by dogs and they too strutted, high off their paws, shoulders up, though the women grumbled that pheasants would need to boil or to hang overnight and would feed no hungry children's bellies now.

The other men and lads returned with rabbits. Some of the boys carried sparrows, netted or shot with catapults. These they and their sisters plucked and skewered and roasted over the fires.

There was no sign of George. Grandpa Samson Orchard leaned against a wheel of his vardo, lit a pipe and called the boy over.

'Leo, is it?' he said. 'You're travellin with us now, boy, and a band of vagabonds is what we are. We'll not stay long in no place. Myself and me Kinity, we wouldn't even stop for you. Our boy George, though, is a soft-hearted man who's saved your life. But you'll pay us back now, won't you, Leo?'

The boy nodded. Samson Orchard was a stoutly built, ruddy and glowering man. He had black hair, though his walrus moustache was nearly white, and black hooded eyes. 'Let me tell ye, Leo, people will treat ye bad while you're with us. You being a gentile, t'will make no difference to them. You're one of us now as far as they're concerned.' He sucked on his pipe then removed it and it was as if he had a stove inside him that he'd lit with his pipe for he seemed suddenly to glow with heat. 'I've been done for drunk and riotous,' he said. 'I've been done for disorderly conduct. For breach a the peace in four counties. For assault. I've never laid hands on no one who didn't ask for it, do ye hear me, Leo? Look at this.'

Samson Orchard gripped the stem of his pipe between his teeth and undid his jacket. Instead of buttons it had sovereigns, holes drilled into them to take the thread. He opened his shirt. 'Will ye

36

look at that?' he said. Leo came closer and saw that the letter D had been branded on the old man's left breast. 'I'll bet ye thought there's no man alive carried a brand like that, Leo,' Samson said.

The boy had never heard of such a thing on any man, alive or dead.

'Must be nigh on thirty-five year ago,' Samson said. He refilled his pipe.

The women skinned the rabbits and butchered them with long knives and threw them in big pots over their fires, and cut vegetables they'd pilfered from fields along the way. They scraped a little salt from the large blocks each possessed, and threw in handfuls of barley. The warm day waned. The sparrows the boys had caught were readying. Children tore the roasted carcasses apart and ate the flesh off the bone. The smell of roasting meat made Leo salivate, but no one, not even Keziah, invited him to join them and he did not ask. Pheasants hung at the side of Samson's vardo. Blood dripped from their beaks onto the dry grass.

'The Battle of Majuba Hill,' Samson said. 'We occupied the hill, see, Leo, and for what reason? There was none. And who were we? Most of us was raw. Even the few old soldiers had seen little action since the Crimean palaver. When the Boers came forward we still could have held the hill, but they wouldn't engage, see, Leo, they wouldn't come hand-to-hand with us. No, boy, they kept well back, didn't they, and picked us off one by one. They was only Dutch farm boys but, by God, Leo, they was good shots.'

The old man yelled something at one of his sons a good distance off. Some words Leo did not recognise. The aromas of the food cooking made his stomach grumble, and it occurred to him that he had fully recovered from the beating his father had given him.

'I don't know who ran first . . . it wasn't me, honest to God, Leo, but then we all did. We fled. It was a rout. We fled for our lives, Leo. Afterwards a few of us was shot by firin squad, they'd to make an example, but they couldn't shoot all a what was left of our company. And we was all out of the Transvaal by the end a the month and on our way back home, Leo, the lot of us. Why they branded me a deserter, I believe it was a joke, Leo. They thought it comical to brand the gyppo. So they did.'

Samson puffed on his pipe. Again it seemed to stoke the bellows of some fire inside his ample chest. 'We came to this country from Hindustan. Over five hundred year ago.' He paused. 'Six hundred now. The first king a the gypsies was a man by the name a Zindl. I wear the golden sovereigns on my jacket, Leo, but I'm no king a the gypsies, no matter what anyone says . . . don't believe them, boy. We've not got one now.

I'm only the shero of my tribe. We're vagabonds, that's what they call us. Priggers and pilferers.' He opened his shirt once more. 'Have a good look, Leo, you'll not see it again. I was told I'm the last man alive from the British Army to carry this brand, and I believe it.'

It was dusk when George came out of the wood, his two rough-coated dogs barking about him, carrying what looked like a bundle of grey fur. In a moment all stopped what they were doing and looked to the big man coming into the clearing. George's wife Rhoda stood up beside her fire and said in a loud voice, 'There's my man, isn't he, there's my man. Truly I've married meat and bread. And don't you all worry, there'll be a piece a meat for every pot.'

They gathered around the fires in the dark. They had to wait longer than they would have if George had not caught the badger but George and Rhoda's children assured Leo that it would be worthwhile, for the rich dark meat of a badger was far superior to rabbit or pheasant, almost as good as that of a hedgehog.

When they'd finished eating, the women washed their cutlery and plates and other implements. The men gathered around Samson and Kinity's fire. They passed a bottle round. What it contained Leo had no idea. The old woman and then the old man sang songs unaccompanied. Edwin produced a fiddle. He was almost as tall as his brother George but thin as wire and nervous where George was calm. Yet on the fiddle he played lilting lullabies. Children crawled into the benders and slept when they chose. The women came over to the fire. Some smoked clay pipes with longer stems than Leo had ever seen before. Edwin upped the tempo on his fiddle while his wife Arabella beat a tambourine and a lad who was perhaps his son set a dinner plate upside down and danced upon it.

When the tune ended the lad who'd danced stepped off the plate. He bent and picked it up and backed away from the fire.

Of the three brothers, Belcher most resembled their father, Samson, thickset and swarthy. He stared at the fire, then spat into the flames. 'He's not broke the plate, Edwin,' Belcher said, 'and that's good. He can step-dance to yer fiddle, but it's only single-steppin.'

'Aye,' said Edwin.

'I could dance the double-steppin to yer fiddle, could I not? I danced the nails out a my boots to yer fiddle, brother. I licked em, didn't I? I beat em all. There was none so light on his feet as me.'

The women smoked their pipes and the men gazed into the flames.

'Now listen here, Leo,' Samson Orchard said. 'See yon brother a mine.' He nodded towards the

40

horseman, old Gully. 'He was born in the sawdust and brought up on the back of a horse. Our parents had a travellin circus, see. They trained me in vaultin and globe jugglin, and then the boxin after. Young Gully there was a trick rider. Bareback and all. There was no money. Circuses got bigger, see, people could watch all manner of amazement of an evenin. Why'd they go to a teeny family circus like ours? But what I'm tellin you, Leo, is my brother yonder could ride a horse . . . he could make a beast do things you wouldn't believe. I've seen none since as good.'

'What stopped you dancin, then?' Edwin said. He addressed his brother. 'If you was so fuckin good? If you was so fuckin better'n my son.'

'I don't know, brother,' Belcher said. 'Yer fiddle playin, was it? Did it lose its soul there? You played it out of tune, did you?'

Edwin stood up and stepped across to Belcher and raised his violin and brought it down upon his brother's head, shattering the delicate instrument. He walked away towards his tent. Belcher removed his crumpled hat and rubbed the crown of his head, grinning, his teeth bared in the firelight.

The boy grew sleepy, but he saw Gully rise stiffly from the ground and turn and walk away from the fire and disappear into the dark. Some little while later Leo heard one of the draught horses neigh. He rose and followed the sound.

His eyes adjusted to the darkness and he was able to see all that was not in shadow for there was sufficient moonlight. He followed the sound of hooves and saw Gully lead one of the big horses towards a high hedge. It was Samson's, the largest, sixteen hands high by the boy's reckoning. Gully did not stop or turn but walked on into the hedge. He disappeared. The horse did not hesitate but followed the man leading it and the hedge swallowed the great horse too. Leo stared. Gully soon re-emerged alone. He fetched another horse and led it in the moonlight through the hedge as he had the one before. He left them grazing in some farmer's field.

Leo stood waiting for the old man to request his help but he did not do so. When Gully had taken all the horses and ponies into the field he returned to the fire. Leo took his blanket and laid it on the ground beneath George and Rhoda's waggon and slept.

In the morning, with much yelling and commotion, the gypsies went to work. Now they had a base women gathered certain objects and implements about them and, with their baskets, headed off along the lane; others remained in their roadside camp making things. Old Kinity, Samson's wife, carved walking sticks. Edwin cut withy saplings and from them two of his children made clothes pegs. Girls gathered wild flowers and strung them into bouquets using bramble twine. It was as if all awoke from a dream of indolence to fanatic industry. Leo watched in amazement. All, even young children, had a job to do. One of the girls filled her basket with boxes of matches and shoelaces stored in the waggon, and set off. Gully gathered two ponies and led them away by their bridle straps.

Edwin's son Henery told Leo he must be shown the best way to collect firewood. He said that he had seen Leo twisting saplings and bending branches full of sap that made smoke when they burned and he felt pity, that's what it was. Henery was a young version of his father, a lean and jittery youth not many years older than Leo but able to grow a thin moustache. He applied some kind of pungent pomade to his black hair and plastered it down close to his skull. His dogs were never far from him. He told Leo to watch. He slid a long pole with a hook on the end off the side of his father's waggon and led the way into the nearby wood. 'You look around,' he said. 'This is you.' Henery leaned his neck forward and adopted an imbecilic expression so that he resembled a backward member of some jungle race other than man. He walked in deliberate circles, saying in a slow, deep voice, 'Wood. Wood.'

Henery resumed his normal posture. 'You're gropin in the wrong direction, see,' he said. He lifted his head and Leo did likewise. They looked up into the branches above. 'There,' Henery said. 'That'll do us.' He raised the pole and hooked a length of dead wood from where it had been caught, and tugged it loose. Leo jumped back as it fell at their feet, breaking. 'The trees store their rejects up there for us, see, ready-dried and all,' Henery said. He handed the pole to Leo and walked back to the encampment.

Leo collected wood in this manner for the campfires and left a stack beside each one. He then took buckets, emptied them of any residue, and refilled them from the spring Rhoda had told him of. He understood what he now was. A hewer of wood and drawer of water. This was how he should repay the favour of having his life saved. Otherwise none enquired where he came from, who were his kin, how he'd come by the bruises that were almost healed now. A lack of curiosity or a surfeit of discretion? The boy did not know but he was glad. He did not wish to speak of Lottie, or of his mother, for he missed them too much.

The gypsies returned to the camp in twos and threes throughout the afternoon. The man of each vardo took the money that was handed over but gave his woman some back. Gully appeared without the pair of ponies he'd left with but one other instead: a squat and muscular chestnut cob Leo reckoned fit for pulling one of the trolley carts.

In the evening they ate the pheasants, which, hung overnight, had been boiled for much of the day. A layer of yellow fat was lifted off and new-caught rabbits put in along with onion, carrot, potato, swede. In her pot Rhoda made dumplings too and when it came time to eat Leo thanked her and said he had never eaten such tasty food.

'It's not me,' she said. 'It's bein cooked outside that does it. I'd never cook inside if I'd a choice. George'll tell you, it needs to be bloody cold for me to use the stove in there.'

On the morning of the day following Leo rose early and helped Gully open up the gap in the hedge and retrieve his horses from the farmer's pasture before the sun came up. The new chestnut cob stood some way off. Gully brought the draught horses one after the other through the hedge and, attaching a rope to their halters, the boy took the ponies alternately. They left the cob till last. A little light had come, enough for him to see as they approached that the cob was injured. A triangular flap of skin had been ripped from his hindquarters. When they got too close he took fright and turned and trotted away across the field.

'They've turned on im,' Gully said quietly. They were the first words Leo had heard him utter. 'Gyres will do it to a stranger sometimes. One a them's give him a good kick.'

'One a the big horses?'

'More likely the ponies.'

'Why?' Leo asked.

'I've wondered that myself many a time,' Gully told him. 'I've not quite worked it out.' He watched the frightened animal come to a halt and stand still as before. 'Strange beasts,' he said.

Leo walked across the field. Some yards short of the cob he stopped. 'It's all right, young feller,' he said. 'Don't be afeared a me. I won't kick you and you don't have to kick me neither.' The boy did not know whether his gritty voice was capable of calming a frightened horse but he spoke to the cob anyhow for it felt natural to him to do so. 'I'm a comin over to you now, old boy, and I'm goin to come and greet you.'

The sun was rising and the sky was blue but with the last stars still visible. Gully had disappeared. Leo put his hands behind his back and walked over slowly to the horse, speaking all the while of his intentions, and of his wish for the cob to trust him and to be not afraid. The cob stood still, shivering as if cold. When he reached him, Leo leaned forward and blew softly into the pony's nostrils and stood back. The cob raised his head towards him and Leo blew into his nostrils once more. The animal was still trembling but the boy spoke to him and in time raised one hand and stroked him. 'It's all right, old feller, you're all right now, they've had their fun. You're good again, old boy.' The horse trembled less. Leo tied the rope he'd been using to the cob's halter and led him across the field and through the hedge.

Gully had rekindled his campfire. In a pan of boiling water he was sterilising needles and gut. Leo held the cob steady. Gully poured some anaesthetic solution over the wound, then threaded a needle. Leo spoke to the cob. He told him quietly what the old man was about to do and that if he felt a twinge or two of pain he should abide, for they intended only to heal him and could do so if only he let them. Then Gully lifted the loose flap of skin and began to suture it back in place.

Afterwards, Gully told Leo that it was good to have someone else with a feel for horses. 'None a this lot do,' he said. 'They're my blood, but they don't have it.'

3

On the morning of the third day in that spot Gully harnessed one of the draught horses to a trolley. Henery told Leo to help him lift a strangely configured contraption onto the trolley. They could not. It was too heavy.

'Wait up, lads,' someone called. George strode over. Most of the gypsies were shorter than the average man. George was six inches taller. He was like a being from a different race walking amongst them. Leo and Henery stood aside and let the giant lift the machine on his own, with little apparent effort. It resembled a bicycle in that it had a frame and seat and pedals. There were no wheels, but rather a stand, and the chain was attached to some other axle, on each end of which was a circular stone. Gully led the horse and the lad Henery accompanied him. Leo looked around the camp, where those who had not yet left bustled around as on each day. There was wood and water stored. Leo ran after the trolley cart.

On the outskirts of a village they came to the rectory. Henery knocked upon the door. A woman answered and the gypsy lad told her they had the finest grinding barrow in England here if she'd cleavers or cutlery or carving knives to sharpen.

'You'll know us from last year, missus, we're the best in the west.'

'It's you,' she said.

'Hedge clippers and cutters,' he told her. 'Shovels and spades, all your gardener's tools. Your cook's finest knives . . . where is she now? She'll be wantin to see us. Your husband's razors we'll edge for him, don't worry about that.'

The Rector's wife sent them round the back. Old Gully and the lad and the boy lifted the grinding barrow off the trolley cart and set it on the ground. Gully filled a bucket of water from a pump in the yard and poured some into a can attached to the machine. When the maid brought the first implements out of the house, Henery climbed onto the seat, put his boots in the stirrups, and began to work the treadle. The shaft turned. On each end was a grindstone, one fine, the other coarse. Gully held a coal shovel to the rough stone. It made a screech like that of an angry seagull. Henery pedalled a little harder. Sparks flew from the shovel blade. The maid reappeared with a tray of small tools she must have collected from around the house. Scissors, penknives, razors.

Henery pedalled at a steady rate. He began to sweat. Gully held each implement with his right hand and pressed it to the stone with his left. Water dribbled onto the fine stone. Periodically the old man felt the tip of each blade with the callused nub of the index finger of his left hand. After a while Henery climbed down and said, 'Your turn.' Leo took his place. It took a little time to find a rhythm, and the speed Gully wanted. 'Faster,' he said. 'Slower.' A gardener wheeled a barrow full of tools into the yard.

In due course a woman came out with a tray of knives. She greeted Gully and told him she was glad to see them, twas about time. All her kitchen knives were blunt, she could no longer get an edge on them with her steel. Also upon the tray were three glasses of rosehip cordial and biscuits, which the gypsies and their gentile consort stopped working to consume. The cook spoke with Gully, telling him of the problems she had.

'Talk about the taste a bread,' she said. 'My old mum says German flour ain't the same as ours and never will be. No one never ate white bread in the old days.' She leaned forward and glanced behind her before continuing, more quietly, 'And you'd think old Ed was still on the throne . . . oh, yes, the Rector and the missus do crave their patisseries. Out a fashion in London, I heard, but down here we takes years to catch up, don't us? I likes to bake but does they have any idea how fiddly they patisseries is?'

The cook rambled on in this manner. Then she asked Gully about him and his tribe and where they'd been. 'Here and there,' he said. 'All over, mostly.' He resumed sharpening the knives. The cook watched while hers were done then took them back inside upon the tray, along with empty plate and glasses.

In the afternoon they called on smaller houses around the same village. As they travelled from one to another Henery spoke. 'We're hawkers of brushes and baskets, Leo. Peddlers of ladles and pots. We're sellers of matches, and laces for shoes or boots. Gully here's a horse trader. Me father's a chairmaker and mender. He'll bottom a chair for you, no problem, any kind. Take it away and bring it back like new or do it on the spot, it makes no difference to him. Me . . . I love dogs, don't I, Gully? I'm a dog clipper. Catcher or killer. I'll destroy a litter if it has to be done, but me, I'm a dog fancier, am I not, Gully? A dog thief. He'll tell you, Leo, that's what I am and no mistake.'

The old horse plodded along pulling the trolley cart. The boy came to the conclusion that amongst the gypsies some spoke and some did not. Those who did could not stop. Henery orated with a cadence akin to singing.

'We're drain cleaners and chimney sweeps. We're goat trainers and pickpockets. You wait till we get to Okehampton Fair in the spring, you'll see. Our women are midwives. Me Grandpa Samson's a ballad singer a the old school. We've been a buskerin from Barnstaple to Brixham.

Me uncle Belcher'll make you a beehive fit for a queen. We're clairvoyants and clowns, Leo. Me uncle George is a fairground boxer like his father before him, only George is twice the fighter Samson ever was—Grandpa will tell you so himself. We change our names to stay one step ahead a the law, but we're all of the Orchard tribe, Leo, don't you fret about that.

'Me aunt Rhoda's duckerin through the villages now, she's readin palms and givin out zodiac advice. The girls'll be with her learnin, but you can only learn the talk. You can't learn the gift. You've got it or you've not. Foresight. Me aunt Rhoda has it, Leo, it's uncanny—I've seen it. What she tells comes to pass, good or bad, she can't help it. She'll not tell fortunes for the family, no, she won't look into our futures. No, boy, she won't. She won't do it.'

So Henery spoke as they walked along the lanes. He kept the stub of a pencil behind his ear and on occasion took it and made a swift inscription on a door or gatepost. He did so when they were turned away from a house by a woman who said she wanted nothing to do with scoundrels such as they, and if they did not leave forthwith she would call the constable. As if some such were waiting on her word in the vicinity.

Gully turned the horse and led the trolley out along the drive of the house. Henery told the woman they'd be on their way, then. They'd be taking their leave, if she didn't mind. Going out into the lane he scrawled a sign on the gate, the letter X. 'No good,' he told Leo. 'Warn the others. No good at all.'

When they returned to the camp, Samson called the boy over. 'Ye went out, Leo. Ye went out with my brother and the lad there. But be careful, boy, we keep an eye on you, all of us. Do you understand? You're ours, aren't you? With your debt to pay. You'll be with us till your debt's paid, won't you?'

The boy nodded. He did not know how long such repayment would take.

'No ideas now, Leo, you don't want any a them. We saved your life, we can take it back any time.'

The pregnant woman went into labour. Leo had taken her for Edwin's wife or one of her sisters. But Keziah told him that she was one of Belcher's daughters, by the name of Augusta, and that the father-to-be was Augusta's cousin, Henery. While the girl wept and yelled, the camp grew quiet. The older women went in and out of the low bender. A boy was born in the night. In the morning his grandmother took him out and washed him with dew. When on the day following Augusta emerged from her confinement, the men avoided her. They burned the bender, and moved on.

The boy got to know the horses, though none had names. He spoke to them. His favourite was the chestnut cob that had been attacked. When he entered a field where the horses were grazing it always spotted him and came over. Leo kept an eye on it but it did not seem to suffer further. The others had accepted it. They were a small draught breed, cobs with broad chests and powerful hindquarters, strong pulling horses. Most of them were piebald. They seemed even-tempered, unbothered by the children. 'We bred them from cast-offs,' Gully told Leo. 'Can you believe it? We used to use mules . . . my grandfather told me that, I never saw it. He was a boy then himself. Then coloured horses went out a fashion. Overnight, gentiles that owned their coloured horses sent them to the knackers, Shires included. We took them, interbred the Shires and Clydesdales with Dales ponies. To make these good pullers, see, strong but small. You don't have to feed em tons a food.'

When they settled in one place for some days, the boys rode the ponies bareback. Leo did not ask to ride, and no one invited him. Gully would stand and watch. He seemed glad to have Leo beside him, someone who was interested in what he saw. This pony's effortless flowing movement. That one's abundant feathering. He pointed out a heavy and clean bone in the leg. He'd lift a horse's foot to show Leo the strong walls on its hoof, the well-shaped frog.

'Me,' the old man said, 'I like a cold-blood horse.'

In one village when it had not rained more than a feeble spattering for weeks they jacked up the vardos and rolled the wooden wheels into the pond to soak.

On what he announced was the first day of October Henery sharpened an old rough-handled knife on the grindstone. He told Leo he'd one small dog, akin to a terrier but with some other unknown breed in him, who waited all year for this. He found a canvas sack for Leo, and a single, left-handed glove made of leather. Before they left, Henery informed his family he was taking Leo with him so none should abuse the boy for his absence from the camp.

They set out into the fields, keeping close to the hedgerows. There was dew on the grass, on sloes in the hedge, on fallen crab apples. The leaves of maple and sycamore were turning from green to russet and yellow and falling from their branches. The dog was an odd little beast, with a terrier's snout but slighter body and long thin legs. He was neither as strong as a terrier nor fast like a lurcher, but eager. Henery called him Strip. He explained that hedgehogs decide about now to hibernate.

'He drops his prickles, see, and drags his self along and spikes up a heap a leaves and grass all about him. Then he'll scrat his self up a hole and roll around in it, and you won't see him all winter. Only Strip here can sniff him out, Leo.

Every dog shall have his day and this be his.'

The dog might have had a nose but he needed his master, for Henery studied the ground as they walked. 'Here, see,' he said after some minutes. 'I reckon there's been one here.'

Leo looked hard but could see nothing but the leaf-strewn ground. Then he could. A line where the leaves lay differently, less thick or uniform or some such.

'Find, Strip,' Henery said, putting his foot to where the faint track began, and the dog followed it and pawed at the earth in the hedge, barking. Henery kicked him out of the way and reached his gloved hand into a mulch of leaves and grass and soil and brought out the hedgehog curled up asleep. He slit the animal's throat with his knife then held it up by one leg and with the same sharp knife scraped off the bristles.

Leo opened the sack he'd been given. Henery dropped the hedgehog inside and they set off searching for the next one, and so continued. By the end of the morning they had a dozen animals and returned to the encampment. Edwin greeted his son and asked where he'd been. Henery said that a hedgehog had laughed at him.

Edwin nodded. 'That's a good sign,' he said. 'You'll find luck today.'

'I already have,' Henery told his father. 'I caught the bugger and half his mates and the boy's got em in his sack here.'

Henery burned off any obdurate stubble and when all the hedgehogs were thus singed he scalded them in a pot of boiling water and skinned them. The process took hours. He told Leo that this was the method he had been taught, though there were others. While waiting patiently for certain parts of the process to be completed he prepared long hazel sticks, and when the hedgehogs were ready he skewered each one and placed it over the fire. They began to roast. Beneath them Henery placed tins and soon fat began to drip from the carcasses. Leo asked what this was for. Henery told him that he would give most of this lard to Gully for the horses' harnesses, but that his mother would keep some for she believed it to be a balm for children's earaches, and he would keep a little for himself to use as a hair oil. Of course if his Augusta wished to have a bottle, he must give it her.

They'd nick a chicken from a farm. The women carried long knives in their skirts, ready to kill a stray goose or lamb. One evening Samson said, 'I've a taste for pork. Will you give me some a your pig juice, Gully?'

The horseman climbed into his vardo and came out with a small bottle he gave to his brother, who put it in his jacket pocket and disappeared into the night.

The next day when the women set off hawking, Samson went with them. He came back with a dead pig on a trolley cart, a large castrated boar, fattening nicely. The boy did not understand.

'I asked a farmer, Leo, if he'd any dead calves I could take off his hands,' Samson told him. 'That I could skin for the hide, to make vellum for banjos. Would you believe it? The farmer said he had a pig must have ate summat poisononous and died overnight, and I was welcome to the whole bloody carcass, for none could eat it now.'

Leo still did not understand. Samson told him that farmers were fools. The boy did not agree but held his tongue. Samson said, 'I have a taste for pork, Leo. I like my rabbits fried in pork fat. I like mushrooms fried in pork fat with a pinch a salt when you take em out a the pan. And tonight my juval's goin to fry me some pork chops, are you not, Kinity?'

George's wife Rhoda wore long boots, laced to the knee beneath her ankle-length black dress that had deep embroidered pockets on the outside. She wore a stook around her neck, a brightly coloured square of silk, as did all the women. She was strong and stout. Her black hair was shiny with a pomade made of hedgehog fat and she cleaned her teeth with soot and salt.

One morning Rhoda asked the boy to light her fire, for her hands were full with Keziah and Lewesa, the younger girl, ill. He did so. The act was witnessed and Leo was soon given to understand that this was henceforth to be added to his chores: stoking or relighting each of the six campfires in the morning.

One damp December day he struggled to ignite kindling. Edwin's wife Arabella was outraged to find her drinking water bucket not yet replenished. She picked it up and tossed its remaining contents, yesterday's water, over the boy. Her children, Henery's younger brother Thomas and sister Priscilla, were gleefully amused.

At mealtimes Edwin and Belcher both ate first, before their wives and children. They did not like to be watched. Only after they had wiped their plates clean with bread were the others served. George did not obey this custom. He and Rhoda ate together. She cooked all manner of dishes in her pot. A black pudding made of the blood of a goose. Gypsy cake of flour and dripping, baked in the fire's ashes. When her man went out to graft she sent him off with onion sandwiches flavoured with brown sugar, vinegar and salt. Leo tried to guess ingredients by smell or taste, and Keziah told him right or wrong. It became a game between them. Rhoda used dandelions to flavour soup. She and her daughters searched for snails on walls and trees and cooked them into a broth, or boiled them and then fried them in herbs. Leo could not believe how tasty these oddities were.

'My juval here worked in the kitchen of one a the big houses,' George told him. 'I was hired by his lordship to fight one of his men on the lawn at a party they held for the Coronation. She saw me and run away with us, is that not so, sweetheart?'

'Don't believe a word of it, Leo,' Rhoda said.

'She only became a gypsy when she married me. Don't make my mistake, Leo,' George advised the boy. 'Never choose a wife by candlelight.'

Rhoda shook her head in reproof, trying not to smile. She cooked whatever game George brought to her and any vegetables filched from the fields. She used nettles like cabbage or kale. Her sons caught pigeons and she made a pie. Lewesa found watercress in a stream and her mother was overjoyed, for she said it was the perfect tonic for the blood.

One morning George whittled pegs while Leo oiled harness nearby. The big man looked across the clearing at his wife, and sighed. 'She walked so light, Leo, I thought she was a wind passin over the field.' He shook his head. 'She was quick as smoke. She's the most beautiful gypsy woman I ever saw. I don't mind. Let other men lust after her. Let them stare themselves blind, Leo, she's my woman.'

It was not easy to imagine Rhoda years younger and slighter. Once beautiful. She and George already had five children. Usually they all slept together in the bender, but some nights George and his wife climbed into the vardo and Leo heard them above him endeavouring to make one more.

'Have you a larkin yourself somewhere, Leo?' George asked him one evening.

'Leave him, George,' Rhoda said. 'He's too young for all that nonsense.'

'One day some girl'll stir his loins, and it might a happened already.'

'Will you leave him, I said, the poor boy. Ignore him, Leo, he's a big fat puddin with a brain no bigger than his mouth.'

George laughed, and so did their children within earshot.

There was a girl, but Leo would not speak of her. Not to these folk, nor any other. One day he would see her again, he did not know when.

Of all the women in the camp Arabella treated Leo most harshly. She expressed the belief that a gentile would bring them bad luck. Others told her they did not know of such a prohibition and she said they should not blame her when he did so, that was all she had to say. The boy lit her fire and refilled her water buckets and stacked her wood before anyone else's, but she discovered errors. The water was not clear. If wood was too young, she beat him with it. Her daughter Priscilla enjoyed such chastisement and

61

though a year younger than Leo administered it herself. She whipped him with a switch of hazel. He resisted the temptation to take it off her and withdrew, but she pursued him round the encampment. No one came to his aid. He tried to steer clear of her. She tripped him up or came up behind him and pushed him over. Leo did not respond. Priscilla explained to him that there was plenty more where that came from, and offered to sort him out whenever he so wished.

Priscilla's brother Thomas was a further year younger. One evening as Leo walked past their family, Thomas leaped to his feet claiming loudly that the gentile had passed between him and the fire. 'I'll call you out for that, you bastard,' Thomas said in his childish voice, removing his jacket. Then he took off his shirt. He was a small, thin boy but he'd been taught by his father Edwin to fight since the day he could stand, and he put up his fists. 'Come on then,' he said, 'we'll do it here and now.'

Leo was mystified. There were many strictures in the gypsies' daily life but none told him what they were. Here was another rule he had broken. He looked to Edwin in hope of a reprieve but was only told that he'd best put them up himself.

Leo wrapped his arms about his head, with his fists up by his ears and elbows out in front of his face. He could see between his arms the bare-chested child coming for him and closed his eyes.

Thomas's small fists pummelled him, first about his head and then the body. Leo did not know what to do. If he fought back and hurt the child he feared the consequences. More likely the child would hurt him anyway for though Leo's father was a fighter of sorts he had never trained his son to emulate him. Nor had Leo wished to.

The blows he now received to his midriff decided for him. He doubled over and the child Thomas rained blows to either side of Leo's head until he went down. Thomas stood above him and said in his thin unbroken voice, 'Let that be a lesson to you, gentile. Mess with me again, you'll get more a the same.'

4

So the gypsies and their unindentured servant travelled in the autumn of that year, 1912, and on through the winter into the next. They journeyed south, along the Teign valley, then headed west and up around the edge of Dartmoor. One day Henery and other lads came back from hunting with their dogs and said there were troops out on manoeuvres on the moor. Rhoda took the girls of the tribe, laden with all the sweets and fruit they could find, and followed the army. When the soldiers fell out for a rest the girls sold them what they had. Henery told Leo it was called troop-hawking and never failed.

That was also the day deemed sufficiently distant from childbirth that Augusta posed no danger, and she and Henery were married. Kinity baked a loaf of bread. She gave it to Samson, who told the assembled company that bread was God's food. It kept away evil spirits. He broke the loaf open. Kinity took hold of each lover's thumb from their right hand and made a small incision in them with a sharp blade. She held them over the bread and their blood dripped onto the loaf. They ate the bread where the other's blood had mingled with their own and so were married. They were invited to kiss, which they had not done before. Though as Leo overheard Edwin tell his brother Belcher, they had done a good deal more.

When the weather was bad the Orchards stayed wherever they found themselves and emerged from their tents only for the barest necessities. They as good as hibernated in their benders. When the weather improved they came out and put in the hard graft hawking and moved on to another valley in their peregrination around the county of Devon. Leo lost all sense of the calendar. One day it occurred to him that Christmas might have come and gone. The gypsies ignored the date. They made no mention of months, or of days. The boy felt as if the calendar and the clock, the normal measurement of time, even time itself as he had been taught to understand it, had been left behind. It still existed, elsewhere, but he had joined the gypsies in their waggons as they moved into a parallel time of no past or future but only an ever on-rolling now.

Leo spent whatever time he could with the old horseman. He saw that Gully Orchard was known to certain grooms and carters, and traded his good horses for their lesser ones, taking the difference in value in cash. In this way his troop became one with a variety of equine defects. In Chagford he acquired a carthorse that had the staggers. The farmer shook his head as Gully led the horse away, perhaps amazed to have outdone a gypsy. Back at the encampment Gully told Leo to give the horse no food or drink for twelve hours. He invited the boy to enter his vardo and watch him mix and roll six cricket-sized balls of liquorice powder, ground ginger and castor oil. Leo inhaled the musty sharp smell of herbs, and a more aromatic odour of oils, with which the very wood of the waggon seemed to be infused. The following morning they fed the mare one of the balls. Gully told the boy to repeat the dose three times a day, with nothing else to eat, but plenty of warm water on hand at all times. The horse recovered.

Leo had never heard his father speak of gypsy horsemen. 'Do you want to know the secret, Leo?' the old man asked. 'It's not the medicine. Yes, I'll bleed em or purge em. But the medicine don't cure a horse. It's me givin it encourages the beast in the healin of itself. Do you see?'

Gully spent hours with the horses at their pasture, clicking his teeth or whistling softly to them. He moved slowly so as not to frighten them. Though he was old now, Leo suspected he had always moved at that speed around his animals.

One afternoon Belcher sickened and took to the bed in his vardo. There was no apparent cause for his condition but it appeared grave. His wife Betsey lit the stove in the waggon and sat beside her man, who lay with his eyes closed and a frown of pain or perplexity upon his face. Rhoda took him medicines of her own devising made from herbs. He sipped a little.

In the night Leo was woken periodically by cries from the direction of Belcher's waggon, whether from the man or his wife he was not sure. In the morning the sick man was no better. Leo asked George if they would fetch a doctor from the town.

'A crocus can't help him,' the big man said. 'Old Allace Penfold put a grudge on him. Them Penfolds is always after us Orchards.'

The boy did not know of whom the big man spoke. Neither could he understand why if this were so she would have picked on Belcher and not his father, the chief, Samson. Or indeed George himself.

George nodded. 'Aye, she no doubt did. A curse is no different to a germ, Leo. Some people it infects, some it don't.'

As the day wore on members of the family gathered around Belcher's vardo. They did not speak more than a few words but leaned against the wheels or sat upon the damp ground, whittling a stick or smoking or gazing at no particular object, like those desert monks who sat in contemplation of the fragility of life.

In the afternoon Betsey's sisters and sisters-in-law helped her down out of the waggon and accompanied her to her bender. Edwin went to find a priest. Henery was sent to order an oak coffin from the local carpenter. Little was said. No one spoke aloud the name of the deceased. The women washed the dead body and dressed him in fresh trousers and a clean white linen shirt. They pulled his old dancing boots onto his stiffening feet.

That evening the adults fasted. Children ate their meal in silence. Dogs did not bark. Leo lay down on his blanket beneath George's vardo in a camp unnaturally silent.

On the morning following George went with Henery, the horse and trolley, to fetch the coffin. They carried the dead man's body out of the waggon and placed it in the coffin on the trolley. Samson put a sovereign in one of his dead son's trouser pockets. 'Buy yourself somethin to eat,' he said. 'Wet your whistle on the way there, boy.'

George and Edwin sifted through the waggon with the help of their wives, removing things that belonged to Betsey or had been acquired during their marriage and would be useful to her and their children. They removed also certain possessions of the dead man and placed these beside him in the coffin. An extra suit of clothes, a handkerchief, the hammer he used for splitting stone. His favourite knife they put on his right-hand side. The coffin was left open. Members of the family placed tokens such as a flower or a leaf upon him. Leo watched the gypsy children climb up on the trolley to peer down upon their father or uncle.

In the afternoon, under a light drizzle, Gully harnessed Belcher's draught horse to the waggon and led it into a nearby field, accompanied by the men and boys of the family. Leo followed. Gully cut some hairs from the horse's mane. He put these in his pocket. He unharnessed the horse. Then he took a rifle from the waggon where he'd hidden it and pointed the barrel at the horse's forehead and pulled the trigger. The powerful horse's four knees buckled and he collapsed.

George and Edwin climbed inside the vardo and set inflammable material alight and came out again. Samson said in a loud voice, 'Look, all you people, the countryside weeps. The hedges, the trees, the stones. All is weeping for the death of a good man. His woman there is weeping sorrow. My son is dead. My God, look down upon me.'

Then the flames began to rush and crackle and soon to roar as they caught the wood of the waggon. The harness was thrown inside. The men and boys stood and watched. When the roof of the waggon fell in, the men lifted the dead horse with strenuous difficulty and awkwardly added him to the pyre.

In the evening the adults still fasted and were

quiet. Gully sat alone, weaving a plait from the hair he'd cut from the carthorse, weeping silently to himself, whether for the horse or for his nephew Leo could not tell. When it was done the old man rose and went over to the trolley and laid the plaited horse hair in the coffin. Then he lifted the lid up off the trolley and slid it over the coffin and nailed it shut.

Early in the morning Samson and Gully, and George and Edwin, took the trolley to bury the coffin in the local graveyard. The women followed behind, consoling Betsey, who cried unrestrainedly in a manner indicative less of grief than of insanity. As soon as they returned the women cooked, and all ate a hearty breakfast. None spoke of their deceased relative but much was said of where they would go next, and who they hoped to see. Then the gypsies packed up their belongings and pulled out of the clearing.

5

As they approached Okehampton in March of the year 1913, Leo asked Gully what he planned to do there. The old man said that he would sell some horses and maybe buy one or two. He would watch George in the fighting booth. And he would see some races. Leo asked him about these races— were they a part of this Okehampton Spring Fair?

Gully laughed and said no. These races were run with other gypsy families, who would meet up some days after the fair was over. Some came up from Cornwall, others down from the north of the county. There were two kinds of race. 'Horses trottin, one leg after the other.' Gully put his hand out shaped like a claw and twiddled the fingers. 'One, two, three, four. Pullin a sulky—a two-wheeled cart. It's an odd way a racin to my mind, Leo. Trottin's a slow gait but the horse is trained to do it awful quick. It's unnatural if you ask me, but there's many swear by it. They go mad for it in America, there's money to be made with a good trotter there, dollars aplenty. And I've heard tell that on the island of Iceland the ponies strut about like that all the time.'

Leo asked Gully what the other kind of

race was. The old man said there was a single competition, a series of heats between each family's nominated horse. With a final between the two fastest. 'Which is when the big money will go down.'

Leo looked around. He studied Gully's ponies, unable to decide which one was qualified for such a competition.

Gully shook his head. 'I wouldn't put tuppence on one a my horses,' he said. 'The Hicks are bringin a fine horse. They're a family that's a part of our tribe.'

'Do they bring the rider?'

'No, the deal is we provide the rider. We're the Orchards. The obligation is on us.' Gully stopped speaking. He raised his head and studied the sky. Perhaps searching for signs of impending weather. The boy wondered if the conversation was over, but then the old man said, 'It's Henery. He's not a bad rider, Leo, he's the best we've got . . . only between you and me, he's no good. He's good but he's fearful.' Gully explained that Henery possessed a modicum of dread. He could not rid himself of it. 'You can see it in his eyes. He's got a decent seat but he can't trust a beast with his life. You have to. He'll ride but he'd rather not, do you see what I'm sayin?'

At the beginning of April they reached Okehampton. 'The Hicks will be there, Leo,'

Samson told the boy. 'We'll have a good rokker for sure.' He repeated that the Hicks were members of their tribe. They would meet them where they always did, away from the town. 'There's a little lonely, out-of-the-way place. I don't even know how the Good Lord found it before he put his plants and trees there.'

Leo laughed. He told Samson that he was learning to like their way of life. He could see it had advantages over the one he had grown up in.

The lane was a crooked dead-end track with high hedges either side and a large space at the end, and the Hicks were encamped already. Rhoda and the other women rushed forward to greet their brethren. Children followed, the men after them. The boy helped Gully stake out the ponies. 'Do you see that, Leo?' the old man asked. 'By yonder tree? You see a white horse in the morning, you'll have good luck all day.'

The boy had already seen the horse. It was all he saw, for he knew it, of that he was certain. It was the colt he had ridden for Lord Prideaux one year before at Bampton Fair. A horse he had ridden and known what speed is. A horse that flew like the wind.

Through the afternoon the gypsies set up their tents and campfires. Leo gathered wood and collected water. Gully intended to sell some of his ponies and these Leo brushed down and groomed. Gully fed them chaff as he did not usually do. He took his wife Caraline's block of salt and scraped a handful into each bowl and mixed it, and he tethered each animal within reach of the stream that ran between their camping ground and the high hedge. Beyond the hedge lay a field the farmer let them use for the duration of their stay, in return for Rhoda telling the fortunes of his wife and all her family. Gully planned also, he said, to sell an old Suffolk Punch. He'd bought it for chicken feed yet the farmer who sold it could not hide his glee. Leo was not surprised. He wondered who on earth now would pay one penny for such a nag.

'When a gentile buys a poor horse,' Gully told him, 'he shouts blue murder. Me, I'll keep my mouth shut, and pass it on to another fool.' He grinned. 'One such as I,' he added.

Leo groomed this carthorse as he had his father's Shires. Gully looked over periodically from his own labours to watch. The horse stood dumb and grateful and perhaps, it seemed, a bit surprised for she was not used to such tender treatment. When Leo had brushed the horse's tail and was washing the implements he had used, Gully came to him and said that it had not been unknown for a gentile to become a member of a gypsy tribe. There was a ritual.

The old man wished to share some arcane knowledge. Leo asked Gully to tell him of this ritual. Gully said he could not remember it in detail. He shook his head. Perhaps to loosen some mechanism inside. 'The chief of the tribe, my brother Samson, or his wife Kinity, they'd slit your arm for you and mingle your blood with two or three of us. Such as myself and George and Henery, do you see?' He lifted his floppy hat and ran his fingers through his hair. 'You'd need to fast some days.'

'I believe a person could do that,' Leo told him. 'It is not pleasant but it is possible.'

'You'd still be an outsider, though.'

Leo understood that Gully was addressing him directly.

'Until you married a gypsy girl. Some girl like Keziah.' The old man put his hat back on and smiled. 'And there'd be a task or two before you could get near to that.'

Leo's lips moved. 'A task?' How could he tell Gully that this was the last thing he wanted.

'Aye. Set by the girl's father. George.' Gully considered what he had said. He pondered what he might say next. Then he nodded. 'If the task was of my choosin, Leo, you'd need to steal a horse before you could have any daughter a mine.'

In the evening when all had fed, Henery told Leo that there would be a trip to a certain public house forthwith, for the purchase and consumption of alcohol. 'You should come along with us, Leo, I'll see you get a bottle a pop or two.'

They walked back along the lane and on to the outskirts of the town. All came, every member of the Orchards and of the Hicks, and soon were strung out. The men strode forward, their thirsty women matching them. The old men and women and the young ones such as Augusta, carrying their babies in their shawls or dragging dawdling toddlers, fell behind, like some tribe wandering in the wilderness. Had the gypsies done something to kindle the anger of the Lord or had they chosen to live the way they did? Leo did not know.

The public house was empty as if cleared for this jocular influx. They crowded into the bar. Most ordered beer but Kinity demanded a mixture of claret and whisky, which she said she savoured as had the poor old lady herself—and hadn't she lived over eighty years, most of them on the throne, and many alone?

Samson raised his mug of beer. All were quiet and he said, 'Here's to thy health, you Hicks, may you live until a walnut shell will make a coffin for you, every man, woman and child.'

They cheered Samson Orchard, then the Hicks's chief stood and raised his mug and said, 'Thank you, Samson. And here's to prosperity for my wife's husband.' There was silence for a moment, then much laughter. In the midst of it Leo heard someone say, 'Nippers outside,' and found himself bundled out.

The gypsy children milled about. Some were

brought a drink by older kin. Leo was not. They found things to do to impress one another. One Hicks boy could throw a stone an unlikely distance. Others tried to match him but could not. A girl sang a song at a higher pitch than anyone else could equal. Each time the door to the house opened the noise in the bar, of raucous talk and laughter, escaped with a roar. Then the door opened and Gully came out, and Leo ran after him and walked back to the encampment beside him.

'I saw you through the glaze,' Gully told him. 'Stood there on your own.' They walked back in the cool darkness. 'I'm not one for the crowds, boy,' the old man said. 'My Caraline's happy as a sandpiper with the rokker back there. It's too loud for me.' He stopped and looked up at the stars in the black sky. 'I just have to get the noise out a my ears.' They walked slowly on. 'They say a gentile's ear is so full a noise in the towns, Leo, that when he's in the forest he can't hear the trees speakin.'

The boy asked him if the family had ever been, or were likely to go, to a town by the name of Penzance.

'I heard of it,' Gully admitted. 'Way down in Cornwall. We don't go there and we never have done. We're Devon gypsies.'

When they reached the camp Leo went directly to the white colt. The old man came with him for

Leo wished to introduce Gully to the beast. There could be no doubt this was the one the Hicks had brought for the race. The horse was tethered close to a hedge. His silvery form stood out in the moonlight. Leo spoke to him. 'Tis good to see you again, my friend,' he said. 'I never expected it. That was some ride you give me.' He blew into the horse's nostrils and stroked him and inhaled his lovely tart smell. The colt stood perfectly still, poised, attentive to the boy. Leo knew the horse could not remember him. It was not possible. Yet did he? Did each know the other? Then he told Gully what a horse this was, for his size the swiftest Leo had seen or could imagine.

'He is a fine beast,' the old man said. 'I can see that, even in the darkness.'

Another man's voice spoke from behind them. 'It's you, ain't it?' Gully turned to acknowledge this member of the Hicks family, but he was facing Leo. 'I thought it were. Yes, and I were right, weren't I? I knew twas you.' He turned to Gully. 'Have you seen this nipper ride? You must have. Why else would you bring a gentile among us?'

It was the lad who had been riding the colt at Bampton Fair, who on Lord Prideaux's orders gave way to Leo. The man and lad and boy looked at each other in the pale moonlight. It was not possible to make out the expressive features of each other's faces, it was like looking through a veil of milk. But the lad could see enough.

'You've not, have you?' he asked Gully. 'You don't know what we have with us here? I thought I could ride, Gully, but this nipper can *ride*.'

'You still haven't sold him then?' Leo asked the Hicks lad.

The lad laughed. 'He tells jokes as well,' he said. 'A course I sold him. I've sold him near enough a dozen times now. He will keep makin his way back to me, though, won't he?'

In the morning at first light the boy went back to the horse. He spoke to him quietly as he ran his hand over the colt's body, pausing at the joints, checking for any swellings or lumps. He found none. The horse became still under the boy's fingers. He felt under his palm the pulse of the veins between the animal's skin and flesh beneath. So far as Leo could tell there was nothing wrong with this horse anywhere in his conformation. He stepped back and beheld him. He figured the colt to be full-grown now, and wondered at his parentage. He was not tall as a racehorse or a big hunter. He was thick-boned, and strong, yet possessed a certain elegance, though perhaps that came only from Leo knowing the speed of which he was capable. Perhaps this colt was the miraculous white offspring of a gypsy horse and a thoroughbred of some kind. It was a mystery the depth of which he had not the knowledge to fathom.

Leo made his way back to the Orchards' vardos. The mood in the camp was subdued. Many slept, for they had not done so all night, coming back from the pub and drinking more and telling stories around the campfires. Those who emerged from their benders were grim, scowling. Leo thought it must be the alcohol, but Gully said there was more to it. 'The Penfolds are here, the bastards. Okehampton is ours, always has been. They know that. They're lookin for trouble and they'll find it soon enough.'

Leo asked who the Penfolds were. The old man explained that they were related to the Orchards and the Hicks, not to mention the Isaacs and the Smalls. All were once of the same tribe, but the Penfolds had broken away. He could not, he admitted, remember why, his brother might, but it was a terrible thing for sure, whatever it was. A grievous offence.

'They follows us around like fuckin cuckoos,' Gully said, unusually vehement. 'We get glimpses a their ugly mugs, but they've never come out like this. Samson will be thinkin hard on it, Leo, thinkin hard.'

That afternoon Gully told the boy he wished to show him something. They walked down the curved, sloping way into the town. There were many people, on the pavement and the road. Gully said it was so busy on account of the Fair taking place tomorrow. He entered the shop of James Wright, ironmonger. Out front were baskets, brushes, buckets, brooms. The boy followed him inside. Receptacles of zinc, tin, copper, hung from hooks on the ceiling joists. There were shelves of nails and screws of every sort and size. A back room full of tools. Gully bought eight twelve-bore shotgun cartridges and a pint of linseed oil.

Back at the waggon Gully extracted the black shot powder from the cartridges and mixed it in the oil. Leo fetched the old Suffolk Punch out of the field. He did not believe that anyone would buy her. She was on her last legs. When he brought her back Gully had uncoiled a length of rubber tubing. Leo held the horse and Gully fed one end of the tube up her left nostril. 'You has to get it down the gullet,' he said. 'Not the windpipe. If I put the tube down her trachea and then the oil into her lungs, I could kill her. Drown her.' He continued to feed the tube up the carthorse's nostril. She remained calm, as if this strange procedure were an everyday ritual, some part of her equine ablutions. 'I think I got it,' Gully said. He told Leo to blow down the tube. 'If I did put it down the windpipe in error, you'll get her breath back from her lungs.'

Leo tried to do as he was asked, but he could not. There was a resistance.

'That's good,' Gully said. 'It's about in the

right place.' He asked George to join them and to hold the end of the tube up in the air. 'Put this funnel in. Higher! Over here.' Gully climbed on to the nearest wheel of his vardo. Once he was stood steady he poured linseed oil into the funnel. When the oil had all gone he pulled the rubber tube carefully back out through the Suffolk Punch's nostril.

Gully asked Leo to let the Punch out in the field to stretch her legs then bring her back for Henery to take to the farmer who might buy her. Leo wondered why Gully would not do that himself. The old man shook his head. 'I'll buy but I'd rather not sell. Me, I'm not much good. You've seen yon lad. He's got the gift a the hawkin. The bluster. He's full of it.'

The boy thought that Henery would need to be. He led the carthorse into the field where the gypsy horses grazed, those of the Orchards and the Hicks all together. He untied the halter rope and stood back. And then to his astonishment the Suffolk Punch put her head first down, then up, and without further ado she set off and trotted away across the field. At some point she broke into a canter. She kicked her heels and galloped from one side of the field to the hedge on the other, turned and cantered back. Years fell away from her. Leo had never seen such a transformation in a horse. It was as if her ancient form had all of a sudden given birth to some younger version of herself. An act of magic, or miracle, but from some other Bible than the one he knew. It came to him that he wanted to share the experience, and realised that it was Lottie Prideaux he wished to tell.

In the evening George soaked his hands in petrol, as he had been doing every night for some weeks. Rhoda complained of the stink but George told her he had grown to like it and planned to give her some as a gift in the form of perfume.

Samson came over. He informed Leo that he would ride in the bareback races for them, it had been decided. Levi Hicks had told them how the boy could ride. It was a great honour for him. Leo nodded. He did not know about the races but he could not wait to ride the white colt.

Then Samson reached up and touched his giant son on the shoulder. 'Will you look at him, Leo?' he said. 'He's a freak a nature, honest to God. He come from my loins and those a my juval there, but would you look at him?'

Leo asked the burly old man if he'd been a fighter himself, as people said. Samson filled his pipe with tobacco and lit it. 'I was a pugilist, for my sins,' he said. 'I fought all sorts. All over. I fought with Welsh mountain fighters and cockney practitioners a the fistic art. I've beat em good, Leo, till they was washed in their own blood, and I've been beat bad myself, make no mistake about it, and I never backed down, Leo, never. But my boy's twice the fighter I ever was. He'll fight tomorrow, he'll fight the locals, and if there's a gentleman turns up with his fighter and wishes to make a wager, we'll have George fight him for the purse. But I wish he'd fight a Penfold.'

Samson stared at Rhoda's fire. He smoked his pipe, eyes narrowed, his body hunched tighter into itself.

'Mendoza Penfold was the biggest bastard of the lot, God rest his soul,' he said. 'I couldn't stand that man. I fought him three times and I'd a liked to fight him three or thirty times more. I'd fight him now if he was not beneath the mud. He bit the top a me ear off, Leo, do you see that there? He bit it off and spat it into the long grass, the bastard. We never found it. One a the dogs had it, most likely.'

Leo inspected the old man's truncated ear where he had held his hair aside for the boy's scrutiny. Samson grinned. 'We all used to take a bite back in them days. Me, I'd take a bit a yer ear, yer nose, yer fuckin cheek. And I wouldn't spit it out, boy, I'd swallow it.'

As he lay in his blanket under the waggon that night Leo heard voices coming from the direction of Gully's campfire. Henery spoke loudly. 'To be replaced on the eve a the race!' he cried. 'By a fuckin gentile? How can you all do this to me, Uncle?'

Gully spoke in reply but much more quietly, his voice indistinct. Leo lay in the darkness. Surely he was not making another enemy?

On the day following, some of the men went to set up a boxing ring in the Okehampton showground. The moor rose up to the south. To the north lay rolling hills of green fields dotted with white sheep or red cattle. Samson proclaimed that in the afternoon Gentle George the bare-knuckle champion would take on all-comers. This Leo did not see but had explained to him by George back at the campsite, where the big man whittled clothes pegs from hazel for Rhoda to sell as if this were any other day.

After he had completed his chores, Leo rode the white colt. Levi put on reins. Gully stood back. Henery lurked in the background with three or four others. Leo took off his boots and rode the colt bareback in the farmer's field. He made it trot in large circles and turn about. He wished to judge its mouth. It resisted him. He brought it over to Gully and the lad Levi who owned it, and told them the colt felt all wrong, or rather he himself did, it was not the fault of the horse. He did not believe he could ride it as he once had. Another rider would not destroy their chances in the race as he would. He was sorry.

Gully stood there mystified. Leo passed the reins to Levi, slid off the horse and walked barefoot out of the field. Back at George and Rhoda's waggon he was tying the laces of his boots when Henery stood before him. He said nothing but loomed above the boy. Leo tied his bootlaces carefully, methodically. He glanced up. Henery was looking at him. Waiting for his attention.

'You don't fool me,' he said. 'You might a fooled them, I can't say, probably not . . . give em a little while . . . but you don't fool me for a minute.' He shook his head. 'Leo,' he said, 'I'd rather be insulted than thrown off that fuckin animal. Have me bones broke.' Henery grinned. 'And I'd rather make some tin out a you than lose it on meself. Do you see, Leo? Now get them fuckin boots a yours off again.'

Leo rode the white colt. There was nothing stiff or awkward in his comportment. He sat the horse like some languid companion of the animal. When he kicked with his bare heels and the horse galloped from one corner of the field to another, the boy and the beast seemed to conjoin one to the other. The faster they rode, the more snug the fit, as Leo's body and his limbs adapted themselves to those of the colt in motion.

He knew this horse would beat whatever was put up against it. He knew it. The animal became more alive as his blood warmed. When his blood was hot, galloping, the colt was most fully himself. And the boy astride him felt himself carried into the same fire-filled realm of existence. Yet the faster they flew, the cooler his brain. Ease the colt round, dig your heels into him now, pull him back. The ground, the hedge, the people watching, blurred past him and the horse but he did not seem to be afeared or even aware of the danger. He could think clearly. Perhaps he was stupid. It was very strange.

In the afternoon they went to the showground. Leo carried George's water bottles and a bucket. At the boxing ring Edwin had taken over the hawking and a crowd milled about. The ring consisted of four heavy posts driven into the ground, one at each corner of a fifteen-foot square, with three cables of rope strung tight around them. It was open to the air. The gypsies had not erected a tent but rather a canvas fence or screen around the outside of the ring. Each man who paid a shilling received a blue ticket as he passed through to the space between screen and ring. A tanner for lads. No children.

Those who wished to challenge Gentle George paid five shillings, customarily from their pals who formed a syndicate for the purpose. All those who survived three five-minute rounds would receive their money back plus the same again. Any who put George down would win a prize of ten guineas, a man's wage for a year. Was that not worth a man of courage bravin a bruise or two? So Edwin sold the show. Punters jostled to get a ticket, ardent for blood. Whether that of those they knew from hereabouts, their friends or acquaintances, or of the gypsy fighter, the boy did not know. He followed George through the nervous, surly throng.

George Orchard undid the buttons of his shirt with a dainty, deliberate precision belying his thick fingers. Then he stretched both arms out behind him and his brother Edwin pulled the shirt off. The crowd grew quiet. The big man had no discernible muscle that the boy could see. His ribs were lost in solid flesh. He was made of great slabs of meat any butcher would be glad of, no more man than beast, half-bull, half-human, just risen on his two feet.

The first punter in the ring was tall and brawny, but facing Gentle George he looked puny. Warming up, he threw quick jabs in the air as if a wasp was bothering him and came forward ducking and bobbing like a man whose nerves had been shot. Long ago or perhaps just now, when Edwin removed the big man's shirt, it was hard to tell.

Gentle George advanced ponderously, clumsily, leading from the shoulders. The punter took some wild swings but even as his fists flew he was already retreating from the big man's retaliation. One or two blows landed and were lost in flesh. Gentle George kept coming. He raised his hands, gathered loosely into fists. He didn't throw punches like the tall punter. It was more like his fists were solid objects or tools he carried at the end of his arms. The big man gently swung his huge fist at the punter. He pawed him like a bear. The right hit so slowly it seemed like an affectionate gesture, a stroke of the cheek, and that was why the punter had not avoided its foreseeable trajectory. Yet his face distorted strangely. Then the left came around in like manner from the other side, a slow hammer swing. The tall man's jaw cracked and blood exploded from his ruined face.

They dragged him out unconscious. Leo poured water from a bottle into the bucket. Edwin raised the bucket to his brother. George lapped from it like a beast of burden. The next punter came forward, a fat, belligerent little man with eyes set close together and misshapen ears. Perhaps he thought he could keep low enough, out of range of the big man's blows.

Leo looked up. Dotted around the top of the screen were faces peering over. As if a band of Cornish giants with small heads, perhaps that county's fabled wrestlers, had turned up to watch. Then he realised they were all boys much the same age as he himself, sitting or standing on the shoulders of friends.

In the early evening back at the camp they counted their earnings from the boxing ring. In addition, the women had done much hawking of goods and telling of fortunes. Nimble-fingered boys and girls had procured money by other means. Henery had sold a couple more of Gully's ponies.

'We'll not be short a tin for the winter,' Rhoda told the boy. 'The winter will tell you what you did in the summer, see, and how we do in Okehampton is a good sign. We should be bok but we're not, on account a those Penfolds. We have to do somethin about it. And we will, Leo, don't you worry about that, you'll see.'

Leo believed her. The men acted each as if someone had just insulted them. Samson sat staring into the fire on which his Kinity had set a pot stirring. Every now and then she muttered, 'So you'll do nothin, is that it? Getting old, are you now?' Samson sat hunched over as his wife continued to goad him. 'You'll let it go, will you? You're no husband a mine, are you?'

All of a sudden Samson clambered to his feet. 'Right. I've had about enough,' he yelled. 'That's it.'

The others must have been waiting for this word for as Samson walked out of the camp all the men, of the Hicks as well as the Orchard family, gathered in his wake and followed him. Leo stood watching them. Gully turned and nodded to him to join them and he ran to catch up.

They skirted the town. Gully told the boy that

the Penfolds had not even set up camp on the opposite side of Okehampton but just a short way around it on the southern side. This supposedly was further evidence of their perfidy.

The Orchards' arrival appeared unexpected for it caused panic in the Penfold encampment. As Leo approached he could see women crawling into their benders, calling their children after them. Men stood in the clearing, backs against tree trunks, or at the wheels of their waggons. They might have been kin to the Orchards yet everything about them was different. The men's faces were darker. Their clothes were in tatters. The waggons were ramshackle. The fires smoked without visible flames. A pony stood roped to a tree, its skeleton discernible beneath its sorry skin.

Samson took up position facing a man of a similar age. The family arrayed themselves around him. 'I'm callin you out, Naylor Penfold,' he said loudly. 'I'm callin you out, you filthy, dirty, thievin bastard. You're not fit to wipe a pig's foot on. I've a crow to pick with you, Naylor, you nasty scum. You're the dregs. You've been followin us around, stealin our patch, sullyin our name, and I'm callin you out.'

Samson paused, to take a breath or perhaps to remember his lines rehearsed over the days preceding. All were quiet around and before him, intent upon the performance.

91

'Ye'll never amount to no more'n a piece a shite—and the same goes for the lot a you. You're the biggest liar that ever stood on two feet, Naylor Penfold. Look at you . . . chewin your tobacca like a sheep chewin its cud. Your old woman there looks as sour as a crab apple tree. All your women chatter like magpies.'

Samson paused again and the man Leo took for Naylor Penfold stepped forward. 'Look at yourself, Samson Orchard,' he said. 'You're a big man with a small heart and you're good for nothin. You're a large puddin with nought in it, so you are.'

'Aye, and you're an ugly bastard, Naylor Penfold. Ugly enough to frighten the Devil himself. I'm callin you out here and now for all to hear. I'll fight you meself like I fought your father and I'm nigh on sixty year of age, an old man, but I'll fight for me and all a my breed.'

Edwin put his hand upon his father's arm and stepped up beside him. 'To be a Penfold?' he said. 'I wouldn't wish it on a dog. I feel sorry for your horses, they don't deserve it. We'll fight you, any one of us, any one of our breed'll take you on. The Orchards or the Hicks, the Isaacs or the Smalls if they was here. We're the tribe of Orchard and we're callin you out.'

Gully and Edwin stepped aside from Samson, and George took their place. Though he had meted out much punishment in the show field

92

that afternoon, he had taken some too. Gully explained to Leo that it was only the sight of blood, of blows landing on the big man, that beckoned punters into the ring. His eyes were swollen and there was a purpling yellow bruise on one side of his face, and his lower lip was misshapen. Leo could not tell whether this made him look less fearsome or more so to a prospective opponent.

Samson put his hand on his son's shoulder. 'My boy George here,' he said, 'will fight any one a your boys. He's a bare-fisted fightin man. If you like, he'll fight em one after the other. I tell you what, Naylor, he'll take em on all at the same time. Or you can put em on a rope and he'll take em on in a tug a fuckin war. There's not one a you's fathered enough sons to beat him. Look at your boys. Will you look at em there? They've seen our George and their hair's liftin the hats from their heads. You're a bunch a miserable cowards and we'll see you in the mornin in that field yonder.'

Samson turned and walked through the middle of his family, who followed likewise and formed a phalanx around him, and so they returned to their camp.

In the morning the Orchards and Hicks rose and went all together once again to the field Samson had stipulated. The Penfolds were not there. They

93

went back to the Penfolds' camp. The people, the animals, the waggons, the tents, all were gone. They had vanished. Stolen away in the night. One or two fires still exuded a weak plume of damp smoke. Scraps of metal and wood and clothing lay around. There was a smell of rotting food and shit, whether of dogs or people Leo could not say for sure. 'They've left nothin but a load a junk to give us all a bad name,' Samson declared. The mood was exultant. To have the Penfolds run was even better than to fight them.

6

On the days following Leo rode the white colt. He would have liked to gallop on the open moor but they would not let him take the animal out of the field so he practised there. Often there were others besides Gully watching him. It rained almost every day, and the horses obtained what shelter they could from overhanging branches of trees in the hedgerows, but the colt was always eager to exercise.

Leo recalled the sight of Lottie suppling her blue roan in the paddock and tried something of the same exercise to see how the colt responded. He took him alongside the hedge on their left-hand side but with the front right leg, followed by the head, neck and spine of the horse, arching as if about to make a circle and the back legs keeping the line along the hedge. The horse did not like it, resisting the pressure Leo exerted, with his legs or on the reins. It was difficult for the colt to bend his spine and as he understood what his rider wished him to do he created the illusion of doing so by bending his neck only.

The boy did not expect immediate acquiescence, nor wish it. He liked the feel of the colt's resistance; there was something subtle and articulate about it, as if the boy had spoken and the horse disagreed, as if they were conducting a conversation in some arcane language each understood.

Leo still had his chores to run, but now he had assistance. Others helped him gather wood and stack it beneath trees to dry. Even Priscilla, his chief tormentor, aided him in lighting damp kindling, and Thomas the little pugilist carried water.

The gypsies possessed no timepiece yet seemed to know when their brethren would gather for the races. 'They'll be here tomorra, the Burtons, up from Tavistock,' Samson declared. On what evidence, the boy could not tell. On the morrow it transpired that something unforeseen had delayed them. 'But the Francombes down from Barnstaple, we'll see them soon enough.'

7

In due course four bedraggled families gathered on the eastern side of the village of South Zeal, east of Okehampton. Men bought jugs of beer at the Oxenham Arms and carried them back to camp. There was singing and dancing around the fires. A Burton girl of not much more than Leo's own age danced to music three men of her family made on a banjo, a violin and an accordion. She danced on a board put down for the purpose. Her black hair swung about her head. She held her arms aloft like a soldier in the act of surrender, yet there was no trace of submission in her expression. Perhaps the opposite. Sweat glistened on her brow in the firelight. All were quiet, watching. She swayed her hips in a manner Leo was sure he had never seen before, and he realised that his body wished for things his mind had not decreed. This was new to him.

Then the girl rapped her feet hard upon the board and grew hot and more ardent and whirled about. The spectators were stilled save for older women sporadically yelling or yelping encouragement. The musicians sped the music up. The girl's black eyes widened like those of the colt galloping as she spun, in a furious vortex, until all of a sudden the music ceased and she did too, and knelt on the board bowing for the applause.

In the early morning they had trotting races on the open road but the boy did not attend for Gully had no interest in them. He told Leo of a Scottish island where gypsies ran bareback races but not with their own horses. Instead they had to steal a neighbour's, and ride it with their wife or girl behind. The old man took a miniscule bag from his pocket and loosened the string. He drew from it a single tooth. 'I took this from the mouth a the best horse I ever had,' he said. 'A skewbald she was. A small, sweet head but a broad chest, well muscled. Flashy action.' The old man gazed at the tooth in his hand, as if he could see in its place the horse it had belonged to. 'A proper cob,' he said.

The day of the first bareback races dawned cool and clear. The sky was a sheer unblemished blue as if it had been rinsed clean. They walked from their encampment to a stretch of the road to Whiddon Down that lay straight and flat before them.

The first race was between the Orchards' and Hicks' white colt and the Francombes' big grey mare. Some kind of committee made up of men from each family examined the horses. Then the riders. They took Leo's boots and his jacket and shirt. Gully had given him a pair of gypsy trousers, high-waisted, narrow-legged, that would not flap around as he rode. These were all the clothes they were allowed to wear. The other rider was a much older youth, wide-shouldered and muscular, and he regarded his slight, pale opponent with a look of incredulity as each was inspected and patted down for concealed whips or spurs with which they might provoke their own mounts or attack their rival's.

Edwin and Henery took money for wagers. Samson came over. He grasped hold of each of Leo's ears with either hand and brought his face close. 'My brother says that this horse of ours is fast,' he said. His breath smelled of stale beer and rich meat. 'He says that you can ride. Well, boy, here's where you begin to repay your debt. Number one you win. Number two you make it look lucky. That way we'll get more money put down on the final race. Do you understand?'

Leo nodded that he did. Samson squeezed his ears in his rough hands. 'Good,' he said. 'Good.'

Then the riders stood side by side facing the crowd of spectators as a pot-bellied man explained that the turnpike would forthwith be closed off. The horses would be ridden west to a post the keen-eyed among them might discern in the distance. They should go clockwise around the post and back here. Between these two poles, planted either side of the road, which formed both the starting and the finishing line.

The riders were helped aboard their mounts. The big grey mare was two or three hands taller than the white colt, statuesque and powerful. Leo studied her. If God had designed her for a purpose it was not for speed. At least not speed alone. Her rider needed his strength for he had to manhandle her up the road and turn her and force her back towards the starting line. He was already a-sweat himself. Leo waited for him. The white colt did not seem concerned by the bustle of human beings nor the grey mare but let Leo turn him this way then the other in a slow circle, on a tight rein.

A man beside the pole on one side of the road removed the red scarf from around his neck and held it up above his head. When the two horses were more or less abreast before him he swept his arm downward and yelled, 'Run.'

The Francombe youth uttered a great roar as if to frighten his horse to action and Leo's to the spot, but they both took off. The mare forced herself forward and into the lead. The colt followed in her wake. He seemed uninterested, yet though both horses sped up, once the mare was at a full gallop the colt continued to accelerate. He almost overtook her, then settled back behind. Leo did not know what else to do. If he did not hold the colt back they must win easily. He had to restrain him. But surely it would be clear that he was doing so. Clear to any horseman. He glanced to his left-hand side as if inspiration might lurk there. He saw a stand of oak trees. Dartmoor rose in the distance, up over the curved horizon.

They galloped along the road. Up ahead Leo could make out a post stuck in the middle of the turnpike. Then it came to him. He let the mare turn first around the halfway point, but kept the colt going another ten or twenty yards. Ahead of him half a dozen gypsies stood across the road. Beyond and above them a single farmer stood on the seat of his waggon, baulked of his passage on the highway but keenly watching the spectacle.

As he slowed his horse Leo looked back and saw that the mare was only now completing her own clumsy pivot about the post, her hooves ruining the patch of shingle and rough tarmacadam. He turned the colt and pursued them. Francombe jerked back and forth on the back of his horse and threw the reins forward and kicked the mare, his exertions as great as those of the animal beneath him.

Leo took the colt as wide as he could, out to the right-hand verge of the road. He still held him back somewhat with the reins and felt sorry for doing so. He hoped that none would realise, that they would see his arms and shoulders flailing and not notice the grip of his hands, distracted by his gradual improvement, the prospect of victory in an ever-closer race, and be caught up in the excitement. His colt overtook the big grey mare a few yards from the finishing line. Leo did not see the crowd on either side nor hear them. He kept the colt reined in even now. There was no alternative for if he let him go all would glimpse his true potential. Leo cantered the horse up the road, trotted him, turned and came back, shaking his head. He could feel the colt resentful beneath him, angered with this rider he'd thought would give him the freedom he desired.

They passed the Francombe lad, bent forward over the neck of the grey mare, breathing hard. As they approach-ed the crowd of gypsies Leo rolled and slid down off the colt and let his owner Levi Hicks take the reins off him and walked, still shaking his head, towards Gully.

'I'm sorry,' he said as he reached the old man, in his voice that was like honey rolled over sand. He knew only one or two could hear him and hoped that was enough. 'I couldn't turn him. Like you said, he don't want to turn. He's fast enough but he's no good.'

The second race immediately followed the first and was won by the Burtons' horse, a palomino mustang of great beauty. The deciding, final race was set for the following morning. During the day word spread through the gypsy encampments and beyond. The Burtons' palomino was fast and dependable, a sure-fire winner. The lad who rode him had won the year before. The titch riding for the Orchards and the Hicks was not strong enough. That white horse had speed but was wilful and the boy could not turn him. He could neither speed him up nor slow him down. The horse did as it wished. Worst of all, the boy was said to be a gentile, and this was the Orchards' most grievous error. The rules forbade them from changing rider at this late stage. Arabella's prediction, that Leo would bring them bad luck, was made more widely known. Edwin and Henery moved gloomily about, accepting wagers reluctantly but trying to haggle the pot down. But they were poor at it this day, downhearted or lackadaisical, and often came away with the price of the wager not lowered but raised. They wrote nothing down, were bookmakers who remembered each figure for each person.

In the Orchards' camp Samson spoke with great vehemence, yet in a whisper. 'Did I not tell the boy?' he said. 'A stroke a genius if I say it myself. Make it look lucky, I said, did I not, boy?' The old man took hold of Leo's hair and pulled the boy to him and kissed him on the forehead. 'You're learnin our ways right beautiful, boy, is he not, Gully? But by God this boy can ride. And that horse! After this we're leavin the West

Country, I'm tellin you, Gully, the Orchards have been down here too long. We're goin up country now. We're takin this horse to the Kilsney races and the Appleby Fair and who knows where else. Wherever there's races and tin. We've been waitin for this moment, have we not, Gully? A horse and a rider together. And the moment's come to meet us.'

In the evening the boy went into the field. He found the colt and fed him some carrots and spoke to him. He apologised to the horse for holding him back this morning and promised that on the morrow he would not do so. He had a debt to repay and though he did not see how they would ever give him his freedom, for the more valuable he became so the longer they would wish to keep him, still he believed that he would gain his freedom and the horse would too.

'What say you to that, old fellow?' Leo asked the colt as he stroked him in the dying light of the spring evening. A smell of mint rose from the grass and mingled with the sharp sweet smell of the horse.

In the morning, none in the Orchards' camp wished the boy well. All but Gully ignored him, skirted his presence, looked away when they glimpsed him. Gully told him he'd rubbed the colt down, he was in fine nick, but he reminded

Leo that he had only galloped this course the once and on that occasion shot right past the half-way mark. Horses are slaves of habit. The colt might think himself obliged to repeat the manoeuvre today. Leo nodded. The Hicks lad Levi walked his horse up to the road. Gully and the boy walked behind. All the others came after. Then George was beside the boy. He put his meaty hand upon his shoulder and spoke softly.

'I've seen me gettin hit, Leo,' he said. 'I've seen me goin down, and I've laid there on the ground, Leo, and I thought the clay is nice enough. The soil. The mud. I could lie on it or under it, I don't mind, there's no need to get up. But I got up. Yes, I did. Every time. I always got up, Leo, I seen it, I seen myself get up and raise my broken fists and finish it.' He squeezed the boy's bony shoulder. 'Never give up, Leo. Never.'

They walked up through the crowd. Perhaps the Burton dancing girl was among them. It would be her turn to watch him. Not all were gypsies. Gentiles had come to place their bets, from the villages of South Tawton and Spreyton. From Okehampton town. Word had spread and many regarded the boy with pity. Leo bowed his head. George kept one of his great hands on the boy's left shoulder, Gully on the right, like the seconds of some diminutive parody of a prizefighter approaching the ring.

The riders removed their clothes save for the

trousers and as before were examined to make sure that neither concealed whip or weapon about their person. The Burton lad had long black hair pinned up behind his head, and black eyes. He was leanly muscled, with no soft trace of fat beneath the taut skin of his torso. He offered his hand to Leo, who took it and yelped as he felt the bones of his fingers being crushed in a brief, fierce grip. The lad let go, smiling, and turned and walked to his horse. Leo shook the pain out of his knuckles and took the reins of the white colt from Levi, who cupped his hands. The boy stepped into them with his bare left foot and sprang up and astride the horse.

Perhaps the Burton rider had taken note of Leo yesterday, or been advised, or come up with the notion himself, but as they waited at the starting line he turned the mustang round in half-circles, one way then the other, as did Leo a few yards away. The same man as before stood beside a pole, removed the red calico scarf from around his neck and held it aloft. The riders turned their horses. They might have been winding them up like clockwork toys. Both men and animals were ready to go. The starter held his red scarf up, staring intently from his side of the road to the pole on the opposite side. He would not bring the scarf down. He waited for the horses to align themselves, each facing the right direction, dead abreast. The riders turned their horses with the reins held tight, the animals' heads high up, their hooves pawing the gravel. They rotated in increasing agitation and the men in the crowd screamed, but what they said each individually in the roar of men and women shouting no one could say. Were they telling the starter to wait a second longer or to proceed now, this instant? All were yelling, each convinced of the impassioned truth of his own opinion.

But perhaps the starter held his flag precisely to prolong the excitement, and the boy was glad, for he could feel his blood warming within him, and the horse's likewise. When the starter dropped his scarf and opened his mouth to yell something none heard, Leo let the colt go. The race might as well have been called off within yards, for though the palomino began well enough the white colt bolted ahead.

The boy clung to the galloping horse. The colt was beyond his control. Any number of catastrophes could occur now and each would mean his injury or death. He did not care. How could terror contain such joy? There was no place on this earth he would rather be, no person, than a bare-chested barefoot bareback rider on this white horse.

Some way to the marker in the centre of the road Leo glanced back and saw the palomino mustang four or five lengths behind. The colt sped on. As they approached the marker Leo slowed him, to a canter, to a halt, and they waltzed together around the post. As they came about the mustang approached. The rider was obliged to turn clockwise around the post. Yet for some reason Leo could not fathom, the gypsy on his mustang came careering towards him, on the wrong side of the road. The rider took his right hand off the reins and reached up behind him and pulled something from his hair. His black hair loosened and fell long and wild around his shoulders. He came veering towards Leo with his right arm extended behind him. Leo walked the white colt forward. The Burton lad leaned out as far as he could towards Leo and as he came past swung the blade in a wide arc across Leo's torso. Leo leaned away. He walked the colt on and out across the road in a diagonal from the left- to the right-hand side. He turned his head and watched the Burton rider struggle to slow the mustang and bring it past the post on the correct, left-hand side. He saw the thin blade fall to the ground.

Leo felt like he had been scratched, as if he'd been fool enough to go blackberry picking bare-chested. He bent forward and looked down and saw a thin, darkly reddening line drawn aslant his chest. What was it? He took a hand off the reins and spat on a finger and wiped the cut with saliva. It was nothing. A slight incision in his skin. He looked back. The black-haired gypsy lad had finally coerced the palomino mustang around the pole and was turning to come back home.

Leo squeezed the colt's ribs with his bare heels and in a moment the white horse was cantering. Leo did not wish him to go faster but he could not stay him for he had given the animal his word. He would not slow him now. Yet the colt did not gallop. Instead he cantered easily, as Leo wished he would. Somehow the colt knew. The boy sat high up on his back and the horse bore him like some imperial hero coming home. They cantered, waiting for the palomino mustang and its rider to catch up with them, and when that pair came abreast some yards away across the road Leo looked over at the Burton lad and waited for him to glance back. When he did so, the gypsy's black eyes seemed blind with hatred. Leo smiled, and held out his hand as if to offer a sardonic handshake to the older youth. He saw the eyes fill and widen with darkness, before the palomino galloped on ahead.

The boy turned back and kicked the colt and leaned back down into his rider's clinch. The white colt accelerated out of his canter and within yards had overtaken the mustang. Leo hung on. Ahead of him the crowd on either side of the road was a heaving throng of bodies, as those behind jumped up for a better view and fell, and many waved their arms and shook as if riding some invisible horse themselves in their wish to encourage their rider. He could make out one among them, a giant at the front, George, who had lifted the boy and carried him and brought him back to life.

Leo glanced back. The palomino mustang was falling behind. The gentile boy and the white colt rode clear, coming to victory. But then they turned inexplicably away, off the road. Towards a stand of oaks. The crowd went quiet. As the pale, half-naked boy, with nothing but the trousers he wore, the reins in his hands and the white horse beneath him, struck out for the distant moor.

PART THREE
THE DERBY

1

Lottie, June 1913

The point of the handicap,' Lord Grenvil told his daughter, 'is that the weight a horse carries determines the speed at which he can gallop.'

'No, no, Duncan,' said Lord Prideaux. 'That is merely a description. The point, Alice,' he said, leaning forward a little from his seat in the carriage, 'is that without a handicapping system, everyone would know which horse is likely to win. Obliging the faster horses to carry weights makes for more even, unpredictable races.'

Alice Grenvil nodded. 'And how is the handicap judged?' she asked.

'That's simple,' her father said. 'The handicapper has the results of every race run during the season so far.' He held up his left hand and with his right counted off the fingers. 'He knows what weight each horse carried. The distance of the race. The condition of the course. The form of each of the runners. He'll have a report on the pace of the race and the distance between each horse at the finish.' Having no more fingers, Lord Grenvil sat back.

'For every race?' Alice said. 'Sounds like a doddle, dear father.'

Arthur Prideaux smiled. 'In addition to all that information,' he said, 'the handicapper will want to know of any incidents that might have occurred to impede this horse or make that one's position better than it deserved.'

The girl, Charlotte Prideaux, gazed out of the window. Fields of ripening corn and grazing beasts racketed through her field of vision; dense pockets of woodland.

'It sounds to me,' Alice said, 'like an impossible job. The handicapper must have to be some kind of mathematical genius. I can't begin to imagine his desk, covered with sheets of scribbled calculations.'

'It's even worse than that,' Duncan Grenvil said. 'Yes, he needs to assess the factual information, but he has also to interpret it. A horse came third in a race but the handicapper learns that the ground was soft, and he believes this horse likes hard ground.'

'I suppose he'll have help from the owners and trainers in that regard,' Alice suggested.

Both men found this speculation amusing. 'A good handicapper is inherently suspicious. He doesn't trust a soul,' Arthur Prideaux said. 'Not owners, not trainers. Jockeys least of all.'

'Why not?' Alice asked.

'Because, Alice, they're all hoping to pull the wool over the handicapper's eyes. Not to mention those of the bookmakers and the ordinary punters. In order, quite simply, to get long odds for a good horse, which they can then gamble upon and make a fortune.'

'Or more likely lose it,' Duncan Grenvil said. 'Talking of reckless gentlemen, did I tell you that Hugh Lowther invited us to pop into his box tomorrow for the customary plovers' eggs and champagne?'

The girl knew the man of whom they spoke, her father's friend Hugh, Lord Lonsdale. When he travelled by train to visit them he reserved two sleeping compartments, one for himself and the other for his dogs. Her father and Duncan Grenvil spoke for a while about extraordinary sums of money won and lost on horses, agreeing with each other that the great plungers were extinct. There were no true gamblers left.

The train braked sharply as they pulled into a station. Westbury. They idly watched the commotion on the platform. Some travellers left the train, others joined it. Porters wheeled their trolleys to the luggage van. Doors closed with reassuringly conclusive percussion. In due course, their carriage creaked as the locomotive pulled on it.

'It's awfully good of you to join us, Alice,' Arthur Prideaux said. 'Lottie's wanted to come for years, haven't you?'

'Yes, Papa.' The girl gazed out of the window. On the estate, human beings and animals cohabited the landscape. You were never far from another person, working, for all the fields, fences, ditches, hedges, lanes, culverts, drains, copses, had to be kept up. Yet this land they rolled through, this England, was huge and barely populated.

'You could hardly have come without Alice, could you?'

'No, Papa.'

'So when I decide which horse to back,' Alice said, 'I should look at what weight the handicapper's saddled them with, but I should also study their form and so on, and come to my own conclusions?'

'Very good,' her father said. He paused to light his cigarette.

'I shall be glad to advise you, Alice,' Arthur said, 'should you need it.'

'She won't,' her father said. 'As I've told you, Arthur, in a healthy bloodline each generation's brighter than its predecessor.'

'Indeed. *Das Ei will klüger sein als die Henne.* Though possibly not as difficult in your case, Duncan, as in some.'

The girl turned from the window. 'It's not a handicap race.'

Alice returned her gaze. Lottie shook her head. 'Most flat races are, but none of the Classics.' The two men and the young woman looked at the girl, who turned back to the window.

116

'It's gratifying to know that one's offspring does listen to what one says,' Lord Prideaux said. 'Occasionally.'

'Yes, Papa,' Lottie murmured, the glass misting from her spoken breath.

There was a knock at the door of their compartment. The train attendant informed them that lunch was being served in the restaurant car.

In the third-class carriage Lord Prideaux's valet Adam Score offered the maid, Gladys, a cigarette. She took it and put it between her lips. He lit a match and held it up to her cigarette but the yellow bulb of flame at its tip would not stay still.

Gladys pursed her lips around the cigarette so that she could speak. 'Your hands is tremblin, Mister Score.'

'It's this bloody train, it's bouncin all over the place.' The match burned down.

'As long as it ain't me makin you nervous.'

Adam Score flinched as the fire reached his flesh. He shook the match out. He put it in the ashtray beneath the window and lit another.

'You'd make any man nervous, Gladys,' he said, holding one hand with the other to steady it.

Lord Grenvil's valet stood to fetch his pipe and tobacco from his bag in the luggage net. 'Will you be havin a flutter, Gladys?' he asked.

The maid sucked on the cigarette and blew the smoke instantly out of her mouth. 'I'm hopin

Mister Shattock might give us a tip or two.' She turned and spoke across the central aisle, to the man seated on his own. 'Won't you, Mister Shattock? Give us a tip for the gee-gees?'

The master's groom smiled. 'I shall,' he said. 'And I'll give it now. Put your tin on the favourite. A little each way.'

Alice Grenvil's maid passed round the luncheon baskets they'd bought at Taunton station. They opened the baskets and inspected the bread and butter and cheese. There were various meats. Adam Score said he could not eat tongue, it did not agree with him. Gladys said there was an answer to that but she would not give it in polite company. She agreed to swap her slices of ham for the valet's tongue. Herb Shattock had ordered beef sandwiches. Others had chicken. The men had purchased in addition a bottle each of stout. The women drank ginger beer.

Gladys asked Mister Shattock more about the bookmakers. Were they bent? Could you trust them? It was true, he said, that in the old days there were those who would take punters' money then try to slip away during the excitement of the race. Welchers. He'd seen the odd one caught and badly beaten. But all was in better order now.

Adam Score said the problem with betting was the dope. 'The Yanks brung it over,' he claimed. 'Got some old nag and give her a shot a cocaine. She run as if possessed a the devil, eyes startin

118

out of her head, sweat pourin off of her. She raced past a field a the finest thoroughbreds and won her crooked owners a pile a loot.' He told them of one who crossed the finishing line in first place. The jockey dismounted and the horse took off again and galloped straight into a brick wall. 'Killed outright,' he said. 'That's true, that is. I heard it from the master his self.'

The maids agreed how scandalous the dope was. They asked how it was administered. Were the horses injected?

'No,' said Herb Shattock. 'They was given this poison from a bottle.' He told them that doping had been banned long ago. In 1904. Those caught doing it were warned off. Perhaps it still went on. It could give a bad horse energy, but made a good horse run itself out too soon. He said Americans were not all bad. He himself had learned much from them concerning the ventilation of stables. 'We leave our doors open now. The horses is much cooler than we used to keep them, and they're much happier,' he said.

In the restaurant car the two friends were also reminiscing about Americans they had known. Their daughters sipped Brown Windsor soup.

'You girls have heard, no doubt, of the new style of riding they brought with them at the end of the last century. The forward seat. We called it "the monkey on the stick".'

'The trouble is, they did win a deuced lot of races.'

'That has nothing to do with it, Prideaux. It was ugly then and it's ugly now.'

'The odd thing is,' Arthur said, turning to Alice Grenvil, 'that they used to ride with even longer stirrups and straighter backs than we did. Your grandfather, Lottie, do you remember him?'

'No, Papa.'

'I suppose not. He travelled in America. Saw some racing in Kentucky. He told me they were most beautiful horsemen. What happened was this. What you have to remember is that America is vast. A continent. There used to be a good deal of remote, up-country meetings—primitive affairs with barely trained horses and local riders. Now Johnny Huggins told me this himself, Duncan. He used to send a decent old plater round, and if a young, local horse beat his, he'd buy it and bring it home. Under his training and his jockeys these horses often improved enormously. But then the trick stopped working.' Arthur shrugged and opened his arms to demonstrate the depth of the mystery. 'Johnny couldn't fathom it.'

Arthur Prideaux stopped speaking in order to consume his soup before it grew cold.

'Well?' Duncan Grenvil said. 'You're going to tell us these up-country horses were being ridden by the Rieff brothers?'

'I suspect,' Alice Grenvil said, 'that the horses

120

were getting thinner. They'd been following these faddish Yankee diets.'

Lord Grenvil laughed at his daughter's joke. Arthur Prideaux choked on his food. Duncan slapped him on the back. There were certain qualities that were particularly welcome in a woman. Intelligence was one, that was true, but wit was surely another.

'Good try. Both of you,' Arthur said. 'Do you care to hazard a guess, Lottie, since this seems to have become a parlour game?'

'No, thank you, Papa,' the girl said.

Arthur Prideaux raised the side of his bowl and scooped a last spoonful of thick soup. He swallowed it. 'One day,' he resumed, 'Huggins bought one of these winning horses, and the nigger boy who'd ridden him begged Huggins to take him too, for the boy loved this horse so. Huggins took him on as a stable hand.' Arthur paused to take a sip of claret. 'Now, Johnny Huggins raced this horse and the damned thing lost, to the very plater he'd beaten up country. Huggins couldn't understand it. The black boy asked to be allowed to ride the horse. Sure enough, the boy won. In fact, he won on whatever he rode. He was the most successful jockey Huggins had ever had, though the boy claimed that riders just as good were ten a penny in the state of Georgia.'

'And he rode in this manner?' Alice asked.

'Indeed. The reason being that no one had ever taught these boys to ride. They were thrown up on old broncos, without a saddle or even reins. So they held onto the mane and crouched up on the withers and held on as tight as they could. They found their balance and it turned out to distribute the rider's weight upon the horse better. It wasn't long before most of the top American riders were black. The very first Yank to come over here and win a race was a nigger—Willie Simms—almost twenty years ago now. Funnily enough, we had a boy on the estate rode like that, a ploughman's son.' Arthur sighed, lost in his memory of Leo Sercombe riding at Bampton Fair. 'A sight to behold,' he said. 'Ugly, perhaps, but thrilling.'

Lost in thought, Arthur Prideaux seemed suddenly to realise where he was and that his daughter was there too, sitting next to Alice, beside the window. He looked over at her. She gazed at the passing landscape, giving no indication of having been listening to what he said. He shook his head, took another sip of claret.

'And we'll witness this style of riding in the Derby, Arthur?' Alice said.

'Not quite,' he said. 'You'll see Danny Maher. Your father won't agree, but I consider him the finest jockey we've ever seen. He told me that the good American courses are much flatter and more even than ours. Here, once a horse's footing is disrupted, it's almost impossible to get its balance back when you're stuck up on its neck. So he rides a little lower and further back than he would in America.'

'Arthur's right, dear,' Duncan Grenvil said. 'I do disagree. There's been no one to touch George Fordham. Not before him, not since. The greatest exponent of the waiting game we ever had. Another facet of the art of horsemanship I fear you girls will not see. Nowadays they're all off and away and just dash em round like brainless whippets.'

'True enough, Duncan,' Arthur said. 'I'm just old enough to remember Tom Cannon. So stylish a rider that during a race he had time to check how finely polished his boots were. No, the Derby's not what it was. The House of Commons used to go into recess for the day, so that members could attend. It really meant something then.'

After lunch, as they made their way back to the compartment, Lottie visited the lavatory. She did not hurry. The hot and cold water in the wash-basin impressed her, the flush toilet too. She wondered where the waste went. She switched the electric light on and off. The illumination was feeble and yellowish. When she came out, her father was waiting for her in the corridor, smoking at a window.

' "Yes, Papa," ' he said. ' "No, Papa." How long

do you intend to continue this performance? It's been almost a year now.'

Lottie looked up at him. 'I don't know, Papa.'

They stood aside to let a conductor pass. 'Could we not call a truce?' he said. 'That we might all enjoy this excursion? Do you think it's fun for the Grenvils?'

'Will you have them back?' Lottie said.

Her father smoked his cigarette. He leaned his head back and blew the smoke up to the open window. 'The ploughman and his family?' he said. 'I don't know where on earth they are.'

'You could find out.'

Arthur Prideaux nodded slowly. 'Yes, I suppose I could. But I cannot have them back. Nor the boy. If you truly do not understand that, all I can say is that one day you will.'

'And one day, Papa,' the girl said, 'you will understand how wrong of you it was.'

Lord Prideaux shook his head. He turned and walked along the corridor, swaying with the motion of the carriage, back towards their compartment. His daughter turned and made her way in the other direction.

There were first-class and third-class carriages on the train. Second class did not exist. Perhaps it never had. Or perhaps an entire category of people had vanished. Second-class people were shipped out to man the Empire shortly after the railways were invented. That was probably it. The girl could not come up with a more rational explanation.

The third-class carriages were open. There were more people to look at, as an alternative to staring out of the window. She saw their party of valets and maids but passed them without a word. She walked along, counting the carriages. There were seven. The luggage van was the eighth. She walked along the corridor. A crewman sat upon a suitcase, dozing. When she reached the end of the train she gazed out of the back door, at the parallel lines of the track spooling out behind, converging in the far distance.

'Are you all right, Miss Charlotte?'

The girl turned. The figure of her father's groom filled the corridor.

'I saw you walk through the carriage,' he said. 'I trust that nothin is amiss.'

She assured him that she had merely wished to stretch her legs. He said that he too found the confinement difficult to deal with. It made him uneasy. To be seated while hurtling across the fields at a speed impossible by any other means—it was strange and disagreeable. He believed the speed of a horse was as fast as man was meant to go. The girl smiled and Herb Shattock acknowledged the partiality of his opinion.

'The first horseman must a been a mighty strange sight,' he said. He bent forward and they watched the view out of the back window together.

'Can I ask you something, Mister Shattock?' Lottie said, turning from the window. 'You come to the Derby with my father every year.'

The groom straightened his back and stood up. 'I do.'

'Why?'

Herb Shattock smiled. 'A fair question, Miss Charlotte,' he said. 'Few would ask it quite like that.'

'I know you're his groom,' she said. 'But from what he's told me, he spends all his time with Lord Grenvil. He's already got his valet to look after him. Do you love the Derby, Mister Shattock?'

Herb Shattock took a deep breath and gave out a long sigh. He pondered the question. Perhaps it was more difficult than Lottie had intended or realised. Then he nodded. 'Your father,' he said, 'has a stake in a stable. It is only one of his business interests, he might have many for all I know, but I believe this one's dear to his heart. The stable is known as Druids Lodge. You might have heard of the Druids Lodge Confederacy?'

'No.'

'Known also as the Hermits of Salisbury Plain?'

The girl shook her head.

Herb Shattock frowned. 'There's no one owner,

126

but the ringmaster, if you like, is a Mister Cunliffe. It was he what brought the master on board. They was friends at school, as I believe.' The groom paused, and pondered the matter a while, as before. 'I don't know as I should tell you all this,' he said.

Herb Shattock had taught Lottie to ride. He'd chosen her ponies, first the little Welsh dun mare, then Embarr the blue roan, then Blaze. It was said he'd been particularly fond of her mother, a fine horsewoman and side-saddle rider; had been almost as heartbroken when she died as Lord Prideaux himself.

'As you know, I go to Ireland periodically to buy a hunter for your father. I found your Embarr there. The Druids Lodge Confederacy buy their horses in Ireland. I am a scout. I meet Captain Forester and the vet Mister Pearl there, tell them if I seen any promisin foals for sale. They brings their purchases back here and trains them in seclusion up on the Wiltshire Downs.' He raised his chin and gestured out of the window, as if should they look now they might see these gallops as the train passed close by.

'Do they have a horse running tomorrow?' the girl asked.

Herb Shattock nodded. He confessed that they did. It had been a lovely bay colt he himself had seen two years ago and recommended. Mister Cunliffe bought him, in a group of three yearlings. It was always a lottery buying yearlings, of course. 'And unfortunately that colt has grown into a savage beast,' the groom said. 'Aboyeur by name. You'll see him. And you'll see Mister Cunliffe too. You can't miss him. You might think the farmer Amos Tucker, on Manor Farm, is a weighty man, but Mister Cunliffe must be twenty stone.'

'So Aboyeur won't win?' Lottie asked.

'No chance at all,' Herb Shattock said. 'Except the outside chance that every horse has. And at the long odds he'll be on, he'll be worth a shillin or two of any punter's money. But do not mention that to anyone, Miss Charlotte. Anyone at all. Not Lord Grenvil. And not Miss Alice, neither.'

The girl looked up at the stocky groom. He looked suddenly worried. He had said more than he should.

'I won't.'

'Good. Now how about I escort you back to your carriage? The master'll be wonderin where you've got to.'

2

On the day following, the party left the Grenvils' town house in Belgravia and took a cab to Victoria Station. Arthur Prideaux and Duncan Grenvil wore morning dress, with silk top hats. Alice Grenvil wore a pale yellow gown of organdie, with a high-necked yoke and sleeves of transparent net. Bodice and skirt each had wide fluffy tucks. She wore long white gloves, and a hat decorated with flowers made of coloured material, and one enormous white feather. Lottie marvelled that it stayed upon Alice's head. She herself wore as plain a dress as she'd been able to find, blue and white, made of dimity, with a minimum of lace trim around the skirt. Her own hat was really a straw boater adorned with another of those ridiculous feathers, and she had constantly to hold it in place for a breeze or the jostling throng threatened to upset it.

The Grenvils' valet had all their tickets and they boarded the train. Herb Shattock was not among them. He had spent the night elsewhere. The maids were on holiday, and could barely contain their excitement. The heaving crowd in the station concourse appeared desperate to flee the capital. It might have been on fire again. All London, it seemed, was headed for Epsom.

3

The girl watched the jockeys come out of the weighing room, carrying their saddles. They walked along the path to the parade ring. Together, they were of a similar size and unremarkable, but as they entered the ring their lack of height became evident in comparison with other men. All were small and slight as boys, though they were of varying ages. Some were old, wind-wizened horsemen. The smallest looked particularly young. The boy had dark eyes, seemingly focused on something no one else saw. He reminded Lottie of Leo.

A pale-faced jockey passed close by them and Lottie saw that his teeth were chattering. Alice said she felt sorry for him, for what he was about to do was exceedingly dangerous. But Duncan Grenvil claimed that nerves were a good sign in a rider, just as they were in a horse, an indication of pluck.

Arthur Prideaux assured the girls that the man was the king's jockey, Herbert Jones, and he always looked like this. They should not be concerned. Jones had won the Derby for the Prince of Wales at his first attempt and again, when Teddy was king, four years ago, on Minoru. That was an unforgettable occasion. 'When the king led his victorious horse into the parade ring, right here, people threw their hats into the air, it was like a flock of birds taking off. Do you remember what Granville said about Teddy?' he asked Duncan. 'That he was loved because he had all the faults of which an Englishman is accused.'

Alice said it was a fine sentiment. Duncan wondered whether Teddy's son, though blessed with countless virtues, could hope to match his father in the affections of the nation. Lottie said that she could scarce remember the old king.

Her father appeared to know half the people milling around them. She wondered how, for at home he led a socially isolated life and showed no apparent wish for more company. She thought they had come for the races, yet he was constantly stopping to chat with his fellow spectators. Some people studied their racecards, others strode purposefully though it was not clear where they were headed. Many wandered around, looking for faces they recognised in the crowd. Alice was most concerned with the women and their attire. The day was becoming increasingly warm but all were committed to whatever they had chosen to wear. Alice shared her observations with Lottie. That there could be such subtle variety of material, colour, cut and trim, was it not extraordinary?

Arthur Prideaux gave his daughter pin money, Duncan Grenvil likewise. They introduced the girls to a bookmaker who would take their bets. They bought Dorling's Correct Cards, with their lists of runners and riders. Arthur Prideaux whispered information to Alice Grenvil: 'This horse has a mouth like silk.' Alice took note of what she considered relevant and ticked off her fancies on her card. She wondered what would happen to her money in the case of a dead heat. Arthur Prideaux said he did not know. Long ago there was a tie and the two horses were sent back later in the afternoon to run the course again. A dead heat occurred once more, at the very first Derby he himself attended, in 1884, at the age of fourteen, the same as Lottie here. On that occasion those involved agreed to share the prize money and the crowd complained vociferously.

'We all wanted a winner,' Arthur said. Whether the bookmakers paid out he could not remember. He suspected not, for bookies never would unless they had to.

Lottie preferred to watch the horses in the paddock. They were extraordinary creatures, all taller and more elegant than the best of her father's hunters. A beautiful blood-chestnut horse. A big lengthy filly, with glorious shoulders, straight hocks. A washy chestnut had four white legs. Lottie could not take her eyes off a great raking bay gelding. But beyond their equine beauty—the nap of their coats brushed till it shone, their manes plaited—it was as if she could see into them, their skeletons, their bones moving in the articulation of their joints. The girl wanted to know more, about their muscles, ligaments, blood. How everything worked.

Knowing that she was going to put money on them, Lottie estimated their likely prowess and found the prospect mesmerising; watching how a horse moved but also gleaning or guessing what one could of its character. Some of the animals were excited or made irritable by the crowd close around them; others remained placid. There was a little mare, all wire and whipcord, barely over fifteen hands. Lottie placed a bet on her to win the first race, the Woodcote Stakes. The mare came in last.

Alice had taken Arthur's advice, placing an each way bet on a horse whose jockey's colours she liked, and won. She wondered whether fillies as well as colts would run in the Derby, or whether men had barred them as they did women from the more important races of this world. Her father reprimanded her but Arthur Prideaux said that Alice had a point. Duncan Grenvil said that a filly had won just last year. Tagalie. Ridden by the Yank, Jonny Reiff, who was on the favourite today.

'If a filly is entered,' Arthur Prideaux said, 'the colts have to carry an extra weight.'

'Don't you think,' Alice said, 'this principle might be applied to human affairs? A little handicap where necessary, so that men and women may compete for the same prizes?'

'For the more significant prizes,' Arthur said, 'there need be no handicap.'

Lottie watched them. She did not quite follow their conversation. It occurred to her that her father and Alice Grenvil were speaking in some kind of code. She saw Alice blush. And all of a sudden Lottie understood that Alice was not the chaperone here. Lottie herself was. The girl turned and pushed her way through the throng, away from the stand and across the course to the vast and bustling interior of the horseshoe-shaped track.

4

Though the first race had already been run, people were still flooding in. Lottie watched the free-for-all between vehicles drawn by horse and those powered by combustion engine. Four-in-hands driven by military-looking men in boldly checked trousers. Landaus, brakes, broughams, chaises, gigs, brightly painted dog-carts. Open-topped omnibuses, their jostling passengers swaying on the top deck. A convoy of black taxicabs. A motorcycle ridden by a man wearing goggles, with an enclosed sidecar, presumably bearing his passenger, weaving in and out of the other vehicles, startling horses.

The smells of cooking drew Lottie on to the food stalls. Hot fat sizzled and spat, savoury sausage fried in one pan, onion in another, over gas-powered flames. She swore they used methods of cooking that intensified the smells for they were unbearably enticing. The stalls were in reality ingeniously constructed carts, only the wheels betraying their mobility. They sold beef-steak pies and kidney puddings. Ham and beef, pork pies, cold sausages, hard-boiled eggs. One advertised baked sheeps' hearts. Another stall called itself a *delicatessen,* and sold sandwiches made of sardines, smoked salmon, German sausage.

Lottie watched customers purchase penny slices of batter pudding, over which the stallholder poured a spoonful of pork gravy. People turned away to eat their pudding and how gravy was not spilled upon their clothes or shoes she did not know. She could resist no longer and bought a slice. It tasted coarse and delicious.

The smell of fish mingled with that of meat. There were oysters and fish sandwiches. Fried fish, and fried fingers of potato, wrapped in paper. When people had paid they took salt with finger and thumb from a box on the counter and sprinkled it on their food. The girl had not heard of many of the delicacies offered. Tripe and onions. Eel jelly served in a cup with a spoon. One stall sold eel pie. The proprietress lifted the lid of a metal bin before her and took a hot pie, ran a knife around its dish and turned the pie out on to a piece of paper for each customer.

Some food vendors had no stall but merely a barrow. One sold peanuts, another baked potatoes. Had they walked all the way from London to Epsom?

There were drinks—yellow lemonade, ginger beer, coffee and tea—and sweets. Hot apple fritters. Candy floss being spun from pink sugar, the air around sweet and sticky. Dark red-coated toffee apples. Lottie bought herself a bag of bullseyes.

There were beer tents. Marquees. Boxing booths. A sprawl of tents across the Downs. She heard a snatch of military music from a brass band in the distance. A barber had a stall composed of a small banner on which was painted his prices, a box for the implements of his trade, a bowl of water and a single chair. Upon this sat a customer whom the barber shaved. Lottie looked down and saw straps hanging from the two back legs of the chair and understood the barber carried it from place to place upon his back.

A lunch party sat on chairs around a dinner table. They had eaten well. The table had been laid with a full service on a white cloth, but now empty wine bottles stood amongst the detritus of the meal. A man dressed as a clown entertained the diners with slapstick, though he appeared to have drunk as much as they and was not funny.

In the middle of the carnival was a fair, far larger than the one that had visited Taunton last year. Carousels, boat swings, dodgems—all powered by steam engines that hissed and whistled with a smell of hot oily vapour in the air. They issued without warning small black clouds of soot that settled on the summer dresses of those who passed too close by. Lottie forgot about her companions, and the races they had come to watch. There were sticks to be hurled at coconut shies, a penny a throw. Rifle ranges, darts aimed at playing cards, hoopla stalls. There were bearded ladies. Snake charmers.

'Guess your age, darlin?'

The man had a drooping moustache.

'Give us a penny . . . money back if I get it wrong.'

The girl was sure that he would for she was tall for her age, taller than most full-grown women. She took a penny from her purse and handed it over. He looked her up and down, then stared into her eyes. Less judging her physiognomy than peering into her mind and finding there what she hid. Mesmerism, it was called. He said, 'Fourteen.' Lottie nodded, and moved away.

A woman in some kind of uniform handed the girl a leaflet for the Temperance Society. Perhaps Lottie looked like a precocious sot. She joined a group who stood before an Open-air Mission. A woman held a placard that stated, *Behold the Lamb of God*. A man with a bulbous nose stood on a crate and promised eternal life to those who gave up drink and gambling and took up the way of the Lord. A punter yelled out if he was so wise, did he have a tip for the Diomed Stakes about to be run? Another, did he wish to be stuck for eternal life with a mug like that? And other such ribaldries. People's smells—perfume, sweat, tobacco smoke—grew stronger as the crowd pressed upon her.

Two children stood, seemingly on show, the girl's dress and the boy's suit decorated with lovely patterns made of mother-of-pearl buttons. A woman festooned likewise passed a box around requesting contributions for the London Hospital. The children appeared bemused by the attention though they must have been used to it.

When she saw Herb Shattock pushing slowly through the crowd towards her, the girl thought that he would see her. But he was deep in conversation with the largest man she had ever seen. This must be the one of whom Shattock had spoken. Though so large as to appear an invalid, the man walked with a comfortable gait, his body rolling from side to side, and people parted to make way for him. The pair passed close to Lottie without seeing her and she watched them disappear.

Gypsy women sold lucky charms, nosegays or posies of wild flowers, purple heather. One stood in front of the girl and handed her a sprig of white flowers. 'Tell your fortune, love?' she said. She wore a blue and yellow skirt, and a red shawl wrapped around her shoulders. 'Real Romany, mind, not like half a them there, only the likes of us've got the foresight, love.'

Lottie felt impelled to pull away but equally to stay. 'All right.'

The woman took her hand. She studied it. She shook her head and looked up and into Lottie's face. They were the same height. The gypsy woman had black eyes. She said, 'You'll see him again.'

'Who?' the girl asked.

'There's no doubt about it, he'll come back. It's not over, not by any means.'

'Who?' Lottie said, but the gypsy let go of her hand and said a penny would do it, she was glad it was good news she could see. The girl gave her a coin.

She climbed the hill. Families with prams and baskets and umbrellas sprawled on rugs with their picnics. Many had come the night before, her father had said, parked their carts and pitched their tents on Epsom Downs.

Some spoke with an accent the girl supposed they'd brought out of London. She had heard it the night before, on arriving at Paddington, and again this morning. Unlike the West Country burr of those on the estate and round about them, whose words issued naturally from the speaker's lips, it seemed to her that these cockneys, if such they were, had to contort their lips to force the words out in order to sound as strange as they did.

At the top of the hill Lottie looked down on the carnival below her. Turning east, London sprawled across the land. She could make out Big Ben. And a great church . . . was it St Paul's? She could see the Thames, threading its way into the city. And that was surely Windsor Castle, to the west.

'Ere, darlin, you lost, are ya?'

The young man stood swaying on the sloping ground. His friend pulled him upright and said, 'Come with us, girl, we'll take you ome.'

The first man appeared to find this suggestion hilarious. 'Yeah, we'll take her ome, Billy, won't we?'

Lottie turned and walked away. Within a few strides they had caught her up and now accompanied her, one on either side.

'You don't want to be on your own up ere, girl,' said the comedian. Billy. 'You can stop worryin now, though, you're safe with us. Ain't she, Tommy?'

'Yeah, you stick with us, darlin.'

'I'm all right, thank you,' Lottie said.

'No, you come with us, girl,' Billy insisted. He had hold of her right arm. The other man, Tommy, gripped her left arm, pinning it to her side. If he had been drunk, he was no longer. They marched across the hill, through the crowd, where to she could not see and did not know. She was not sure if she was walking. It might have been that they had lifted her from the ground and carried her away, and her legs though moving had no say in her ambulation.

The girl attempted to struggle but her body would not obey her. She wished to cry out for help but she could not. Her voice did not work. She saw men, women, children as she passed them and implored them to come to her aid, but the plea went unspoken. They did not see her, or if they did saw only three friends strolling.

Lottie could not understand it. She had not known fear of this kind before: induced by human beings. She had not thought that she could be scared of other people. Only of death and who it took. Yet this was a paralysis, and she was terrified. The men smelled of beer, their clothes reeked of tobacco and sweat. Then it was as if she had come to life, yet without knowing it, for she felt the men beside her shoving and writhing. Then suddenly she was free. Stumbling forward, the girl turned and saw Herb Shattock holding each man by the hair of his head. He swung them towards each other, letting go of their hair and sliding his meaty hands around their skulls before he cracked them one against the other. The impact made a sound like that of croquet ball and mallet meeting. The two men staggered. One bled. Shattock struck one upon the chin with his fist, then the other likewise, and each fell to the ground and lay inert.

The girl stood and stared from the bodies on the ground to her father's groom. He breathed deeply, his mouth closed, chest rising and falling, as he surveyed his victims. Then he looked at the girl.

'Let's get you back,' he said. 'The master'll be wonderin where you is.'

Herb Shattock indicated the direction in which they should walk. He headed that way and she followed and walked beside him.

'I heard rumours a trouble,' he said. 'More layabouts than usual, that's for sure. There's more bobbies but not enough. Down the Rubbin House more n likely.'

Lottie's legs felt weak but as they descended the hill her strength returned. So too did her voice. 'I don't want to go back,' she said, and stopped walking. Herb Shattock did likewise. 'Not yet.' She frowned. 'I want to watch the Derby with you.'

'We should get you to your father.'

'Please. Nothing will distract him from the race. We'll go directly after.'

Herb Shattock looked around him, as if one amongst the crowd might arise and offer him the answer.

He nodded. 'All right, Miss Charlotte,' he said. 'Come along. They'll be almost off.'

5

They walked fast down the hill, through the crowd, past the tents and food stalls, hucksters and entertainers, Herb Shattock not breaking stride and Lottie having to trot periodically to keep beside him. As they drew closer to the racetrack the crowd thickened, and he forged a path through the throng that she could not. She found it more sensible to drop behind and follow in his wake, holding on to his jacket. She glanced up and saw the sky had clouded over somewhat, though the afternoon was still bright and there felt no chance of rain.

They approached the course. The groom did not slow down but pushed on, easing people out of his way, the girl clinging on to him. Some complained at being so manhandled or of the breach of etiquette but Shattock paid them no mind. Soon they reached the rails and he turned aside to let the girl squeeze past him. He stood behind her. The stand containing her father and the others was on the opposite side of the track. A line of horses and riders had come out and the first walked past directly in front of them.

'The king's horse,' Herb Shattock said. 'Leading

them out onto the field. Ridden by Herbert Jones, what won it twice before for Teddy. You might recognise His Majesty's colours.'

The royal silks: the purple body of the shirt, with scarlet sleeves. The black velvet riding cap with a gold fringe. White breeches and white silk scarf. Lottie watched the horses walk up the course, one after the other. There were fifteen runners. She asked the groom which was the one her father had a stake in, and he said it was the one in blinkers. He might not look like a savage but he was, and had no chance. The jockey, Edwin Piper, was good but not top notch. He was due to ride a different mount, Knight's Key, but that horse was scratched. Shattock did not know who had been jocked off Aboyeur to let Piper ride him.

He gave a commentary in Lottie's left ear. The favourite was that beast, Craganour, ridden by the Yankee Johnny Reiff, glaring at the crowd as if to defy them to boo him. Both he and his brother Lester had been warned off some years previous, had had their licences revoked, for pulling their horses or some such dishonesties, and were disliked by a good few punters. But Johnny was not merely a good rider. He knew how to win, and that made him popular with many more.

Lottie asked Mister Shattock to point out others. Which jockey was her father's favourite, another American? That was Danny Maher, there on Lord Rosebery's horse, Prue.

When the horses had passed out of sight the groom and the girl studied their racecards. She said that Aboyeur was a beautiful bay colt. She liked the white streak down his face, and did not believe a horse was made bad. Trainers made them so. The groom smiled and allowed she might be right. Aboyeur and the favourite Craganour, of which he had heard nothing bad said, were sired by the same stallion, one Desmond by name.

'Then they are brothers,' the girl said.

Herb Shattock nodded. 'Half-brothers, yes.'

'Then I should like to bet on both of them.'

They squeezed back out of the throng and he took her to a tic-tac man who stood beneath a large banner bearing his name, Henry Bradberry. He stood making hand signals like some kind of dance designed only for the arms. She could not see to whom he gesticulated. Mr Shattock took her money and put it down for her equally on her father's horse and on the favourite, half a crown each way.

They returned to the rails near the finishing line, the swarthy groom once more pushing his way through, to the consternation of those ahead of him, and waited. The horseshoe-shaped racetrack stretched for almost one mile and a half. The groom told Lottie that from the start it bent slightly to the right but then curved around to the left, rising over one hundred feet. Then it would come down again a little to Tattenham Corner, the first place they would be able to see the horses. The girl leaned over the rails and peered to her right. Herb Shattock said that, as she could observe, the surface was cambered, the inner rail upon which she leaned, appreciably lower than the far one. Then the track came downhill from the Corner until the final half-furlong, where it rose a fraction once more towards the finish right there in front of them.

Lottie could not make sense of what he said nor what she saw. She turned and said, 'But why? Why do they not flatten the course and make it perfect?'

Herb Shattock smiled and said, 'Then it wouldn't be the Derby, Miss Charlotte.'

Lottie looked around her. All were excited as she was. An odd agitation shared by so many strangers. The groom reached over her shoulder and gave her his binoculars. She thanked him and looked through the lenses for her father and Alice and Duncan Grenvil, in the stand on the far side of the course, but could not find them. Then she realised that those around her had gone quiet. All were facing to their right. She looked too but there was nothing to see. Then she heard a sound. It was that of people shouting, yelling, cheering, in the distance. Then she saw movement on the track, blurring into view down around Tattenham

Corner. She raised the glasses to her eyes and adjusted them and saw the horses coming.

For a long time they did not seem to draw closer, whether because they were coming more or less directly towards her or by an effect of the glasses she did not know. There were many of them, nine or ten, seemingly all packed together. Then she identified her father's horse, Aboyeur, in the lead. Herb Shattock told her he thought that was Craganour coming up outside. Others were gaining on the inside. By now spectators all around them were yelling but the girl could not hear what they said for she was too intent upon the sight in the circular frame of her vision. Suddenly Craganour lurched across, bumping into Aboyeur, causing him to veer towards the rail, hampering those coming up the inside.

Was that allowed? Surely it was not. She watched. The jockey Edwin Piper struck Aboyeur with the whip in his left hand, causing his horse to lurch to his right and into Craganour. As he did so Aboyeur reached out his neck and bit or attempted to bite his brother.

Now the jockey of Craganour, the American, whipped his own mount. He held his whip in his right hand, and so drove his horse back towards Aboyeur. The horses' hooves disappeared as they hit the dip, and then they came rising up for the final hundred yards, both jockeys thrashing their horses, bumping them repeatedly against each other even as others on either side drew closer to them.

The riders worked furiously but it seemed to the girl that they and the horses were slowing on the incline as they came to the post. By now they filled the lens and she lowered the binoculars and looked up to see them flash past just yards away from her, the sound of their hooves thundering loudly into the turf even with the crazed yelling of the crowd around and behind her. The huge beautiful beasts with their small jockeys like insane parasitic creatures, past her and gone at a speed she could not fathom. She turned and watched them, now slowing to a canter, the jockeys' backsides lifting clear of their saddles, easing their mounts down.

A second pack of also-rans followed, one of them riderless, and behind them the crowd spilled onto the track and rushed to the finish to see the winner in the ring. Herb Shattock and the girl did likewise. She had no idea who had won in the blanket finish, it had happened so fast, but he said it was Craganour for sure. Who came second or third he did not know, and did not envy the stewards' job.

They found Lord Prideaux and Lord Grenvil in the crowd around the winner's enclosure. There was no sign of Alice. If the girl or the groom thought that her father might be relieved to see her they were mistaken, for all he said was, 'There you are, Lottie, did you enjoy the race?'

The stewards had put Craganour first by a head from Aboyeur and a neck from Louvois in third. There was no objection made by the loser, though some expected one, for all the rough riding in those final furlongs, so the clerk of the scales gave the instruction that the winner was all right, and the flag was hoisted. There was a great roar, for Craganour being clear favourite had the most backers amongst all those punters present, and many rushed to the bookies to collect their winnings.

Duncan Grenvil was dejected for he had put his money on Danny Maher, riding Prue, swayed—so he claimed—by Arthur's eulogies of the American rider. Arthur Prideaux said that his friend was surely swayed more truly by the winnings he'd made on Maher in the past, but though once a great jockey he had not won the Derby in almost ten years.

Then there was unrest among the crowd. The flag had been taken down. This, Lord Prideaux said, was unprecedented. He sent Shattock off to find out what had happened. Some around them gabbled their own theories but most were simply confused, and gaped, waiting for enlightenment.

Meanwhile Alice Grenvil appeared. She was in a tearful state. She told Lottie that she had gone out looking for her and seen a terrible thing.

Right in front of her. Directly across the course a madwoman had bobbed under the rails and calmly walked out into the middle of the course. The first group of horses had already passed and the second group bore down upon her. One missed her. She tried to grab the reins of another. 'The king's horse,' Alice said. 'Anmer. I saw the rider's silks.'

The groom returned and said that one of the stewards, Eustace Loder, had demanded an enquiry. This Loder claimed Craganour had jostled Aboyeur and a stewards' adjudication was necessary. The girls' fathers and the groom went to stand amongst those milling about outside the stewards' room.

Alice held Lottie's arm and stopped her following them. She said that Anmer hit the madwoman at full gallop head on with his shoulders, knocking her with great force to the ground. 'She rolled over and over and lay unconscious,' Alice said. The horse had stumbled, pitching the jockey clear over its head.

'Anmer missed her somehow. And the horses following swerved by and missed her and the jockey too. Anmer rose up and went on.' Alice took out her handkerchief and wiped her eyes. 'The poor jockey, Lottie. His foot caught in a stirrup and he was thrown. He didn't move. They brought a stretcher for him and when they lifted him up, it was like they were lifting up our Lord for the Deposition. The poor, poor man. I pray to God he lives.'

Then the verdict of the stewards' enquiry was announced. Craganour had bumped and bored Aboyeur and interfered with other horses too and so was disqualified. Herb Shattock came over and told the girls that the jockeys had all spoken out against Johnny Reiff and his use of the whip. Arthur Prideaux and Duncan Grenvil were in contrasting moods. Lottie's father had won more money than ever before today, it was a miracle. Duncan Grenvil said it was a poor show that Prideaux had failed to advise him to put money on a horse he had a stake in. A very poor show. 'They didn't even let the beast into the parade beforehand,' he said. 'They saddled him separately from all the others.' He looked to the girls for support.

The fat man Lottie had seen on the hill with Herb Shattock passed close by, but neither her father nor the groom acknowledged him, nor he them. Alice tried to tell her father and Arthur Prideaux what she had seen, but neither paid her any mind for there was so much to ponder and to argue over, which they did all the rest of the afternoon, and upon the train back into London, and on into the evening of the day.

PART FOUR
COPPER

1

Leo, June–July 1913

The boy rode the white colt to the moor, up on to the granite massif. The tors loomed on the horizon, small in the distance but when he came to the first one he saw the great weight of granite. Once upon a time volcanoes had bubbled and erupted here and left huge boulders on the hillocks and ridge crests, the tors of Dartmoor, like the ruins or relics of some geological religion, as if an enraged earth had erected monuments to itself.

He rode on, bare-chested, barefoot, saddleless upon the colt. He knew that none of the gypsy horses could catch him and did not believe they would try. But they might. The tors had patches of moss or lichen but were mostly grey. Yet somehow, coming closer, he fancied one was blue, and rode up to study the rock. The closer he came so the tinge of blue was lost, in the manner of a blue roan horse. Perhaps not like a roan exactly for he touched the granite and was able to trace the veins of some finer-grained and lighter rock. It was curious.

Leo rode on. He turned the horse westward, across purple grass and bog cotton, searching for

157

paths over the wet moor. The horse trod warily on black soil, sodden, soft and springy. The moor was empty, and quiet save for a light soughing wind.

The day was cool but the noon sun warmed his white skin. He came across a circle of stones, granite obelisks planted at two- or three-yard intervals. For what purpose it was not possible to say. Beyond it was a small herd of ponies. They were like Exmoor ponies but had more variety of colour. They had small heads and large, wide-set eyes. They watched the pale rider, or more likely his mount, like plain maidens at a village dance into which a beautiful visitor has trespassed. Their ears twitched, suggesting that listening to this passing vision was as important as seeing it. They had strong bodies, with broad ribcages, well-muscled hind-quarters. Their manes were full and their tails long and flowing as they turned as a group and moved away.

The ground dried and Leo and the colt crossed heather and the dark leaves of whortleberry bushes. The moor opened out and he could see the full extent of it looking westward laid out before them, sloping away into the distance. He saw a man digging on his own surrounded by nothing on that windswept heath. No horse or cart. No dwelling, not a tree. Only the lone labourer, who dug narrow spadefuls of black earth that did not crumble but cohered in rectangular tablets, which he removed and laid down to one side in a row then dug the next. The man stopped working to watch the shirtless and unbooted rider pass, each an apparition to the other on the empty moor.

Leo rode down past gorse bushes studded with yellow flowers whose pungent scent reminded him of something he could not specify, through green, aromatic bracken, and on into a steep valley, its bevelled sides ridged with buttresses of rock. In some of these granite was visible in black seams. In others, sparkling quartzite or some such mineral. The horse walked on silt, then sand, then on to valley gravels. They came to a stream in which cold clear water ran over smooth shining cobbles. The horse and the boy both drank deep.

They rode on. Sheep grazed on unfenced grass. Leo smelled a farm before he saw it. First smoke, then the muck pile. A wooden gate hung open, spars bent, split, the lowest rotting. The horse's hooves sounded in the stony lane and a dog barked. Leo walked the horse into the yard. Two muddy geese hissed at them. Grey stone outbuildings were closed or had their doors opened to darkness. Beasts resided within them, he was sure. The dog bared its teeth then slunk away.

The house was a different shape from Amos Tucker's commodious farmhouse. This was long, with a cattle byre evident to one side downstairs. Leo pulled the reins over the colt's head and tied them to a post and stepped forward and rapped upon the dark, heavy door. It opened, inward, almost instantly. A woman stood in the hallway, peering out at him.

'Do you have clothes?' the boy asked.

The woman did not answer.

'I'll work for em,' Leo said. 'Have you jobs? For food as well. I'll do anythin.'

The woman gazed out of the dim interior of her house at the bare-chested, puny boy before her. Then she looked past him.

'I's stronger than I looks, I can chop wood, or carry aught.'

The woman stepped out of the house and to one side and studied the white colt, with the avidity of one long hungry. She swallowed.

'I'll give ye clothes,' she said, 'for yon horse.'

The boy shook his head.

'I'll feed ye up an all.'

'No.'

The woman did not look at Leo. She addressed not him but the colt directly. 'I'll give ye all a my dead boy's clothes. They's in the wardrobe, the lot of em, not that there was many. We buried im in his best. You can have them others. I'll keep the horse.'

'I can't give up the horse,' Leo said. 'Let me work.'

'Ye can ave my old man's too. Ye'll grow into em.'

Leo shook his head. He wished to take hold of the woman and force her to look at him, see his need.

'I'd like that horse,' the woman said. 'I'll feed ye for a week.'

She looked at him now. They assessed one another. Weighed each other up. She was taller than he and rangy for a woman or at least a farmer's wife. He wondered if she had killed the man and the boy of whom she spoke. Or perhaps the man still lived and cut peat up on the moor. The afternoon was cooling. The sun fell. Leo trembled. He had no choice. The woman had white in her hair. She was not as muscled as she might once have been. The boy walked past her, through the open door and into the house.

'Where do you think you's goin?'

'I need clothes,' he said over his shoulder. She came after him. He saw the stairs off to the side and took them barefoot two at a time. At the top were two doors off a tiny landing. One was open, the other shut. He heard the woman climbing the stairs behind him.

'Get out a my house,' she yelled.

He stepped forward and opened the closed door. Some mouse or other rodent scuttled across the floorboards.

In the small room was a bed and a wardrobe, each of dark heavy wood. Nothing else. The boy opened the door of the wardrobe as the woman stepped through the doorway. There was a mirror attached to the door, which swung open and gave him a view of himself, a thin pale wraith with a faint diagonal line etched in pink across his torso. Then a view of the woman as she advanced towards him. Except that it was not her. Yet it was. He could make no sense of the sight. What was she? Leo turned from her reflection to see the woman true. She had lost twenty years, had climbed the stairs and become again the young woman she had once been, swift and strong. He shielded himself with his arms and backed into the corner, flinching. What infernal magic did this house contain?

'Is this he?'

'No.'

Leo cowered yet he was not struck, or seized. He opened his eyes and peered between his fingers. The woman scrutinised him. She now wore, he saw, a muddy smock. And behind her stood herself, aged as she truly was.

'It is,' said the younger version. ''Tis him or the ghost of him.'

'No,' said her mother.

'The white horse brung him.'

'He's a beggar come to steal your brother's clothes.'

'That white horse brung him back.'

The young woman came towards Leo. She placed an arm upon his shoulder and turned him

162

away so that he faced the wall and could not see her. All he possessed were his gypsy riding trousers. Perhaps they would soon hang in the wardrobe of this devilish abode.

He felt the young woman's fingers upon his back. Measuring him or probing his skin. For the point of a blade? Like a butcher?

'Don't pull em,' said the older woman from the doorway.

'I shan't,' said the other. 'I twist em.'

Leo could feel her fingers on his skin but not what she was doing. 'Did ye ride through bracken?' she said. 'Picked yourself a couple or three ticks ere.'

When she had removed the blood-sucking insects she bade the boy sit upon the bed and picked out clothes for him. Her mother had disappeared. She chose a white flannel shirt, woollen socks, and a black serge suit. She told him to take off his trousers. Unabashed by his nakedness she had him put on her dead brother's clothes. They smelled of someone other, yet they fitted Leo well. The boots were too big but he believed his feet would soon grow to fill them.

Downstairs in the kitchen the mother had warm stew. There was no meat in it. Leo ate greedily. The vegetables were soft and collapsed upon his tongue. The bread was hard and tasted stale but he ate all she gave him, and drank the tankard of flat beer too. The young woman had gone. She reappeared and said that the white horse was feeding and the boy thanked her.

The two women watched him eat. The light in the room was fading. The young woman told the boy he should stay the night, but he said that he could not, he must press on. She did not insist, nor ask him whence he came or where he aimed to go. The mother said that if he sought work he should try the mines, though not the one in which her son had drowned. Her daughter said that he'd be lucky to find such work for most of the mines had closed. Wheal Friendship remained, east of Mary Tavy, not two miles from here, he could not miss it.

'There was a man,' Leo said. 'Digging turf. Is he yours?'

The two women looked away from the boy and at each other. 'I warned im,' said the mother.

Her daughter shook her head.

The mother said, 'I warned im for the last time.'

'I knows you did,' said the young woman. She rose from the table. From the corner of the kitchen she took up a wooden post or cudgel the boy had not noticed before and left the house by the back door. The boy rose too. He thanked the woman for the food and the clothes and walked to the front door.

'Wait,' said the woman.

Leo turned and saw her take down a cap from a peg in the hallway. She gave it to him.

He thanked her and put it on his head. Like the clothes it fitted him snugly.

Outside, the colt stood where he had been left. He munched the last of the hay from an empty tub. Beside it was a half-drunk pail of water. The reins had been removed and lain down on the ground by the wall of the house and in their place the colt had been restrained by a halter. Leo picked up the reins and walked the horse out of the yard. He did not mount up but walked on in the darkening afternoon until he saw a barn in a field. Its stone-tiled roof was half caved in but one end of the building was dry and there was straw, many years old by the look and musty smell of it. The boy gathered stalks and wisps of straw into a pile and lay down and slept, the white colt standing hobbled for the night close by, sentinel of his safety and his dreams.

2

In the morning, the boy in his new suit rode the horse bareback. He rode down deep, winding lanes. Hawthorn trees blossomed white, or pink. Crab apple trees likewise. Birds sang of his passing. He rode past white cottages with grey slate roofs. Leo asked their inhabitants where the mines were. All were friendly and assured him how fortunate they were to live here, in this land so rich in minerals. In the coombes and woods on the western margins or periphery of the granite moor, mines had flourished for centuries. They told him of the lead at Florence Mine up in Lydford parish, of silver at Crandford Mine in Bridestowe, of zinc at Wheal Betsy just up the road. Sadly all were closed at present. They directed him to the village of Mary Tavy and Wheal Friendship mine nearby.

The mine was not one pit or shaft but covered acres. Granite buildings shaped in squat blocks. High pyramids of black spoil. Chimneys, from one of which spouted pungent fumes. Others stood unused. There were rail tracks leading out of the earth. Along them a man pushed a barrow filled with some kind of rock, clattering loudly. Many buildings appeared abandoned. The noise of machinery issued from inside one, pumping and stamping. The colt looked askance at it, but let Leo lead him past. One massive waterwheel turned. Others did not, the water courses that fed them blocked or dried up or otherwise defunct.

The boy was directed to an office in the Counting House. He tied up the horse outside and knocked upon the door and entered. One man sat at a desk, writing in a ledger. He looked up.

'Yes, boy?'

'Have you work, sir? I'm lookin for work. I have a horse. He can work, too. The horse and me.'

The man removed his wire-rimmed glasses with long, thin fingers bent like claws and peered through rheumy, grey eyes at the boy. He did not answer but turned to another man, who was reading something at a table with his back turned to the room.

'Did you hear that, Arnold?' he said. 'We have before us an optimist.' He glanced back at the boy and studied him a little longer, then once more addressed the other man, or at least his back. 'The young men hereabouts are leaving or have left already. Gone to work in the iron mines of Cumberland, so we're told. The coal mines of the north. As navvies on those new railway lines in the Home Counties. Yet here we have one hopeful lad, and with his own horse no less, come to offer us his labour. Will you not stir yourself to look upon him, brother?'

The man Arnold was heavyset, unlike his brother, and it seemed to take him a considerable effort to stir from his reading. He tried but could not turn his body much and so was obliged to stand, and twist his chair, and sit down again in order to behold this unlikely visitor.

'Do not mind my brother and his contentious manner of speaking,' he said. 'We can find you some odd jobs, boy. For you and your horse.' He rose once more, took a deep breath, and steadied himself. 'I'll show you round.' He turned to his elder brother. 'You stay there, Captain. Do not stir yourself. I'll show the boy around.'

Leaving the colt outside the office, Arnold Mann escorted Leo Sercombe on a tour of the mine. He explained that theirs was an industry in decline. Tin had been the great product of this moor but when their buyers could purchase cheaper ore from Malaya all did so. It was the same with copper. 'Fifty years ago more than half the copper used throughout the world . . .' the large man stopped and turned to Leo, spreading his short chubby arms '. . . the world,' he repeated, 'came from west Devon and Cornwall. But then it came cheaper from elsewhere.' He shook his head. 'Abroad. So much for the Empire, eh? Does it help us?'

He showed the boy the smithy, the carpenter's shop, the dressing house. In one or two places a man pottered, retainers waiting for work to be brought to them. In the engine house the air was oily. A steam engine pulsated. It raised the tubs of copper ore to the surface, Arnold Mann said. Recessed in the solid walls were bearings for thick axles to turn huge cable drums. The boy had never seen such massive machinery. The metal cables ran over pulley wheels above the pit, for raising and lowering the cages. 'Back in the old days, the men climbed down the shafts on ladders,' Arnold Mann said. One man looked after the engine, his face smudged where he'd wiped the sweat of his brow with an oily hand. The boy was not being shown jobs he might do but given a history lesson. A metal flue from the engine ran through the large shed on its way to the chimney stack. There were wooden racks around the walls. The mine owner asked the boy what he thought they were for. Leo shook his head. 'For the miners to dry their wet clothes.'

Arnold Mann and the boy followed men who pushed trolleys along the tramway, to the crushing and sorting sheds. Here the ore was washed and separated on noisily vibrating tables over which water flowed. Back outside again, they walked uphill, the corpulent man stopping every now and then to get his breath back. He smelled of snuff. He said that a great problem here was water, inundating the sub-terrain, flooding the mines. He asked Leo with what did their clever predecessors solve the problem?

The boy did not know.

'With water!' said Arnold Mann. They built waterways, or leats, bringing water from up on the high moor to turn waterwheels that powered pumps that pumped water out of the mines. 'Was that not clever?' he said. 'All before the age of steam.' He was proud of his ancestors as another might be of his children. 'There are miles of shafts and tunnels underground,' he said, stamping his foot upon the earth. 'Beneath us, all around.' He opened his arms wide again. 'We have maps,' he said, as if the boy might not believe him. 'Our deepest shaft is over two hundred fathoms.' He sighed. 'Closed now, of course.'

Leo followed him back down. Arnold Mann said that what men there still were at the mine lived locally or lodged with families roundabout. In the old days many had kipped in the bunk-house. He did not know how many did so now. Naturally they had a stable but he could not remember where. He and his brother, who was the captain of the mine by virtue of being the eldest and no other reason, lived in the Counting House.

Arnold Mann returned to the office, leaving Leo with no advice or instruction. He untied the colt and led it round searching for the stable but could not find it. Perhaps the owner was mistaken and there never had been one. He found a shed with two dozen bunks. It smelled of old wood and stale sweat. The stove was cool to the touch. All was covered in grey dust. Leo went back outside and walked the colt out until some way distant they found a patch of new wet grass and he let the horse graze. He broke a branch and stuck its sharper end into the ground as a stake and tethered the colt to it. He climbed further up the hill. From a height he looked down upon the mine. There was something strange about it and now he could see what that was. Nothing grew there. Grey stone buildings, ground of cinders or gravel, heaps of black waste.

3

There was no work for the horse. Leo left him in the bunkhouse. There was no food either. Men brought their own and at crib time took pity on the boy, each giving him a morsel of their own, until the Mann brothers had their housekeeper make him pasties. Both the proprietary brothers and the miners treated the boy as a curiosity or mascot. They sent him on errands so that he could exercise the horse. A miner needed matches from the shop in Mary Tavy, paid for with mine tokens. Captain Mann needed a book returning to his friend William Crossing.

On the third day they put him to work in the refining of mundic or mispickel, known also as arsenical pyrites. It stood around in waste heaps. Now arsenic was in demand, for weedkiller, insecticide, medicine, the manufacture of paint. No longer despised. More profitable than tin or copper. On the dressing floor he learned to wash and separate the mispickel from ore.

On Saturday afternoon the men knocked off early and received their wages in the Counting House. They walked out from Wheal Friendship and set off in various directions. Leo was given four shillings and sixpence. He rode the colt out. At a farm he purchased hay and a bag of oats. Back at the mine he poured oats into a bin he'd found. The hay he separated into what he estimated were mouthfuls for a horse and the rest he laid on the floor of the bunkhouse.

On Sunday the mine was silent. Leo left the colt to feed and walked over to the Counting House. The Mann brothers came one after the other out of the front door as he approached. Leo took off his cap.

'We are going to church, boy,' Arthur said. 'You are welcome to join us.'

Leo regarded the two dissimilar men. Perhaps one resembled a fat mother, the other a thin father. Or vice versa. They were dressed as on every day in dark suits, coloured waistcoats and ties, white shirts. But these were clean and pressed, their boots shining. He looked down at his own dusty suit. He raised his head and shook it.

'You see, brother,' said Captain Mann, whose first name was Ernest. 'As I've told you, mining makes heathens of men.'

Arthur ignored his brother. 'You are not inclined to take Holy Communion?' he asked.

Again Leo shook his head.

'A mere lad,' said the captain. 'Been here a week.'

'He's not even gone underground,' Arthur said. He began to walk along the lane out of the mine. 'I thought you said it was proximity to the infernal regions that caused their nihilism.'

Captain Mann carried a stick, which he did not appear to need for walking since he raised it and used it rather in the manner of Miss Pugsley the boy's old schoolteacher, pointing at script on her blackboard, though in his case it was at something in the air only he could see. 'Perhaps he climbed down a shaft in his spare time. Driven by curiosity as foolish people have been ever since the very first.' He followed after his corpulent brother, speaking all the while, emphasising his points with his stick, until the words were lost, and soon the brothers too vanished around the first bend in the lane.

Leo knocked on the door of the Counting House. There came no answer. He knocked again, more loudly. Perhaps the housekeeper had gone to chapel. Or like the miners went home. Could he munch hay? He turned the handle and pushed the door open and went in. Doors gave off the hallway to an office and the counting rooms. The brothers' living quarters were upstairs. He walked quietly along the hallway to the kitchen. It was silent, clean, tidy. There was nothing out of place. No dirty pans or plates or cutlery. The sink was empty.

There was a doorway the boy had seen the housekeeper come out of carrying food. He surmised it led to the larder. He opened the door and stepped inside a narrow room illuminated only by a small square window at its far end. This window was slightly open, pivoting from hinges along its bottom rail, but wire mesh covered the opening anyhow. The larder was much cooler than the rest of the house. Along the two walls were wooden shelves stacked with jars and tins and bags of food. Upon a long granite worktop stood four plates, each displaying a joint of meat that was protected by a wire-mesh hoop or bell put over it: ham, beef, chicken and pork.

The boy returned to the kitchen and found a carving knife. He sharpened the knife with a steel and returned to the larder. He carefully sliced a thin strip off each of the cold joints. Back in the kitchen he cleaned the knife and used it to cut two slices of bread off a loaf he found in an enamel bin. Between these he laid the four slices of meat. The sandwich was too large to fit in a jacket pocket so he cut it in half, put one half in each pocket, cleaned the knife and put it back in the drawer in which he'd found it. Then he took a single carrot from a rack of vegetables and left the house as quietly as he had entered it, as though despite his certainty that it was empty yet someone watched him all the while.

Leo rode the colt up onto the moor. He found a track and nudged the horse in the flanks with his heels, just hard enough to let him know that he could go as fast as he wished to now. The white colt cantered across the bleak terrain. He gave the impression that he could happily gallop if only he had a reason to, was a horse in search of a race.

The damp air smelled of peat. There was some bird or birds hidden in the heather, cheeping persistently. They rode beside a leat, perhaps the same one Arnold Mann had shown the boy. In its bed were grey stones stained brown. As he sat the horse gazing around, a lone sheep came floating along. It looked clever, and smug to have found a novel way to travel from one place to another, saving its frail legs as no other sheep ever had. The ewe lay on its side. Perhaps it was asleep and would at any moment wake up and clamber out of the leat, shake the wet from its wool and totter off. Then Leo saw its eyes were open and realised he was wrong. The ewe had drowned.

Again they came across wild ponies. He stood the colt and watched them from on high make their way down a shallow valley. He counted nine. They paused to graze. One ate thin grass, another chewed gorse, a third pulled sedge from the water's edge. Such was their varied menu. After a brief feed they moved on. They had to be tough to live up here all year round. Leo reckoned the white colt would not last a single winter. The boy watched the Dartmoor ponies until they disappeared. Browns, greys, nondescript, differing yet not easy to distinguish one from another. He rode down to the same stream and dismounted. While the horse drank, Leo dislodged stones from the bank and used one of them as a tool to mix up black mud. This he took up in handfuls and plastered across the hide of the white horse, speaking to him as he did so, explaining the need for disguise since he was such a singular creature and the Orchards would not rest until he was theirs once more.

There was little wind. It was so quiet on the moor the boy thought he could hear his own heart gently beating. Leo walked the horse up to a tor and tethered him in the weak sun for the mud to dry, then climbed the rocks until he found a perch on which to sit and eat the lunch he'd taken. He opened the bread and pulled loose a thin slice of ham, rolled it into a tube and chewed it. The taste and the texture burst upon his tongue like the revelation of some truth that a wise man might express in words but was given to him by this other sense. It was not the Holy Communion of wine or wafer, but it did seem to him like the sacrament of some other ritual, once practised but since lost in time as all things were. He ate the meat and bread, crouched upon the rock in his fine suit, and beheld the horse below and knew not whether he was blessed or cursed. Wealthy or poor. Free or bound. Joyful or desolate. In time he might discover.

The boy looked around. He knew the tors

were long-extinct volcanoes. He imagined them centuries ago waiting for God to light them like fireworks. Then the explosions of stone. Around the hills below them were strewn heavy grey boulders, most of random shape yet some perfect headstones or obelisks. A leat ran like a thread of grey steel around the contour of a hill. He looked out to the west. The land lay in ridges, like the ridge and furrow of the old agriculture, as if a Cornish giant farmed out there. On a promontory of land stood a church like a proud outcast of some schismatic sect, to add to the Baptists and Methodists, the Plymouth Brethren, Salvation Army, and doubtless others the boy had failed to ever comprehend the point of.

When he climbed down, Leo walked away from the rocks, then turned abruptly in order to look upon the horse as a stranger might. It was a feat of magic, no less. The elegant beast had been replaced by a scruffy, uncared for, unremarkable cob. Though his form was unchanged, really. Leo approached. The colt looked mournful, like one standing in the rain, head down, unnaturally still. Downcast, miserable.

'How can you know what you look like?' Leo asked him. 'What do you care?'

The horse would not look at him. The boy shook his head. He peered up at the sky as if beseeching the clouds for assistance, then back at the horse. He threw up his hands. 'I hear you,' he exclaimed. 'You damn beast. I hear you.'

The boy rode his muddy horse down off the high moor, descending some way south to where he'd that morning ascended. There at the edge of heathland he discovered further mine workings. These were entirely abandoned. The roofs of buildings had begun to collapse as the wooden beams rotted. Doors and windows were disintegrating. Grains of soil had accumulated on gravel and spoil; seeds of wild grass or weeds had sprouted therein, giving the landscape a watery wash of green like a first thin coat of paint. A ramp ran down into a large pool. Leo pulled loose some tufts of scratchy heather. He removed his jacket, shirt and waistcoat, then his trousers, and laid them on a rock. He led the horse into the water and stood him there while he brushed and scraped the once again wet mud off, apologising for whatever insult he'd inflicted. The water was horribly cold. Leo shivered as he worked, naked but for his boots, standing in the water up to his waist, his boots drenched but necessary to protect his feet from the horse's hooves. When the white colt was once more clean Leo pulled on the clothes over his damp skin. He rode the horse out of the quarry, trying to eat the carrot he'd taken despite his chattering teeth.

Back at the bunkhouse Leo gathered wood for the stove. The Mann brothers were back in their house and he begged a light. Arthur gave him a box of matches. He lit the stove and hung his wet boots and damp clothes all around to dry, and sat wrapped in a musty blanket close by, watching the flames. The horse too stood there, warming himself, perhaps lost in the fire's display as the boy was, with the same vague ruminations. Who could say?

On Monday morning the miners returned to work. None said a word but moved warily, with eyes half closed. No man worked harder than he had to. Leo did not know whether they suffered hangovers still from Saturday night or had drunk on the Lord's day too.

Three men did not turn up so they put the boy to work in the ovens. These were huge stone-built calciners where the mispickel was roasted. Vapour passed through a huge flue, condensing upon its surface. The men covered Leo's hands and feet. They padded his mouth. They blocked first his nostrils, then his ears. He was given a metal scraper and a bucket, and sent into the metal flue-pipe. He spent that day working hard. They told him that he would be paid three times as much as he had the week before. His eyes stung. When he took the plug from his nose he could smell the sulphurous odour. He looked at the men who worked there and understood that those who did not escape were dead men.

On the morning following, the boy rose before

first light. Rain drummed upon the roof of the bunkhouse. He gave the horse the remainder of the oats and when he had fed led him out of the mine. With the sack of hay tied upon his back like a rucksack, Leo headed west.

4

In the driving rain Leo walked on the leeward side of the horse, using the beast for protection. Still, he was soon soaked. A road curved south around the moor from Okehampton. The boy did not wish to be seen upon it and so kept to back lanes and tracks. Peter Tavy church had four knobbly decorated points at the top of its tower, like the crown of some comical king. A black crow spread its ominous wings and launched itself from the tower as if performing an act of great bravado.

The boy and the colt walked through the sodden land. At a dip in a lane, a run-off of water flowed from a field of red soil and swilled like a pool of blood. They splashed through it.

With no sun Leo had nothing by which to guide the way save for the road to his right and the moor on his left-hand side. The boy soon began to doubt his instinct. When he came to a mine he thought at first it was Wheal Friendship and that he had navigated a convoluted circular route back there, but it soon became apparent that this was a different one, abandoned. He found a shed with its roof intact and took shelter there. He broke up an old cupboard and lit a fire with the matches Arnold Mann had given him, which had kept dry in an inside pocket of his waistcoat.

Around midday, though the sky did not clear, the rain ceased and they set out again. Leo mounted the horse and rode. The sound of water running downhill, along streams, in underground drains and riverlets, accompanied them. The sky was grey but that single word did not begin to describe it. The boy let the colt plod and splash through the puddles in the lanes and studied the sky above him. You could dismiss the firmament as overcast or you could look at it. He did not have the vocabulary to describe the fluctuating shades of grey where the sun tried to shine through thin cloud here or rain-filled thick clouds there. He saw charcoal grey, pewter, ash. He saw slate, granite. But granite itself was not uniform. Neither were the cold ashes of a dead fire. A man would need a thousand words to describe all the varieties of colour upon which he gazed. Only a fool would say the sky was grey.

A wasp buzzed. Close by. It must be flying around his head somewhere. Except that some quality of the sound suggested distance. Not an insect. A machine. Approaching. He stopped the horse. The sound grew louder, coming closer from along the winding lane. Leo slid off the horse and pulled him hard against the hedge and gripped the bridle tight. A horn blew, high-pitched, like the alarm call of a fractious mallard, and the colt tensed. The combustion engine grew louder, then it appeared around the corner thirty yards away, and bore down upon them.

Eyes wide, the horse reared up as motorbike and rider screamed towards them. Perhaps what the colt saw was a grotesque parody of himself. Hooves replaced by wheels. Frame, rods and forks, pistons and pipes, the parts of a skeleton of a creature without flesh, nothing but bone. The colt pranced on his hooves as if the ground were suddenly too hot to stand on. Holding tight the bridle, Leo glimpsed the rider hunched over his motorbike like a jockey, gripping the handlebars with leather gloves, some kind of spectacles buckled to his head beneath a peaked cap, worn back to front.

The bike disappeared around the next bend and the sound of the engine, like the scream of some animal in pain, faded away. When the boy could hear it no more, still its impact remained, some strange resonance, as if it had sucked oxygen out of the air, and the atmosphere would require a period of readjustment.

Leo spoke to the horse, calming him from the terror of this intrusion. Holding the bridle with his left hand, he pressed the fingers of his right hand to the skin beneath the colt's jaw until he found the artery there, and felt the animal's heartbeat hammering, almost as fast as his own.

• • •

They rode down into the town of Tavistock. There was intermittent traffic: traps, a governess cart, carrier carts, drays. He was surely conspicuous amongst them. A number of the large granite buildings in the centre of the town possessed battlements, as if they aspired to the status of castles, yet the crenellations only made them look like children's toys. Like Lottie's facsimile, Leo remembered, of the big house in its own attic. In Tavistock he found a bakery and bought bread. In a provision store he bought a lump of cheese. A greengrocer sold him apples and carrots, and gave the boy a potato sack to carry these victuals.

Leo mounted and rode out of the town. He followed the Tavy river down along a wooded valley. In one stretch all the trees were being throttled by ivy. In another the trunks of the beeches were covered in moss of an intense green, as if these trees had grown themselves an extra skin.

The moist air smelled fresh from the downpour. No more rain fell from the sky but when a breeze shimmered through the valley, water dripped from the leaves. The rain had swollen the river, which ran dark brown. Four men built a wall beside it. Two dressed in waders stood in the water, the other two on the bank above. All stopped working to watch the boy as he passed them on the white horse, gazing blankly at him, none raising an arm to greet him or acknowledge his passing, as if he were some strange child of the woods of whom they had heard tell but never seen before.

He rode beside a stream, through a valley with fields of meadow and marsh grass, no beasts grazing thereon and woods rising to either side. He saw men cutting trees with long two-handled saws.

A chaffinch stood on the branch of a tree and called to him. Leo attempted to whistle back to it in its own language but it took off and flew away. He stopped and ate some bread and cheese. As he ate, Leo stood and listened to the birds. He could hear them calling—small birds, wood pigeons, crows. The air around him was composed of layers of birdsong.

In the afternoon he forded a stream and rode up out of the woods along a lane past large, long, quadrangular fields. Some for grazing, others ploughed. Beneath the young corn the soil was turning red again. As they kept climbing out of the steep valley, he and the horse rose straight up to the sky above, clear blue, washed clean by the rain. Up on the ridge he crossed a single-gauge railway line and then entered a large field across which a flock of sheep grazed. His arrival vitalised them. They came towards the horse, crowding all together, hustling and shoving, noisily bleating. They parted enough to allow passage through their midst then followed the horse and rider across their high field with a plaintive chorus of lamentation, beseeching them to stay. They'd hoped the boy was their Messiah long awaited, come to free them from their sorrow, yet they knew already that he was not, merely another false prophet, and so they wailed loud and resentful once again, a congregation grieving for themselves. If they could betray him to the gypsies they would.

In the cooling evening the boy sat his horse and looked upon the wide valley below, pondering his route down to the brown river, which snaked south, nosing its way towards the sea. Mist rose from the water. There was traffic on the river, boats of different size and sail. He could see one bridge. To the north was a quay with many buildings, and ramps, conveyors, sheds, bustling even at this late hour of the day.

Across a water meadow lay a path. A ribbon of mist formed along it as he watched. He kicked the horse forward. They descended the steep fields, the boy leaning back almost with his own spine along that of the animal, so sharp was the incline.

They rode along the misted pathway like ghosts of those countless animals and riders whose passage had hollowed out their route. As he approached the riverbank, Leo looked up. The bridge was a viaduct, raised on huge pillars, a hundred feet above the river. A train steamed across it. Halfway across, its whistle blew, for the benefit of its passengers, perhaps. Leo watched the plume of white smoke in the wake of the train dissipate in the sky, whose colour was turning to a paler blue before it darkened into night.

He rode on upstream, passing beneath two of the massive pillars.

'An a'penny for you, but if you wishes me to take yon horse twill be a penny a'penny.'

The ferryman was a stout, bearded man with muscular shoulders. He did not look simple but perhaps he was.

'I do wish to bring the horse, sir,' Leo said. 'How could I not?'

The ferryman shrugged. 'Let im swim?'

Leo looked across the river. Some kind of steamer sailed downstream.

'I won't be able to take no one else, see?' the ferryman said. 'They wouldn't want to share the platform with no horse who might turn spooky, see?'

The boy looked around. There were no people in sight, and little prospect of further passengers. He said nothing, but handed over the money and led the horse onto the barge. As the ground shifted the colt skittered, sliding his hooves one way and another to secure his balance. The ferryman loosed the rope coiled around a wooden post on the riverbank. He stepped onto the barge and took up the oar and placed it in a rowlock on the back plate of the vessel and began promptly to work it to and fro in the water, both oar and rudder in one.

Leo held the horse, and stroked his shoulders. The barge moved slowly but unwaveringly towards its corresponding bay on the far bank. The ferryman must have much knowledge and skill to work so consistently against the current. As they came into the middle of the river the boy saw fish in the water before and around the boat, a multitude of them, all swimming downstream. He turned in confusion to the ferryman and yelled to ask him what they were.

'Salmon,' the man called back. 'Come up the Tamar to spawn. This lot was born somewheres up there.' He gestured with his chin upriver. 'Two year old. Now they's headin out to sea.'

The barge progressed through the shoal of fish and on to the far bank. The quarryman turned the barge and docked. He secured the rope to its post. Then Leo led the horse onto the bank, and mounted, and rode on into Cornwall.

PART FIVE
DISSECTION

1

Lottie, July 1913

The lad walked silently through the walled garden, on through the glasshouse and down the steps to open the door. Sid Sercombe stepped into the dank cellars. The girl was there, waiting for him. Often she was not, and he would leave a package for her in the old oak cupboard amongst the stack of stowed furniture. He handed her a small parcel tight-wrapped in hessian.

She took it and did not thank him but said, 'Do you have more or fewer bones in your body now than when you were born, Sidney?'

The lad frowned and said, 'I do not know, Miss Charlotte.' He shook his head. 'I never thought about it.'

'Have you never studied a skeleton?'

'Not a human one, miss.'

'In that case,' she said in a tone of forbearance, 'you might consider the matter a moment now, and favour me with an answer.'

Sid pondered the riddle. 'Well, I never counted em,' he said. 'And I don't know as I've lost any. As I noticed, like.' He bit his lower lip in concentration. 'My brother Fred did push me out a tree when us was nippers and snapped the bone in my arm here. I thought twas mended but maybe there's two bones now where there was one before.' He smiled. 'Yes, tis a trick question, Miss Charlotte, and that's your answer. I has one more bone than I was born with.'

The girl shook her head. 'You have far fewer,' she said. 'You were born with three hundred. A number of bones fuse together in childhood. How old are you, Sidney?'

'Seventeen year old.'

The girl looked up at him. 'By the time you are fully grown, if you are not already, you'll have not many more than two hundred.' She nodded to the small packet in her hands. 'Now, what have you brought me?'

Lottie placed the parcel on a dust-covered table and untied the string. Then she unwrapped the hessian and beheld the contents.

'Oh,' she said. 'Another rat. Is that the best you could do?'

'Her's fresh. Alive not an hour ago.'

'But still. You have given me a number of rats.'

'See how swollen her belly is,' Sid said. 'Pregnant. And well on, I should say.'

The girl gasped. 'But that's marvellous!' she said. 'It's just what I wanted.' She folded the wrapping as it had been before and tied the string. 'Here,' she said, and gave the lad one penny. 'Thank you, Sidney.'

The girl turned and hurried away along the corridor through the cellars. The lad went back out of the door by which he'd entered and walked away from the big house.

2

The girl helped herself from the silver chafing dishes set on the sideboard: poached and scrambled eggs, haddock, kidneys. There were also hot rolls, three kinds of marmalade. A cold platter of ham. She carried her plate to the table. Her father read the newspaper. He tilted his head slightly and looked up at her over the top of his spectacles, and smiled, and returned to his reading. The girl munched her breakfast. The poached eggs were perfectly done, runny orange yolk inside firm white globes, which meant Cook had poached them herself. Anyone else and the yolk was too hard or even worse the white too runny, gelatinous, it made Lottie sick.

'Does it not bother you, Papa,' she said, 'to know that what you are reading about took place the day before yesterday?'

Her father looked at her, then lifted his cup and sipped coffee. 'Your grandfather's copy took not one but two days to reach here. Things are speeding up.'

The girl was unimpressed. 'I don't know how you can stand it,' she said, smiling. 'I could not.'

Arthur Prideaux removed his glasses. 'Much

of what is reported from around the Empire has taken days, weeks even, to reach London. Look at this.' He lifted the newspaper and brushed his fingers against the page. 'Skirmishes on the Northern Frontier district of the East Africa Protectorate. There's nothing there, only arid waste, but the few unfortunate inhabitants are raided for their cattle by Abyssinians. Tribes bring their own beasts in from Somaliland to graze and steal the water from the wells. Ivory hunters cross the border in both directions. It says here a gang of Abyssinian outlaws attacked a platoon of native rifles. Shot the British officer. Murdered the poor fellow. It happened weeks ago. What does another day matter?'

He reached forward and scooped a spoonful of marmalade, dolloping it onto the remnant of toast left on his plate. He lifted the toast and ate it. Lottie could hear it crunch between his teeth. He swallowed, and said, 'One is told that many of the stars in the night sky burned out long ago, they do not exist, their light has taken aeons to reach us, yet still we study them.'

'I don't.' Her father smiled again. Lottie saw and scowled. 'You read the news down here a day later than almost everyone else in England does, Papa. That is sad.'

Lord Prideaux shrugged, with mournful theatricality, as if to say, What can one do? One does the best one can in the circumstances.

'Would you rather live closer to London?' he asked. 'Or Manchester, perhaps?'

The girl shook her head and said, 'I'm sorry, Papa. If being a little out of touch with events is the price we pay for living here, it is a small one. You are right.' She poured a glass of pear juice and drank, then put her glass down and said, 'Where is your heart, Papa?'

'My heart?' He frowned. 'It is with you, my dear girl, of course. It is with your mother and always will be. But time moves on, and—'

'No,' she said. 'I mean, whereabouts in your body? The organ. Touch your chest to show me where your heart is.'

'Oh, I see. Well.' Her father raised his left hand then changed his mind and lowered it and raised his right hand instead and touched his jacket over his left breast.

'That's what everyone does,' Lottie said. 'You're all wrong. Our heart is in the middle of our chests. The bottom of it leans over to the left and the strongest pumps are located there, so that's where we feel our heartbeat. It's an illusion.'

'I didn't know that, my dear.' Her father nodded. 'Thank you. Most impressive.'

'Some of our organs are to the right and the left of our body. Like eyes and ears, of course. And kidneys.'

'I see.'

'Two organs that are almost identical, but not

quite. Have you any idea how many organs there are in a human body, Papa?'

Arthur Prideaux rubbed his eyes. 'I don't believe I do,' he said, but he was already putting his reading glasses back on.

'Almost fifty. Isn't that remarkable?'

'It is,' her father murmured, while glancing at his watch. 'I say, my dear, won't Ingrid be expecting you?'

'Which one do you think is the biggest?'

Lord Prideaux removed his glasses once again. 'What?'

'Which is the largest organ in the human body?'

Her father inhaled deeply, and sighed. 'I don't know,' he said. 'The heart?'

'No. You'll never guess, Papa. Nobody does.'

'Well, perhaps I just might. The lungs?'

'No. Do you give in?'

'Of course not. It's a trick question, isn't it? Some odd thing . . .' He gazed towards the table and swung his head slowly from side to side. Then he looked up. 'Of course! I know, the guts . . . they're much longer than we think. What's it called? The colon.'

'No. Shall I tell you, Papa?'

Her father breathed in and then breathed out, his shoulders dropping. 'Well, all right,' he said.

Lottie grinned. 'The skin.'

'Skin?' her father said. 'Piffle. The skin is not an organ, dear girl.'

'Yes, it is,' she said. 'Nobody gets that one.' She rose from her seat and turned and walked to the door, her father watching until she'd left the room before he returned to his two-day-old copy of *The Times*.

3

The dowager Lady Prideaux, Lottie's great-grandmama, no longer left her bed. In the morning her maid washed and dressed her, changed the bedding, then fed her, one spoonful at a time. Often she needed help with her tasks from Lottie's maid Gladys, for the old lady became distressed. The only one who could reliably calm her down was her great-granddaughter. So this morning after breakfast Lottie did as she always did before her lessons with Ingrid Goettner and visited her great-grandmama. The old lady lay whimpering like a frightened bird and Lottie took her hand and spoke to her until her agitation subsided. Then she placed a kiss upon her powdered cheek and left the room.

The girl studied Latin grammar for one hour then history for one more. While Lottie read of Romulus and Remus, then of William Tell, her governess marked the Latin/German translation she had set her.

At eleven o'clock the maid brought in a tray of milk and biscuits—some flavoured with lemon, others almond. Lottie told her governess that the crumbs would pass from their stomachs to their small intestines. Ingrid grimaced. Lottie said that this organ was twenty feet long. The molecules of food would creep through its walls to tiny blood vessels, or capillaries to be precise, and be carried in the blood to parts of the body where they could become molecules of new human cells.

'Of course what is not needed will continue, to the large intestine, and on to the rectum, and—'

'Yes, thank you, Lottie,' Ingrid said. 'It is very interesting. Just what I am wishing to consider as we take our elevenses.'

'It is natural.'

'It is crude.'

'Oh, don't be such a muff, Ingrid.'

The governess was of indeterminate age. Her unlined face could have been that of a girl but she wore dark, sternly cut clothes with high collars and her hair tight to her head, and her dark tresses had single white hairs scribbled amongst them if one looked at all closely. Lottie did not believe that she herself would become one of those vain, empty-headed women she had met at that summer's parties, yet she reckoned she would pluck such errant hairs if they appeared before they should. She wondered whether Ingrid might be as old as thirty or even forty but had not quite the impudence to ask. Nor had she determined the cause of her governess's limp.

'You are ready to leave, Lottie, this is plain to see. You must be patient.'

'I do not wish to leave. Why should I have to? Other girls don't go until they're seventeen or eighteen.'

'Oh, you will love Weimar, Lottie. Your German relations will amuse and entertain you, I promise.'

'They are not my real cousins. And Papa says I will not be able to take Blaze with me.'

'Yes, but there are muscular horses in Prussia too—the Trakehners. This is I believe the most spirited warm-blood breed in the world. Come, Lottie. Back to work. We shall read some Fontane.'

At lunchtime Lottie went to the kitchen where until this year she had always shared her midday meal with the servants. She understood it was frowned upon now and her meal was served to her in the dining room instead. She went to the larder and returned with a tomato, an apple and a potato of almost identical size. She laid them upon the kitchen table. 'Look at these, Cook,' she said. 'Which has the most water inside it?'

The cook was working at the stove and did not look at the girl or the items, but said, 'I haven't the foggiest, my lovely.'

Lottie shook her head. She turned to the three servants who had taken their places around the table for lunch. She repeated the question. 'It might be important,' she said. 'If you find yourself in a crisis. A person can go weeks without food but you'd never last one week without water. You'd be really up the stick.'

The head gardener Alf Satterley said he would study the matter. He reached over and took up the tomato, rotating it in his hands like a cricket ball. He put it back. The apple he scrutinised likewise, then the potato. 'I should a reckoned, Miss Charlotte,' he said, 'to decide by weight. Water I should say weighs more than the flesh of a fruit or vegetable. The potato weighs the most.'

Lottie made to speak but the gardener resumed. 'Yet I do not believe it, for I consider bitin into each a them. And when I does consider it, I find the tomato has the most water. The spud the least. The apple somewhere's in between.'

The others had followed what the old man said and now turned to the girl to hear her judgement. She frowned. 'You are right. A lucky guess.' She turned and said, 'I suppose I had better have lunch now, Cook,' and walked out of the kitchen.

After lunch, while waiting to resume her studies with Ingrid, the girl sat upon a sofa in the drawing-room watching her maid Gladys cleaning. She bent and dipped a cloth in a bucket of warm water and wrung it out till it was merely damp then wiped around the outside of picture frames. She climbed the stepladder to reach the picture rail.

'Do you know,' Lottie said, 'what most of the grime you're collecting is composed of?'

Gladys looked down at the young mistress. 'I should say tis mostly dust, Miss Charlotte.'

'House dust is largely made up of cells of the skin we shed. That's what you're wiping away.' Lottie closed one eye. She balled her hand into a fist save for thumb and forefinger leaving a miniscule gap between them. She held this up to her open eye and said, 'Thousands of infinitesimal flakes of dead skin.'

Gladys descended the ladder and rinsed the rag in the bucket once more. 'I should prefer to think of dust as dust, Miss Charlotte, if I may.'

'Or hairs,' Lottie said. 'Do you not find human hairs when you sweep the carpets? We lose about one hundred hairs a day from our heads. They fall out.' She saw the look of alarm on the maid's face. 'We grow many more, Gladys.'

'I suppose,' the young woman said, 'that Mister Shattock, the groom, his cottage must be clean's a whistle these days.'

When she joined her father in the drawing-room for afternoon tea, Lottie found Alice Grenvil already there. She was in the act of pouring tea for Lord Prideaux.

'Lottie, my darling,' Alice said. 'Will you have tea or lemonade?'

It was their custom for the maid to leave the

tray upon the table, with cakes or scones, and Lottie would serve her father. 'I shall cut the cake,' she said. 'Which would you prefer, Papa, ginger or fruit cake?' She kept an eye on Alice. 'Papa only takes a dash of milk,' she said.

'I know,' Alice told her.

'He cannot bear weak tea. Can you, Papa? And one sugar.'

Arthur Prideaux asked after Alice's father, his friend Duncan. She said he was well but London life bored him. He wished to come home. 'He says in his letter that the glory of our capital is the Thames flowing through it. But whenever he sees the river all he wants is to get a boat and row into the countryside.' Alice asked Arthur if he did not feel duty bound to attend the Upper House himself. He told her that he felt no such obligation for he had nothing original to say on the sort of matters under discussion and would not inflict his views on other members, but that he did attend if called upon. When there was some abhorrent bill to be resisted, for instance. He relied upon Duncan to let him know if his presence was required.

'Papa is not a country bumpkin, you see,' Lottie said. 'Whatever he claims. He follows events, but from a distance.'

'Through field glasses,' her father said.

'Mama was more involved, wasn't she, Papa? In improving the lives of people on the estate.

People still tell me about her work. And in the village. She persuaded Papa to build the new school.'

Arthur Prideaux accepted a second piece of fruit cake. Alice tried it too and said that she thought their cook to be top drawer.

'She is indeed,' Arthur said.

Lottie stuck with the ginger cake. It was dark, almost black with molasses, and moist. She savoured its texture in her mouth, its spicy taste on her tongue.

'Alice has a present for you, my dear,' her father said.

'Oh, yes,' Alice said. She rose and went out of the room, returning carrying a long box or case. She laid it on the floor at Lottie's feet and, kneeling, unclipped the catches and lifted the lid. She swivelled the case towards Lottie.

'You know what a terrible shot I am,' Alice said. 'And frankly I have no interest in improving myself. Your papa says you almost certainly do.'

Lottie gazed at the pair of light Churchill guns. Then she jumped off her chair so that she too was kneeling on the carpet and hugged Alice Grenvil and thanked her profusely. She let go and studied one of the guns and ran her hands along the stock and the barrel and the decoration around the name E. J. Churchill.

Alice glanced up at Arthur Prideaux and smiled and he nodded to her, smiling likewise.

4

Lottie Prideaux opened the door to the library and walked in. The room was empty. She looked around for the magnifying glass. Her father used it to read the old almanacs and encyclopaedias, whose print was too small to read with the naked eye. The people of earlier epochs had better eyesight. This was, he claimed, but one of many measures of human decline. She found the instrument and removed her jacket. Though she intended only to borrow the glass, she hid it inside the jacket when she left the room. She walked across the hallway and up the stairs. She saw and heard no one, yet felt herself observed. The big house itself seemed to be listening to her, watching her, as she climbed the stairs.

In the attic nursery Lottie laid out the implements she might need upon the table. In the hours between tea and dinner she could expect to be undisturbed. The small hammer she had found in the cellar, amongst a box of tools that she believed might once have belonged to a cobbler, though she was not sure at all. The tiny nails or pins she'd begged from the estate carpenter, who said he used them when glazing windows and gave her a handful. The small, sharp pair of scissors were in the sewing kit that had once belonged to her mother. The slightly larger, blunter pair she'd found at the back of a drawer in her father's desk. She had never seen him use them and did not believe he would miss them. The tweezers or forceps were her own. The board was an old bread or chopping board found in the shed in the back yard. She had two knives, one a penknife, the other a small kitchen knife Cook had missed at once and even now, six months later, would shake her head periodically and bemoan: 'Wherever has it got to?' Sid Sercombe had showed Lottie how to sharpen them, and given her a whetstone, a small bottle of oil and a sharpening steel. The pipette she had been given by the new veterinary surgeon, Patrick Jago.

Lottie unwrapped the parcel the under keeper had given her that morning and placed the rat on its back upon the board. She spread out its four clawed feet and pinned them to the wood with smart taps of the hammer. The creature had been dead no more than twelve hours and smelled strangely like a dog. A sharp but not unclean aroma.

She counted the nipples or mammary glands. A row of five along each side of its belly. There were three openings above the tail: this, the vaginal; this, the urethral; this, the anal.

Lottie gripped the rat's brown hair with her

tweezers and lifted a pinch of skin above the urethra. Using the sharp scissors she inflicted a small wound. Then using her tweezers she lifted the skin and inserted the larger scissors, their blades unopened, into the wound, and poked them in from side to side to rupture the connective tissue and separate the skin from the muscle beneath. One of the scissor blades was rounded at its end and blunt. With this one under the skin and the other sharper one above, she cut the skin of the rat along the middle of its belly up to its thorax.

Holding up the flap of skin with the tweezers, Lottie separated more of the tissue between skin and muscle using the same scissors, lifting the flap away, first on one side, then the other. The world around her disappeared as all her concentration settled on the small carcass before her. With the sharper, smaller scissors she cut the skin in diagonal lines out to each of the four legs, and lifted the two flaps of skin out, and pinned them as she had the claws, with a nail at each corner. Now she could smell the slightly metallic odour of blood.

All the viscera were there dimly visible beneath the encasing wall of muscle. Lottie made a hole in the rat's muscle wall beneath where she had done so in the skin and cut up through it, careful not to disturb what lay beneath. The muscle was thin from being stretched by the rat's pregnancy and easier to cut than normal. She sliced up as far as the ribcage, then cut through the thin bone as well. Cartilage and bone breaking made a faint sound and was soon done. Now she could scent a rank smell of meat. She made diagonal cuts in the muscle as she had the skin and lifted it out in flaps on either side and pinned it likewise.

Lottie had been surprised to discover that she was not squeamish. The inner structures and workings of the small bodies Sid gave her were so engrossing. She picked up the penknife in her right hand with her tweezers in the left and delved into the rat's innards. There was its diaphragm, separating the abdominal cavity from the thoracic cavity. There was the dark red liver. Beside the liver was the rat's stomach. She lifted the stomach and found what appeared to be a further part of the liver, yet it was separate from it so could not be, surely. She consulted the anatomy textbook the vet had given her. There. It must be the spleen.

The small intestine was orange. She did not know why. It was covered by globules of white fat. When people spoke of guts did they mean the stomach only or the whole of the digestive tract? The small intestine fed into the slightly larger intestine. Where they met was an organ peculiar to herbivores, the caecum, where the cellulose they consumed was broken down. Humans possessed one but it had no function and was connected to the appendix. Or was the caecum another word for the appendix in humans? She could not remember. The one in this rat was a tiny lump of reddish matter.

The heart was a compact little fist, with the lungs on either side. They looked like nothing at all but she found her pipette and inserted it into the rat's mouth and pumped in air and saw the lungs bloom. The heart that beat, boom-boom, boom-boom, and lungs that breathed in and out, in and out. How incredible they were. People didn't realise.

Lottie was taking her time, she was aware of that. Affirming what she already knew, putting off the fresh discovery awaiting her. She moved aside the organs she'd identified and found another, surrounded by fat. Using the knife she cut away the fat to reveal a bean-shaped kidney. It was a similar dark red colour to the liver and the spleen. Perhaps a little more purple. There were many miniscule blood vessels attached to it.

The other kidney Lottie would have sought and studied to see how they each connected to other organs but her patience ran out. She beheld the womb or uterus, normally a long, insignificant ribbon of pale flesh; now it ringed the rat's belly, a sausage curled around its innards.

Lottie counted the shapes inside. Six on one side, five on the other. Eleven rat babies. She cut into the uterus and carefully removed one of the foetuses. Attached to it by a pale umbilical cord was its dark red placenta. The foetus was tightly bound inside its amniotic sac. She cut this open and scraped it off, and studied the tiny, strange, embryonic creature before her. She could make out its head, its snout. The forelimbs, the hind limbs, all beginning to emerge from the blob of flesh. Were those not its eyes just starting to form? She could feel a kind of tingling sensation. These cells had multiplied and divided. Life was formed. Did people—her father? Her tutor?—not realise how extraordinary this was? No one had told her. It was something she was discovering for herself. Biology. The science of life. It was more fascinating than anyone could imagine.

PART SIX
ON THE FARM

1

Leo, September 1913–April 1914

The day was Michaelmas, the twenty-ninth of September, 1913. The boy on the white colt rounded up the flock of one hundred and twenty ewes and secured them in a hurdled pen. The horse had taken to the work.

The shepherd put a dark red, powdered iron oxide in an old bucket. He added linseed oil and stirred the mixture to a paste. Leo caught the first ewe with the crook and brought it stuttering on three legs to the old man. He examined each ewe. Some had fared badly in the summer from the fly. Others had damaged udders. Mastitis. He took the boy through ailments from which sheep commonly suffered. What he should look out for. The beasts were prone to scab, mange, worm. They could breed despite such conditions. As he had grown older this was one thing he had learned. Eye disease, foot rot. Another thing was that they could lie down and die from no apparent cause. 'There's naught the little sods likes better an dyin on you,' the old man said. 'I swear they thinks on nothin else while they're grazin.'

The shepherd Vance Brewer wore a coat of dark grey fustian, a hard-wearing cloth with a heavy

217

weft. He had a white moustache, part stained or burned brown from the cigarettes he smoked. His clothes smelled of Jeyes Fluid and cider and tobacco. His breath stank of onions. He doubtless smelled of sheep, too, but so did Leo himself, and was no longer bothered by it. It had only taken him a week or two to become accustomed to the animals' unpleasant odour.

The shepherd mouthed the ewes. As they squirmed in his grip, he winced from the pain in his hip, cursed and kicked them to subservience. The youngest had two teeth. These ewes he told the boy to mark upon the back of their heads. Leo dipped a short stick into the raddle and applied a little of the paste. Those a year older, with four teeth, he marked on the neck. The six-toothed ewes were marked between the shoulders and the full-mouthed in the middle of their backs. All these ewes, marked for tupping, Leo let loose in the field.

As ewes grew older their teeth continued to grow. They became long in the tooth, and often lost one or two. These sheep the old man called broken-mouthed. He told Leo to mark them on the rump, as he did those he knew to be barren.

Leo asked Vance Brewer why he culled every ewe who'd lost as much as a single tooth, even when her udders were correct.

'Broken-toothed sheeps can't eat turnips and that,' the old man told him. 'How's they goin to give their lambs good milk?'

Leo said nothing. He put the ewes marked thus in a different pen. The gaffer would take them to market. Supposedly for slaughter, though Vance claimed that disreputable farmers bought cheap broken-toothed ewes and bred from them for a further year, if not more. Leo tried to imagine such a farm, meaner than this one, but could not.

After some time Vance Brewer asked the boy to tell him exactly how many he had examined. As some of these were already out of sight the boy had to count the larger group still within the holding pen, and subtract this figure from the number of the flock. This he attempted to do but could not, for the animals would not stay still. He climbed into the pen and tried again. They huddled close together and he could not distinguish one from another. His failed attempts amused the old shepherd, watching with an open-mouthed grin. Eventually the boy gave up.

'You has to count em as you study em, see?' Vance Brewer said. ''Tis the only way. No one could do it else.'

'Have you been countin em?' Leo asked.

'I have,' the shepherd said. 'Us have checked forty ewes. That's one-third a my flock and I reckon tis time for our mornin croust.'

Leo shook his head. 'You can count, Mister Brewer, and not just on yer fingers.'

'You has to be a mathematician in this job,' the old man said, tapping his skull, still grinning.

● ● ●

The flock was of long-woolled sheep. They were tough, short but bulky in form. All but two or three of the ewes were placid. They weighed around twelve stone each and the boy could not lift them. Neither could the old shepherd. Together they could.

The ewes' faces were white, though their fleece came down in a fringe, veiling their eyes, giving them a coy appearance. Their fleece was hard-wearing and used in carpet-making. Vance Brewer claimed that Cornish long-woolled sheep produced more wool than any other breed in the United Kingdom. Leo did not know if this was true. The shepherd also said the animals could be sheared as young lambs.

'Beautiful lambswool like you never sin,' Vance Brewer said proudly.

Five days after Vance Brewer's examination of his ewes Leo rode the colt and gathered the flock once more. The shepherd had no dog. There was not one on the farm. By the markings upon their backs they separated the maiden ewes from the rest. The old man wore a pinafore or frock he'd cut for himself from a sack. Again they mixed the red paste, but this time they raddled the rams, upon their breasts or briskets. There were three such. Vance Brewer put the old one with the thirty-two maiden ewes, and the young rams with the rest. 'Eighty-eight between the two of em,' he told Leo. 'Think they'll manage?'

Then the shepherd and the boy left them alone. Periodically over the days following they returned to the pens and released the ewes with the red mark upon them that showed they had been served.

When Leo had ridden into the farmyard and asked for work Cyrus Pepperell, the tenant farmer, told him that his horse didn't look strong enough for agricultural labour and neither did he. The boy assured him that together they were worth more than any other horse or lad. Mister Pepperell narrowed his eyes. He said the boy was lucky, he was looking to take on a new lad, having only just let one go.

'You'll be wantin fodder for yon horse—I'll take it out a yer wages,' the farmer said. 'Let's try you, boy. Learn the shepherdin from my old chap. He was a dab with sheep. As good as any in his time.'

He shook Leo's hand. It was like grasping rough-barked wood. The farmer took Leo to the barn and told the old man to show the boy the ropes. Vance Brewer regarded Leo through narrowed eyes. When the gaffer had gone, he muttered, 'The ropes? Do he want a shepherd boy or a fuckin sailor? I spose he don't reckon I'll be needin many more pair a shoes, do e?'

2

The farm lay in the bottom of a coombe, miles from the nearest village, south of Bodmin Moor. The land was all up and down, nothing level, yet more rounded than steep. It reminded the boy of his mother's bread-making. The earth here had been kneaded into shape. The sloping fields were small and overlooked by woods. Even on clear days the sun found it hard to find the farm. Vance Brewer told him that the water supply was unreliable and dried up most summers, as did the pond across the yard, yet the fields around the farm turned marshy when it rained. Leo looked at the threadbare pastures and guessed they had not been visited by a muck-cart in a long time.

The farmer, Cyrus Pepperell, was a man of medium build, a head shorter than his wife, Juliana, and once he stepped out of the farmhouse he had a harried air. He was always on the move. However hard he worked his men, Cyrus toiled more. He chose the tougher part of any job and sweated at his labour. On occasion, shifting from one place to another, he broke into a run. Vance Brewer shook his head and told the boy, 'Never will catch his self up.'

Vance said Leo should see him in the spring on the vegetable patch, the gaffer scratching the miserable earth with his hoe like some demented cock.

There was a stockboy, too, an ill-tempered lad by the name of Wilf Cann. He was tall and rangy, with straggly brown hair, and wore a permanent scowl as if he was suffering from some irritating pain or insult, but did not wish to share it.

All slept in the small farmhouse, Leo with Wilf Cann in the loft above the Pepperells' bedroom, which they climbed to up a ladder off the landing. The house was odd. Heat was supposed to rise but in this dwelling it did not and on cool nights the attic was shivering cold. The old shepherd slept on the ground floor in a stall on the other side of the kitchen wall from the hearth, partitioned out of an old pantry or stockroom. There were no others on the farm. No children. According to Vance Brewer there were once four, 'two of each', but all had long gone.

It was a poor establishment of a kind Leo had heard referred to but not seen for himself before. They were known as mean farms. The Pepperells provided cider sop, bread soaked in cider, for breakfast. Mustard sandwiches for lunch. Rice pudding for supper. Pastry lard and bread pudding. Tea was offered but neither milk nor sugar. Juliana made no apology for this meagre fare. She was an anxious, fidgeting woman.

She made it clear that she could do better with assistance. Why her daughters had left her she did not say. Her breath smelled of menthol, from some concoction she gave herself daily to ward off the flu. Yet she was often sick, she said, and was obliged to drink beef tea as she laboured, trimming the oil lamps or blackleading the grate.

When Leo and Wilf Cann climbed to the loft at night the lad crawled beneath the unwashed blankets of his mattress, blew out his candle and told the boy to do likewise. When Leo spoke to him, all Wilf said was, 'Why does you croak when you talk? Is you a frog?'

Leo resolved to avoid him but this was impossible for the farm was too small. Every day at some point the gaffer ordered Leo to help Wilf dig this drain or mend that gate. Beside the flock of long-woolled sheep were half a dozen Ruby Red cows, two pigs, geese and chickens, and a single ancient carthorse by the name of Cobby. Wilf was junior stockman, part-time carter, ploughboy. He was three or four years older than Leo and might have welcomed at least one companion within thirty years of his own age, yet did not seem to.

There was no greater cordiality between the lad and the old shepherd. Beyond the most essential discussion they only exchanged jibes and insults. 'A sheep's fart is better than a cow's turd,' Vance Brewer told Leo within Wilf's hearing. 'Cattle does sod all for the land, they gives nothin to it, see?'

'Oh, aye?' Wilf said. 'But at least a cow's breath is always sweet, eh, unlike them fuckin ewes, all shitty one end and sour-breathed t'other.'

Through the autumn Leo watched the woods around the farm change colour. It was as if the trees were singing, not in sound but in their own language that he suspected no human painter could quite equal. None of the others seemed to take any notice. Leo lifted his gaze. He regarded the field maples' flame-filled leaves. There was a chestnut tree. A breeze blew across the hill and a dozen pigeons rose out of the branches, bad-temperedly, as if the tree had tired of their company and shrugged them off.

Some days they hitched the colt to a cart and went up onto Bodmin Moor and cut bracken for cows' bedding, a coarse and cheap equivalent to straw.

Thursday was baking day. Juliana set the dough beside the fire to rise, and on that day the kitchen filled with the odour of yeast, fermenting in the rising dough. On Fridays Cyrus Pepperell went alone to Bodmin. Some weeks his cart was laden with jams and jellies made by Juliana, or eggs and potatoes, or geese for the butcher. Another time it went empty but returned with four sinewy, ill-tempered goats. Leo could see no pattern or logic. The only certainty was that Cyrus would bring back a single copy of the *Cornish Echo*, which in the evenings he read from beginning to end over the course of the week, allowing himself occasional pinches of snuff as he did so.

Leo spent a cold day ditch-clearing with Cyrus Pepperell and Wilf Cann. All three of them worked hard so as to keep warm. The gaffer possessed a pair of oilskin waders and went into the ditch to dig out silt, while the lad and the boy hacked branches and brambles from the banks.

At the end of the day they carried the tools they'd used to the shed and Wilf said, 'Do that again and I'll fuckin trim e.'

Leo asked what it was he should not repeat. Wilf did not answer but dumped the shovel, billhook and slasher noisily and went out. The boy reviewed the events of the day in order to discover what sin or affront he had committed. Had he uttered some insult? Used the lad's favourite tool? Worked in sunshine, Wilf in shadow? He could find none.

Leo's pay was two shillings and sixpence for a sixty-hour week, which Cyrus said he would receive at the end of the farming year, after harvest. He allowed them ten-minute afternoon breaks, which had to be worked off between midday and one o clock on Saturday. On Saturday afternoon Wilf Cann and Vance Brewer went rabbiting. In the village shop they received three ounces of tobacco for each rabbit they produced.

On Sundays Wilf shot pigeons and brought the catch home so that he could enjoy pigeon casserole made by Juliana once a week. One time he saw no pigeons but bagged two hares. Juliana made a hare stew that included their eyes.

Leo took out the white colt. He rode up onto the moor. The miserable farm in its gloomy coombe was a good place to hide, but he had to escape. If only for a while.

Grey sheep grazed on Bodmin Moor, perhaps coloured by the sulphurous smoke that rose from one or two chimneys. Pump houses and engine rooms stood empty, spoil tips around them. He heard the throaty cry of birds but could not see them. Moorland birds were unknown to him. He came to a quarry, now disused and full of water. Promontories ran out, made up of huge rejected slabs of granite. Before he saw horses he smelled their dung. Then he saw them. They were much like Dartmoor ponies but a little less robust-looking and were mostly bay or blackish. They had good coats, manes and tails, and stood around thirteen hands high.

One Sunday in October he rode down off the eastern side of the moor. In the middle of a wood was a barley field, all enclosed by trees like some secret holding. He could identify the crop by its stubble, which had not been burned. Perhaps owing to the danger of a forest fire. He found evidence of the deer before he ever saw them: the twin half-circles, like elongated horseshoes, of their slots in the mud of a ride or fire-break after the rain. Under the trees were small mounds of neat droppings.

On subsequent Sundays he revisited the wood. He saw trees had patches of missing bark, chewed when better food was scarce or else rubbed off by stags scraping the soft skin or velvet off their antlers. He could recall his brother Sid telling him that.

Then he saw them: a group of fallow does with their calves out in the barley field, nibbling at what they could find scattered amongst the stubble. Perhaps this was a Cornish custom: the gleaning was left not for women and children but for deer. He eased the white colt deeper into the wood, away from the herd. Looking back over his shoulder, they did not seem to have noticed him.

The week following he dismounted from the colt and let him graze. Leo sat upon a fallen tree. Some way along the path a doe and her calf appeared. She stared at Leo. Or towards him. He kept still. The doe had large dark eyes. Her ears appeared to have pricked up, alert. He knew she had an incredible sense of smell, and acute hearing. His brother Sid had told him deer could smell a man a mile off, though their eyesight was comparatively poor. The doe lowered her head and grazed.

Other deer came out of the trees and onto the path. Leo reckoned this was the same group he had seen in the barley field. They browsed and chewed the moss off beech roots. One of the does was more alert than the others. They grazed, or even sat down to rest, but this one cast around her, listening, scenting the air. She must have smelled him and sought him out with her eyes, for when his gaze returned to her he found her staring at him as her fellow had done. But this was different. This guard doe held him in a fixed gaze. Leo felt a strange sensation in his stomach. He was an alien passing through their domain. She turned and walked away from the path and off into the trees, and one by one the other deer stirred or rose and followed her.

One Saturday afternoon in November, as Leo was grooming the colt, Wilf came up to him and said, 'I don't know where you go, boy, but I'm prepared to come with you tomorrow. I've had enough a pigeons for a while.'

They rode together on the colt, Wilf behind the rider, at a walking pace. They rode up past the mines and the quarry, and on over the eastern side of the moor. The day was cool and smoky, and still. Wilf declared that this was his favourite time of year. Leo took them to the woods. He told

Wilf that he came to watch deer. Wilf said that if he'd known he would have brought the gun.

Leo tied the colt to a sapling on a long rope and left him to graze. 'This way,' he said, and led Wilf to thick undergrowth in which he'd made a comfortable hide. They could look out upon a wide clearing.

'This is the spot from where you make your observations, is it?'

'Yes,' Leo whispered. 'Now we wait.'

They sat or kneeled and peered out between branches. After a while Wilf yawned and lay down. Some time later he sat up again.

'This is it?' he asked. 'This is what you does on a Sunday? Come all the way up here, crawl into a bush and sit starin at nothin?'

Leo shrugged. 'Yes,' he said.

'The tedium'll kill me,' Wilf said. He stretched out his legs. 'If cramp don't first.'

Leo shushed him. 'Quiet,' he said. 'Look.'

They gazed and saw a doe on her own, walking slowly, her black tail flicking over her white, heart-shaped rump. Her light coat was changing to the dull brown of winter. Then she began to move faster and Leo saw that a buck pursued her. She ran away but not far. The buck trotted after her, and she stopped and waited for him. When he reached her, she stroked his neck with her cheek and rubbed her body along his. Leo wondered whether they had already mated for this looked less like a courting ritual than a marriage. The buck waited to let the doe walk slowly ahead of him and then he rose on his hind legs, his front legs scrabbling awkwardly astride her. But she walked on and he slipped back onto his four feet.

'Poor bastard,' Wilf said.

Leo put his hand on the other lad's arm, to quiet him.

The buck followed after the doe, grunting. Whether out of annoyance or frustrated lust, Leo did not know. Otherwise both buck and doe were silent. The male tried a second time to mount the doe and again she moved away and resumed grazing. He followed her. This time he moved alongside and licked or nibbled her neck, the boy could not quite tell which, for the buck was on the far side of the doe from where Leo and Wilf were hidden. After a while the buck once more mounted the doe and this time she stood her ground and took his weight upon her back quarters, and the buck pressed himself into her. For a few seconds the beast thrust to and fro into the doe, then suddenly his great back arched and his antlered head flew up in the air. The doe stepped forward and the buck teetered on his back legs then fell to the ground.

The doe resumed grazing as if nothing had happened. In seven or eight months' time there might be proof that something had. The male wandered away.

The lads watched them until both animals had moved out of sight. 'That's the thing about fallow deer,' said Wilf. 'And most other breeds too. They split after the rut. The does stay with the fawns. The stags and young bucks form a male tribe, go off wanderin across their territory.'

Leo looked at him, open-mouthed. 'How do you know that?' he asked. 'Was your father a gamekeeper?'

Wilf exclaimed as if expelling breath that had got stuck in his mouth. 'A gamekeeper? No,' he said. 'My old man was a poacher.' He shook his head. 'The worst poacher in the history a Liskeard District. He knew all about deer. He just knew nothin about keepers. Always gettin caught he was. I'm not sure as I've ever tasted venison, even now.'

They crawled out of their hiding place and walked back to where they'd left the white colt.

'Roe deer is different,' Wilf told Leo. 'They's the odd ones out. They lives as families all year round. Father, mother, usually twin kids.'

They rode back to the farm. Wilf slid off the horse. 'That was good, boy,' he said. 'That weren't too bad at all. I'll be sure to bring the gun next time, mind.'

3

In December, wood pigeons ate ivy berries. Against a grey sky, black leafless trees swayed. They appeared to Leo as sentient beings deep in thought. At dusk a flock of starlings swirled overhead. They did not fly straight but changed direction all the time, all together. Thousands of one mind, creating patterns, the birds knitted one to another into a fabric that stretched this way then contracted that. How could they swoop and veer and alter course so swiftly without hitting one another? It was impossible to understand or even believe, only to witness.

Leo stood and watched. When the starlings passed directly overhead the whole world darkened. The sound of all their wings beating was a roar. There was a stand of sycamores and the birds flew there to roost. Some landed and were lost to sight. More came swooping out of the sky.

Something made him look to his right across the field. Out of a lone oak a sparrowhawk appeared. She flew on into the black whirling mass of birds. Leo saw some kind of disturbance and then the hawk came out of the flock with a bird in her claws. She flew back to her oak. The starlings did not show any sign of panic but continued swirling as they had before and settling in the sycamore trees.

The boy stood, transfixed by the brief spectacle of violence. It was a moment before he remembered to resume breathing.

One Friday morning Leo went out with the shepherd to look at the ewes. With no dog to bring them in, the old man stood some way off and regarded them from a distance. 'You'd be surprised what you can learn from watchin em,' he said. Leo did not think there would be much. He remembered little Ernest Cudmore, the shepherd back on the farm where his father was ploughman, always in amongst his sheep. The air was still. Blackbirds sang loudly as if to exclaim at the mildness of the morning. In the east the sun had not yet risen but lit up that portion of the grey sky, turning clouds into pink continents of some otherworldly realm all may go to in time. Soon a watery sun rose, and the sky lost its colour. Rain fell in the afternoon. The water was colder than the air into which it came. They spent the day turning the wheel of the cake-grinder in the granary, grinding up slabs of kibbled linseed and cotton-seed oil cake. Cyrus Pepperell had gone to market.

In the afternoon the rain ceased. Leo walked

across the yard to beg black tea from Juliana for their break. She told him he must not come in the house while Cyrus was away, and that they had their cider. She had no time to make them tea. On the way back, Wilf Cann stood in his way.

'Right,' he said. 'That's it. I've had enough. Put em up.'

Leo tried to walk forward but his way was blocked. He made to manoeuvre around but Wilf stepped across him in whichever direction he began. Leo stood with his arms by his sides, palms forward. Wilf was a head taller. Leo did not look up at him but at the ground. 'I don't want to fight you,' he said. 'I thought we was friends.'

'I don't want to fight you,' Wilf replied in a sing-song childish voice. 'I thought we was friends.' He slapped the boy's cheek. 'Put em up.'

Leo stared at the stockboy's hobnailed boots. He knew he must not cry yet he wanted to. He shook his head.

Wilf slapped Leo's other cheek. Now both cheeks stung. The old shepherd had come out of the granary. He did not intercede but watched mutely as he might two ram lambs.

Why was this happening? Leo did not know. He took a step back. Herb Shattock's stable lad. The maid Gladys, who was his cousin. Lottie herself, for her own amusement. His father. The gypsy boy, Thomas. The gypsy rider at Okehampton.

Now Wilf Cann. Perhaps there was some oddity in his manner that provoked people. Something of the runt about him, of the hen-pecked or nag-ridden.

Or maybe that was not it at all. There was nothing peculiar about Leo Sercombe. It was simply that there existed more violence in the world, in man, than he happened to feel within himself. For it always surprised him. He made his hands into fists and raised them.

Wilf Cann grinned. He put up his own hands and from the waist began to jerk and sway, side to side, as if trying to see around Leo's hands into his eyes. As if one lad was playing some kind of peek-a-boo game with the other. Leo waited. Wilf tossed his left fist out to the side and leaned after it. Leo leaned the other way, to his own left, away from the stockboy's left fist. He watched it hover in the air then drop as Wilf let it fall to his side and took one step back, then another.

Leo didn't realise he'd been hit at first. He'd not seen the blow coming. This pain in the left side of his jaw seemed random, not necessarily connected to the lad stepping away from him, smiling. Perhaps it was coincidental. A wasp happened to have stung him at that moment. A wasp in December? Or the old shepherd had for some reason joined in, pitching a stone in their direction that had struck his face.

It was only when he tasted blood in his mouth

that he understood how Wilf had feinted to the left but slugged him on the blind side. Caught him with a knuckly punch. With his tongue Leo discovered in the blood a loose object. As he identified it as a tooth so Leo saw that Wilf had ceased retreating and was coming back at him, jittering and weaving, hands in compact fists rolling before him. And in the instant that Leo found the tooth so a fire was lit within him. A furnace. His belly was an oven and the heat roared through his body to his brain. He bent his head and, yawing some formless word, ran forward.

The boy caught the taller youth unprepared. Wilf tried to punch Leo's head but it was already through his guard and he staggered backwards. He tripped and Leo fell with him, the two boys locked together as one, rolling, tumbling, towards the pond. On the far side the ground sloped so that animals could walk in to drink but here there was a bank, a foot or more clear of the water.

For a moment the boy and the youth seemed to cease competing and instead collaborated, slowing their momentum, until both were on their knees. But once they had done so each fought to propel the other into the water yet keep themself from it. Such was the conundrum with which they grappled on the lip of the pond. Leo grunted and heaved in his fury. He had his arms around Wilf's body, his hands locked, his head wedged against the larger boy's armpit, the rough material of the suit jacket against his bruised cheek. He could smell Wilf, his fresh and his stale sweat mingled. Wilf could not punch him except on the bony back of the head. And Leo would not let go. Never. Nothing could make him. He could smell the water. He was desperate to force his opponent in. He sweated, pushed Wilf in the direction of the water, pulled himself back. As Wilf did the same to him.

What sent them rolling over the bank together and into the pond? They splashed in the cold water and the shock of it loosened their grip and each floundered separately until he had retrieved his balance. When they stood, the water came above their knees, almost to their waists. Each boy looked down at himself, then at his adversary.

'You looks like a drowned rat,' Wilf said, gasping.

'You looks like a drowned cat,' Leo replied.

The stockboy examined himself once more. 'I does, don't I?' he said. He began to laugh, then so did Leo, even as the cold water made him shiver.

'You is cracked, boy,' Wilf said. 'Or crazed, if you prefer.'

'What do that make you?' Leo asked him.

'Come on,' Wilf said, 'let's get us out of here.' He climbed out and gave Leo a hand and pulled him up. The old shepherd had changed position in the yard and stood suspiciously close to where they had wrestled.

Wilf grabbed Leo in a headlock and held him tightly there as they stumbled across the yard. He could have strangled Leo to submission or worse, yet Leo understood that this hold was not martial but a gesture of affection. While also making clear to him Wilf's superior strength. He had finished the fight on a whim or from an impulse of mercy or even admiration, but it was he who had let it finish all the same. He could continue the fight at any moment and could hurt Leo if he wished. But Wilf did not wish to. This hold was an embrace, and it had a meaning, clear as words, in the language of men.

They sat around the stove in the barn to warm their flesh and dry their sodden clothes. Leo had no other suit and Wilf only one, and that was his best. He asked Vance Brewer if he had pushed them in.

'I did not,' Vance said. 'But my foot might have.'

When Cyrus returned, Vance told him that the lads had had a little bate or squabble. Cyrus said that most lads wait to have their baths in the brook or the river come summertime.

'I never seen the pond used in winter,' he said. 'But there you go, Vance, that's life. The young has their own ideas, there's no helpin it.'

4

On Christmas Eve after supper Juliana cut all the men's hair, beginning with her husband then continuing with their workers in order of age. She gave each man the same look, hair cut close to their skull all round. When it was Vance's turn he sat with his eyes closed and a smile on his face. Afterwards the old chap preened in front of the flawed mirror Juliana held before him. He said she had a talent for the work and could have done well for herself in Launceston or Bude, though he was glad that she had not.

Christmas Day proceeded the same as any other, save for the fact that at breakfast Juliana Pepperell told the men that she would pray on their behalf and afterwards walked out of the yard, presumably to attend church or chapel thereabouts. The men worked as usual. Leo did not notice Juliana return.

Old Vance Brewer was a bachelor and Wilf an orphan, and like Leo had no other place to go. But even before it grew dark Cyrus Pepperell told the men to finish up and come inside. There he poured them a glass each of what he called his best cider. Before he could drink any, Leo had to swallow the saliva in his mouth, caused by the rare smell of meat cooking.

'This be zingin stuff, gaffer,' Wilf said.

'Don't think it means I'm getting soft,' Cyrus said. ''Tis but a Christmas treat for you lads.'

The men smoked. Leo sipped his cider. Juliana peeled vegetables at the table and pulled a pan sizzling with lard out of the oven. She poured the chopped vegetables into the pan, and stirred with a wooden spoon till all were covered in the hot fat, then returned it. Cyrus Pepperell said that there was much sense expressed in the *Cornish Echo*. He explained that there was one reason and one alone for the decline of agriculture, and it was what politicians who regarded themselves as lords and masters nowadays pursued at all costs. 'There's only one word for it, lads,' he said. 'Free trade.'

Cyrus called his trio of workers 'lads', though one was twenty years older than himself.

'I'm a doin my mathematics,' the old shepherd said, 'and I makes that two words.'

Cyrus ignored him. 'The Huns? The Frogs? Do you think they opens theirselves up to free trade? No, lads. They're protectionist and I don't blame the bastards. Excuse me, Juliana. No, we depends on Germany for wheat, flour, even sugar beet.'

'That's wrong, gaffer,' said the old shepherd. 'We should be feedin ourselves.'

'Aye,' said Cyrus. 'Still, I spose there's one

good thing about it. At least tradin partners don't fight each other.'

Juliana called them to the table and they ate as they had not done since the boy arrived. Roasted goose. Roasted potatoes, carrots, parsnip. Brussels sprouts. A thick, dark gravy. This feast was like some kind of mockery of their usual meagre sustenance. They drank the cider and the gaffer refilled their glasses. Vance Brewer said he was having trouble with his water and went outside to piss in the yard.

'You lads might not believe this,' Cyrus said upon the shepherd's return, 'but Vance here was a wrestler in his time. One a the finest in this district.'

The old man nodded modestly, but Cyrus said, 'You don't believe me, lads, do you? Look at him now, I don't blame you. I wouldn't neither. Show em, Vance. He was a young heller, lads. Show em.'

Vance Brewer grimaced in apparent reluctance but bent forward and pulled up his trouser legs to reveal the blue scars of the kickings he'd received, thick upon his shins, such that Leo had never seen the like.

'All right, old lad,' Cyrus said. 'That's enough showin off. No need to put Wilf and the tacker here off of their suet puddins.'

Leo gazed upon the scars. He could not see them well, for the old man appeared to have four legs. The boy blinked and there were once more two, only for his vision to swim again. He blinked once more, and the shepherd had two heads. He looked up at the ceiling and saw it turn around in a full circle, somehow, then the wall came above him, then the floor, and so he slept.

5

Cyrus Pepperell came inside from pulling mangolds on chill winter days with his hands full of deep sore cracks. In the evening, sitting before the fire, he rubbed ointment from a small tin into them, methodically. It smelled of eucalyptus. Out in the field with sacks tied around his legs, another tied around his shoulders for a cape, he was like one of those Syrian hermits who condemned themselves to life atop a pillar or standing motionless or shut in a cell. So Cyrus Pepperell worked himself to his own deluded benediction in the Cornish wilderness.

Juliana did the milking of their cows. 'The gaffer says er's got kind hands,' Wilf told Leo. 'Gets the last drop a milk from them teats. Won't let me near em to learn.'

Leo had seen Juliana in the milking parlour, her posture an insecure squat on a three-legged stool, the bucket pinched between her knees. She had a widespread walk on bandy legs, and a stoop that made her look even more subservient to her husband.

'If tis true about her hands, they's the kindest

part of er,' Wilf said. 'Whatever old Vance thinks.' He looked at Leo, saw his quizzical expression and said, 'Did you not realise? Old Brewer's in love with the missis.'

Leo did not say anything but he allowed that disbelief might be writ upon his face.

'He says er beauty do not come from the paint pot,' Wilf explained. 'He says it come from within and do make her glow.'

'He said that?'

'One time after too much cider.'

Leo shook his head. 'Do the gaffer not mind?'

Wilf shrugged to show he did not know the answer to this question. 'Perhaps it do amuse him. I'm not even sure that Cyrus and Juliana Pepperell is man and wife.'

'What do you mean?'

'They might be brother and sister, I reckon. They looks somewhat alike, would you not say?'

'Perhaps a husband and wife grow to resemble each other.'

'But can you imagine them two ever couplin?'

Leo considered this proposition, and said, 'I cannot imagine any folk so doin, if they does it as beasts do.'

One cold, sunny Sunday Wilf walked Leo around the perimeter of the farm. He said as they walked that he was sorry for their fight. The truth was that the boy had done nothing wrong, it was just

245

that Wilf loved fighting. 'I always have,' he said. 'Don't get no opportunity here.'

Leo said that he accepted the apology despite its taking a month to arrive.

The perambulation took all morning and into the afternoon. The extent of the holding was far greater than Leo had realised. There were fields unused. Crops gone to seed. Grazing turned to tufty wilderness. They sat on a log at the highest point of the top field and looked down into the gloomy coombe.

'The gaffer don't know what he's doin,' Wilf said. 'He's a landskimmer. Old Brewer reckons the soil was plum once upon a time. Not that he's any good.'

Wilf rolled a cigarette and gave it to Leo, then he rolled one for himself. 'Take them sheep,' he said. 'I know I ribs the old fellow but this farm is sheep-sick. Why do you think they suffers so many parasites? Worms and fluke. You just watch and see how many lambs you lose next month. Dysentery.' Wilf felt in his pockets, patted his jacket. 'The old boy don't move the sheep around enough. They need shiftin from one field to another. That's why they get restless, them ewes. The grass is always greener. They need fresh grazin. They've not been up here for years. Ever since it's pained him to walk. Damn it,' Wilf said. 'Someone's took my matches.' He stood up, and cursed loudly at the sky. 'Come on, boy. We better get back. I wants a fag.'

Leo rummaged in his own pockets. 'Here,' he said, and passed Wilf two red-tipped matches.

Wilf grinned and took them. 'Good lad,' he said. He put his cigarette between his lips, sat back down and struck one of the matches on the bark of the log. The flame took and he cupped it in his hands and lit his cigarette. Leo leaned towards him and lit his in like manner.

Wilf exhaled smoke and took the cigarette from his lips. 'What else you got in there?'

One after another Leo emptied the pockets of his trousers, jacket, waistcoat. A knife. The stub of a pencil. He put the contents on the log. Wilf shook his head. Thin copper wire, twine, nails of different sizes.

Wilf ruffled Leo's hair. 'You're a funny one and no mistake,' he said. 'Come on, boy, let's get back.'

In January rain fell, and turned to sleet. One evening Leo went out to use the privy before bed. As he came back to the house he looked up. White chips of snow floated down from out of the grey clouds, flakes of ash from a fire so far away it was long frozen, alighting upon his suit and his skin, and upon the ground.

The snow fell long and thick and stayed upon the earth. All motion stopped. Time floated and drifted. Dusk fell seemingly at random. Dawn likewise. Nothing moved but rabbits, their mouths and teeth all white for there was no grass and they lived off chalk.

On the snow in the mornings were the prints of animals who'd journeyed in the darkness. The slots of deer, scat of rabbit. Badgers' paw prints, fox trails. Leo hitched the white colt to a small cart and took hay to the field, the snow creaking beneath him. The first day he stood on the ground to fork the hay out but the ewes in their hunger overwhelmed him and he fell amongst them. The sound of their bleating hurt his ears as their bodies pounded and squashed him. He grabbed hold of fleece and pulled himself up, and with the fork fought his way out of their midst. Thereafter he stood upon the cart and distributed the hay from on high.

At the end of January, the temperature rose and it rained but then froze again. Trees groaned. An ice storm caught and held rain on to the branches in the wood. At night the weight of the ice broke them off, and they fell with a sound like waves crashing on the shore. In the morning pheasants flew down from their roosts leaving their tail feathers stuck to the branches. The boy found a mute ruddock glued by its frozen feet to its roost. He took out his knife and chipped it free. The tiny redbreast rose and circled above him, and with a shrill cry flew off towards the house.

6

In the second week of February, Vance Brewer prepared his maternity ward. He partitioned the big barn with hurdles, and spread straw. Bottles of medicine and disinfectant were lined up on a shelf beside the stove, along with paraffin lamps. Wilf brought him a cartload of chopped wood and dumped it. The old man spent hours stacking the logs carefully against the wall. He also carried the wicker chair from his room, and dragged the mattress off his bed. These he placed either side of the stove. Leo asked if he should do likewise, manhandle his mattress down from the loft and sleep here in the barn.

'I would rather you did not,' Vance Brewer told him. 'My ewes and me gets along fine. Strangers bother em.'

The boy rode out on the white horse and brought the pregnant ewes to the barn. He slept in the attic and had his breakfast in the kitchen, but most of the day he spent in the barn. He did not believe he was any longer a stranger to the sheep but anyhow the only way for them to become accustomed to him was by his quiet presence among them.

The shepherd closed his eyes and dozed sitting in his chair, a slumber so light the slightest noise from a ewe could wake him. Then he limped among them, holding up a lamp in the gloom, studying their behaviour. One ewe refused to come to the trough. Another stood in the corner of her pen, looking bewildered. Each morning that Leo came to the barn it was to the sound of fresh bleating. The ewes chose to give birth at night. On the third evening he returned to the barn after supper and remained. While Vance Brewer sat in the chair, Leo lounged upon the old man's mattress. Thus they stayed in silence. The smell of the sheep mingled with that of paraffin and woodsmoke. Leo's eyelids drooped of their own accord. On occasion the old man spoke and woke him.

'There's some who shear their ewes prior to lambin,' he said. 'Or crutch em, which is shearin just around the udders and vulva. I never have. You only has to feed em more to make up for their heat loss.'

He gave the boy further advice on shearing sheep. He said the beast should be laid on its rump, and the wool shorn from its neck and fore-shoulders, then laid upon one side and the upper side sheared, then turned. Care must be taken not to cut the skin or the teats. 'If you makes a wound, apply a mix a tar and grease,' he said. 'And one other thing. If you put em out after shearin, make sure they have shelter. The sun can give naked sheep blisters summat awful.'

Deep in the night Vance prodded him awake. 'Come on then, boy. If you's here you may's well make yourself useful.'

The barn was full dark beyond the radius of the light from the lamp on the shelf. Vance told Leo to light another. He did so and followed the old man a few paces, to the pen they brought a ewe to when she was ready. Away from the stove the temperature fell.

'Look at this one,' Vance Brewer said. 'Not hardly a year old yet. Her first lamb.'

As they watched, the ewe lay down and bleated. 'See how er's strainin there,' the shepherd said. The ewe stood up and ran around the pen, then lay down again. 'Er waters broke a while back but there be nothin showin. I be mortal afeared for er.' He shook his head. 'She can't lamb, see? She needs our help. Your small hands might be better an mine. Go wash em with the disinfectant in that bucket.'

Leo asked why labour should be so problematic that animals needed human midwives just as women did.

'It is a good question,' Vance said. 'One I intend to bring up with the Good Lord when I meet im.' He frowned. 'That is, if He's in when I gets there.'

The ewe lay down and the old man sat against her and held her hind legs and lubricated her passage with green oils. He told Leo to slide his hand inside the ewe and find the forelegs of the lamb. The boy did so, and felt around with the trembling fingers of his right hand. It was warm inside the ewe, a pleasant sensation in the cold night, but he had no idea what he was doing.

'I think I have them, Mister Brewer,' he said.

'Good.'

'Wait,' Leo said. He probed the fleshy shapes in the ewe's womb and tried to make sense of what was there, attempting to conjure a picture of what his fingers found, but he could not. 'They's all t-t-tangled up in there,' he said.

The old man cursed. 'They?' he said. 'Twins?'

Leo found it hard to speak. 'I don't know,' he whispered.

Vance Brewer told him to take his hand out of the ewe. Leo did so. 'Help me lift her,' the shepherd said.

They took her by one hind leg each and with a great effort heaved the ewe, heavy with lambs, up in the air.

'Shake her,' Vance gasped. They tried their best. Then they laid her down again. She bleated weakly. Vance said that he hoped the lambs had slid back inside her from the cervix, and might disentangle themselves. He kneeled down beside her and Leo inserted his hand and his arm once more. He found two small, slimy but hard shapes.

'I've got the hooves for sure!'

'Keep calm,' Vance told him. 'Now each time her strains, you pull em.'

'How will I know when she does?'

'You'll feel it,' the old shepherd said. 'Don't fret. You're doin fine, boy.'

A few moments later Leo felt something tighten around his wrist, and he pulled the lamb's feet. When the pressure ceased he waited, still holding the tiny feet. Vance Brewer waited. The ewe also waited, for she did not command the contractions within her. They came again. Soon the boy had the first lamb's feet clear.

'Do you want to finish it off now, Mister Brewer?' he said.

'You'm be doin good,' the shepherd said. 'Carry on. Only those is the hindlegs. Tis a breech birth.'

The lamb emerged by degrees. Vance told the boy he could let go now. The lamb inched out of the ewe, its back legs and half its body, then all of sudden the whole of it slithered out with a squelching sound. Vance held the lamb upside down and rubbed his hand hard down its sides to remove fluid from its lungs. Then he wiped the birthing sac or membrane away from the lamb's mouth and laid it on the straw and it took its first breath. The mother licked the rest of the membrane off and ate it. The lamb soon began to try to stand. It tottered, legs buckling at the knees. The sight was comical and beautiful at the same time. Leo watched it, chuckling, but Vance told him not to get distracted, they were only half-done.

The second lamb came out of its own accord, in the correct configuration. The forelegs and head emerged slowly, then the rest. So it was born. The ewe treated it as she had the first.

The shepherd instructed Leo to guide the ewe into a small hurdled pen. Vance Brewer carried the lambs, one in each hand. The ewe continued to lick her lambs dry of the covering of yellow slime upon their white curly coats. Then she ate the afterbirth. Leo grimaced and said that he had not needed to witness that. Vance said he reckoned it must have something her body required.

Each lamb, once on its feet, sought its mother's teats, and sucked the warm curds of colostrum from her udder.

7

On a Sunday in the middle of March Leo groomed the white horse in the yard. His winter coat came away on the brush. As he shed it, sparrows swooped by and took up hairs in their beaks and flew away. Wilf told him that last year he had seen crows on Cobby the farm carthorse's back, taking his hair and making him bleed.

Wilf once more accompanied Leo on his Sunday rides. The colt was full-grown and strong and the two lads rode him together. They took the gun to bag a pigeon or any other prey. The first time Wilf raised the gun and shot it while still mounted, the horse bucked in alarm and threw the boys off and cantered away. Wilf sat upon the hard ground holding his painful elbow and laughing heartily. Leo told him he was a fool, a man of shocking ignorance, not to be trusted with horses. He said he felt sorry for Cobby. Wilf said that Cobby gave as good as he got and that Leo need not feel sorry for the old jibber. Leo shook his head and walked after the colt.

The next week they rode to the River Fowey, for Wilf said he had a yearning for fish. Grilled fish or fish soup, he didn't mind. Leo presumed he would have a rod and line but he had neither, only the gun. They rode along steep and winding lanes then into a wood. The air cooled. All the trees looked young and slender; their trunks and branches were covered with a skin of dark green moss. Thick slabs of granite lay strewn amongst them and were clothed likewise. A leat like those the boy had seen on Dartmoor flowed through the wood. Stones from its unkempt walls had fallen into the water.

When they reached the river Wilf slid off the horse from behind Leo and said he would find a good spot, they should follow him. He walked along the river. Yet he studied not the water, but the trees. He came to a lone willow. Four branches grew more or less vertical. A fifth grew horizontal, a finger pointing to the far bank. 'This'll do,' he said. Leo watched him crawl out on the branch above the river. There Wilf lay on his stomach, leaning from the neck out to the right side, with his left arm around the branch holding the barrel of the shotgun, the stock against his right shoulder. The sight struck Leo as foolishly precarious. He believed explosives were used to stun fish, and Amos Tucker had once told him of the whaling ships of North America, whose men harpooned those ocean-going leviathans, but he had never heard of any sane man shooting fish with a gun. Perhaps the Pepperells had adopted Wilf from Bodmin Asylum.

Leo staked the colt to graze and took out his knife and found an ash tree growing by a stand of sallow and elder and cut a thin stick. He ripped off the leaves, then fumbled in his jacket pockets and found the thin strip of wire he had remembered to store there. He tied the wire to the narrow end of the stick, embedding it in a notch behind where he had removed a twig. Next he made a noose out of the wire. It slipped back and forth with ease.

Leo looked up at Wilf, lying still on the branch with his gun pointing vertically down at the surface of the water. He appeared to be taking careful aim at his own reflection, like a cat that attacks itself in a window.

The boy crept to the river's edge where the water was clear and flowed over brown mud. He lay down and moved the stick out over the water and lowered the wire. It touched the bottom and a cloud of mud rose, and slowly fell. There he lay. Time passed. The morning was warm and he knew he'd fallen asleep when he woke with pins and needles in his arm and the stick slipped down to rest on the floor of the river. He raised it back. He looked up and saw Wilf lying as before. He too slept and would at any moment fall from the branch. Leo was tempted to watch for it would be a crime to miss such a comical spectacle. But when he glanced down he saw that a trout was drifting straight towards the noose. He could see its jaws moving. He held his breath. The trout eased unerringly forward. Its head, its gills . . .

'The hell with this waste a fuckin time!' he heard Wilf yell. Leo glanced up momentarily, long enough to see his friend now sitting on the log, the gun across his lap, shaking the stiffness out of his arms.

Leo said nothing but looked back into the water. The trout had moved into the noose past its first fin. An inch or two further then Leo would flip the fish up and land it. It pleased him greatly that Wilf could see what was happening, and what was about to occur.

The gun went off and made Leo jump. The ash stick fell out of his hand, the trout swam away and was gone. He looked up. Wilf sat on the branch holding the shotgun in both hands, the gun pointing upwards. His expression was one of unrepentant fury.

They walked along the river, Leo leading the horse. 'I can't rightly believe it,' he said. 'You'd rather have no fish than let me be the one to catch it.' He shook his head. 'I cannot believe it.'

'Twas my idea to go fishin, boy,' Wilf told him.

They walked in silence for a time. Then Wilf said, 'But twas funny, the way you jumped when the fuckin gun went off.'

'Make you laugh, that, did it?'

'Looked like you was imitatin the jump of a

salmon for me. "This is how they leap, Wilf." '

Leo looked at Wilf and saw him grinning in the way he did, on rare occasions. It was a smile that was the grin of a little boy and a demon both at once.

'I spose you think the sight a yourself pointing the gun at the water was a fine one, do you?'

Wilf shrugged. 'I doubt it,' he said.

'So do I,' Leo said.

'Bleddy hell,' Wilf said. 'If you got nothin good to say, you miserable sod, at least it sounds like your fuckin voice is finally broken.'

Leo led the colt. Wilf walked beside him. He nodded and said, 'You ever raced that horse?'

'Yes,' Leo said.

In the distance smoke rose from a bonfire.

The stockboy took another drag of his cigarette. It looked like inhaling the smoke enabled him to formulate his next thought. 'Is he as fast as he looks?' he asked.

Leo nodded. 'He is.'

They mounted the colt and rode him at walking pace. Leo said that as the weather grew warmer he thought he would like to go out on a Saturday and camp out overnight. Perhaps Wilf would like to accompany him on such a venture? Wilf said it sounded like a good idea. Leo said that he had begun to think on the future. When he left the farm, he planned to buy a saddle for the horse.

'I should warn you,' Wilf said, 'he don't plan to pay you.'

The boy asked Wilf what he meant. The lad explained how the farmer took boys on then towards the end of the farming year, once the harvest was gathered, did things such as to cause them to leave early. What things? Leo asked. Arduous work, Wilf said. Even more horrible food. Other cruelties.

Leo shook his head. 'He won't do it to me.'

'No,' Wilf said. 'He likes you.'

'He do.'

'He liked the others too.'

'What about you, then?' Leo said. 'Why has he not done the same to you? How much do you get paid?'

'I gets paid in kind,' Wilf said. 'Clothes is ordered. The rabbits keep me in tobacco.'

'Your master treats you rough,' Leo said.

Wilf grinned. 'He's tight as a duck's arse. And that there is watertight.'

'You should leave,' Leo told him.

'Where would I go? The grubber?' He looked frightened at the prospect, but then he grinned again. 'When we do have meat he carves it so thin it tastes of the knife.'

'I wouldn't mind a slice a thin meat,' Leo said.

'Last year he took two old cows to market. He wouldn't let the missis milk em, so's their udders was full, poor beasts. I said to him, "You must think people is stupid." He said, "They is." And I suppose he must a been right, for he come back without them cows.'

They rode on for a while, then Leo felt Wilf's hands on his shoulders. 'I could leave,' he said. 'If you was leavin.'

'You could get a horse a your own,' Leo said. 'We could ride together.' He tried to turn around.

'Whoa,' Wilf said. 'You'll pitch us both off, boy.'

Leo looked ahead. 'I never ad a friend like you,' he said. He was glad that Wilf could not see his face now. Otherwise, he did not think he would have said it.

'Me neither,' Wilf told him.

Leo felt the older lad's arms fold around his belly. They rode on back to the farm.

8

One morning towards the end of March the boy noticed the old lag Vance Brewer and Wilf look towards him as they spoke quietly together. A quiver of alarm ran through his innards. Some time later when he had forgotten this moment of foreboding and they were picking up stones from the field behind the house, prior to ploughing, Wilf suddenly grabbed him in a headlock. He felt another take his hands behind his back and bind them together and hold him. Wilf let go of his head and walked to a shed. He came back with something cupped in his hands held before him like some precious gift. Leo struggled desperately. Vance had hold of his arms. Leo thought he might be able to twist loose and run fast enough away from him even with two hands tied behind his back. But Wilf would surely catch him in seconds. Even if first he had to hand over what he held to the old boy or even put it back in the shed.

'You've heard a muzzlin the sparrow?' Wilf asked him.

'He probably thought it had gone out with they old parish apprentices,' Vance said. 'Well, it ain't gone out here, boy.'

Wilf held his cupped hands out towards Leo and opened them, enough for the boy to see the grey bird trembling there in its dark cage of fingers.

'You know what you ave to do?' Wilf asked.

Leo neither nodded nor shook his head, but stared up at the older lad. It occurred to him to yell for help, that such might come from the farmhouse. But then the door opened and Cyrus and Juliana Pepperell came out and walked across the yard towards them. They stood some yards away, spectators come for the performance.

'We got im, gaffer,' Wilf said.

'I can see that,' said Cyrus Pepperell.

Vance Brewer kept hold of one arm but let go of the other and stepped around the side of Leo. 'I ad to do this,' he told the boy, grinning. 'For Cyrus's dad. So did this lad Wilf, three, four year ago, and many another in between.'

'Tis a tradition,' Cyrus said. 'What you might call an initiation, boy. Others let em go but we don't. Not this one.'

'I ain't sure as he knows what to do,' Wilf said. 'He won't say.'

'He knows,' said Juliana. 'They all know.'

'Will you explain to him?' Wilf asked.

Cyrus nodded. 'The lad here will place the wing a the bird in your mouth,' he told Leo. 'You has to draw the wing and then the body a the bird in, and bite off its head. If you do that, you stay on. If you don't, you still stay on, but with one difference. I shall sell the horse.'

'Do you understand?' Vance Brewer asked. His red eyes were inflamed with excitement.

Leo nodded. Wilf opened his fingers and took hold of the sparrow. He pulled the tip of a wing out and raised the bird and fed the wing into Leo's mouth, which he reluctantly opened for this purpose. Then he clamped it with his teeth, and Wilf let go. Immediately the bird flapped its other wing, trying to escape. Using his teeth and his lips, Leo drew the wing of the bird deeper into his mouth. It felt unpleasant on his tongue, whether taste or texture, so he folded his tongue to the back of his mouth, for he could not afford to retch. The bird meanwhile pecked at his cheeks and his nose in its frantic attempts to get away. Leo closed his eyes. He had to use his tongue. It was his most significant tool or weapon against the unfortunate bird. He had to gobble it up as fast as he could, using tongue and teeth and lips all together. It pecked at him and thrashed against his face. He pulled the wing into his mouth, bit by negligible bit, dimly aware of new sound, the clamour of people close around him, yelling. He kept his eyes closed. The sparrow pecked his face. He did not wish to kill it but he must, he had to, he could not lose that horse. It was all he had, the only thing and everything. He pulled the whole body of the bird into his mouth, its head too, its other wing, and he did not vomit.

But now the sparrow was struggling inside him, in the constricted space and the darkness of his mouth. He tried to feel with his tongue the shape of the bird, where the parts of it were, but he could not do so. All was confusion. Stabbing pinpricks of pain, fluttering wings, scrabbling claws. The sparrow's tiny beating heart. When he felt it at the back of his mouth he sensed his throat pulsate and the need to retch. He must not let his mouth open. He tasted something odd and it occurred to him that the terrified bird had shat upon his tongue. He kept his eyes closed. He should not have drawn the animal entire into his mouth. He had to let its body out without allowing the head free. No. The other way round.

Leo sought the bird's beak with his tongue. He let his lips open, a little, then his teeth, and pushed the head of the bird towards the opening. The bird struck out for the light, the air. Leo closed his teeth around its neck and bit them hard together. The sparrow was too small, its neck a string of ligament and gristle. No matter how tightly he clamped the two rows of his teeth together there were gaps. Perhaps he could extinguish the life of the bird, but not pull off its head, and that would be enough.

All awareness was in his mouth, and face. Suddenly Leo became aware of somewhere else, another part of him. Behind. His hands. Undone. He lifted them and took hold of the head of the sparrow, and with a great shaking of his own head and roar through his teeth he pulled it away from the rest of its body. Then Leo opened his mouth and puked the body of the bird out. He dropped the tiny head.

Around him the others were talking.

'Well done, boy,' said Cyrus Pepperell. He passed Leo a bottle. The boy drank the cider, washed it round his mouth, and spat it out. 'I wagered on you with the missis here and won.'

'I never thought he would,' Vance Brewer said.

'We'll celebrate with sparrow pie tonight,' said Juliana. 'Nice and sweet, not like robin or tit.'

Wilf patted the boy on the back. 'You can keep yon horse,' he said. 'I knew you would.'

Leo turned and staggered away. He made his way to the stable and went over to the white colt and hugged the horse around its neck, sobbing.

9

One evening a week later Leo went to the loft to fetch some hay for the colt and the carthorse. There was an uncanny feeling in the air, something like warmth yet not of the temperature, for it was still cold. What was beginning deep inside the soil and within the roots of plants and trees was discernible in the atmosphere above. Spring.

Leo climbed the ladder. Just as he put his left hand upon the boards above, the white colt whinnied in his stall below and the boy stopped and looked down at him. He told the colt that he'd be but a moment with the food, he was doing the best he could. He stood on a rung of the ladder, his hand still resting on the board of the hayloft, and thought that horses were strange because they understood some things very well and others not at all. It would take a lifetime to know them, and he was already wasting too much of his with sheep.

The sensation when it came he could not identify. Then he could. Pain, intense and searing, in his left hand upon the loft board. Leo stepped up the next two rungs of the ladder with a sense of dread. He rose and found himself looking into the dark brown eyes of a tawny owl. The eyes were rimmed with a pink or reddish circle and around them were feathers that were like tiny Christmas trees when the needles had dropped. He looked into the eyes and could see nothing but the reflection of himself.

Then he looked at his hand. The owl had gripped it with the four talons of its right foot. Blood appeared around the talons. Leo tried to prise them loose with his other hand but he could not. The owl watched him calmly. The pain was unbearable. The boy gripped his left arm and raised his hand off the board and climbed down the ladder. The owl seemed to expect this for it wrapped the talons of its other foot around his wrist as if it were a branch, and let him carry it.

Leo ran across the yard, calling out for help. He held his left arm out from his side with the owl facing behind him, as if covering his back. He rushed into the kitchen. Wilf cursed in amazement at the sight and Juliana screamed at him to get that creature out of her house.

'Bloody hell,' said Vance Brewer. 'The boy's took up falconry.'

'Help!' Leo sobbed. 'Please.'

Cyrus Pepperell studied the boy's arm and the owl upon it.

'You'm up a tree there, boy, and no mistake,' Cyrus said.

'Come back outside,' Wilf told him. He led the way and Leo followed. His friend walked around the side of the house and told the boy to sit on the bench, facing the wood. 'Put your hand on the arm a the bench and sit,' he said. Leo did so and Wilf sat beside him in the dusk.

'There's nothin to do but wait,' Wilf said. 'He'll let go eventually, but you can't make him.'

'I'll die a pain afore then,' Leo sobbed.

'No, you won't. I know it's bad but, believe it or not, boy, there's worse.'

'Is there?'

'There is. I'll tell you what I can't work out, though. And that's what a tawny owl was doin in the barn.'

Leo glanced at the stockboy and found him looking back. 'I don't know,' he said. 'I didn't invite him there.'

'I never heard a such a thing,' Wilf said. 'Never.' He shook his head. As he did so the owl lifted its wings, as if to hide what it had caught from greedy eyes.

'Now listen,' Wilf said. ''Tis better for you if I leave. He'll be off quicker without me here for him to worry about. You just sit there. Don't make no noise nor sudden movement. You have to give im the time to work out what's goin on. Owls look wise but they ain't.'

Wilf Cann stood up and walked back round the side of the house. Leo let go of his left arm with

269

his right hand and wiped the tears from his eyes and looked at the owl. The bird faced the wall of the farmhouse. It appeared to be studying the brickwork. Leo stopped sobbing and sniffed and his breathing calmed. The pain was still intense but he bore it. Darkness deepened with each passing minute. He wondered how long the owl would stay there. It seemed relaxed and content where it was. Leo remembered his brother Sid telling him that an owl inserted its talons into prey and kept them there without the need for muscular effort. Its bones locked into place.

Night fell. Surely the others would not let him suffer all night long. Could he not kill the bird and cut off the legs? But perhaps there was no way to extract the talons. They would then stay in his hand forever. The brand of a bird of prey stamped into his flesh. The owl gazed at the wall. Leo could not see if its eyes were open. It might have fallen asleep. The night was milder than it had been for many weeks. The last of the snow had melted, Leo could hear water dripping and gurgling underground. The long slow thaw was in progress.

Suddenly another bird hooted from the wood. Perhaps a companion. The owl swivelled its head at the sound. It seemed to reassess its surroundings. To become aware of the open air behind it, of the wood beyond. Leo felt the grip of its talons loosen. After another minute or two the owl began to extract them from the boy's hand. Leo did not move. He waited until the owl had removed his talons and waited longer. Finally, the bird looked behind him again and hopped up on Leo's hand and wrist and turned and took off, and flew towards the trees.

Leo got up from the bench and trotted around the house and indoors, holding his throbbing left hand. Juliana was at the table. 'Come here,' she said. The men had gone to bed. Leo stood beside her. She took his hand and he winced. She placed it on the table. It was already swelling. She poured Jeyes Fluid onto a rag and rubbed it on his skin. For a moment the pain was worse than from the owl but he gritted his teeth and held his breath and it passed. He thought it wrong to be treated with the same disinfectant as sheep, but said nothing. Juliana told him that was it, and sent him to bed.

10

In the old orchard, full of gnarled cider apple and a few pear and one or two damson trees, the grass came up earlier than it did elsewhere on the farm. The ewes and lambs were put there. The boy watched the lambs play. One would climb onto a fallen log then suddenly dash off around the orchard and all the others followed. They came to a stop and walked around in the sun or bleated for milk. Each one's mother recognised the sound of her own and made herself available for suckling. Then another lamb would rush off and all joined in.

'About time to cut em, I reckon,' Vance Brewer told the boy. 'We'll put em back in the big barn.'

That night when they climbed up to the attic Wilf told Leo that he would not be seeing him tomorrow. It was one job he refused to assist with. Leo asked him what he meant but all the stockboy said was, 'E uses his own fuckin dominoes. You'll see. Now blow out the candle.'

The rainfall was so light the boy did not notice it nor could he feel it on his skin. It left no impression on his clothes, only a slight dampness on his hands. They brought the flock into the barn and put them in a pen. The shepherd told Leo to lift the lambs over the hurdle into another pen, while he whetted his bone-handled shut knife. He then tied a sack around himself, as an overall or apron.

On the shelf beside the shepherd's pipe and morning croust and cider was a packet of twist tobacco. This was not his usual weed, he told Leo, it had been bought by the gaffer for veterinary purposes. He pulled loose some threads, put them in his mouth and began to chew. He had a bucket of cold water ready too.

'With a ewe lamb, all we do's dock the tail. Get yourself a tup lamb for us to start with.'

Leo caught a young ram. Vance Brewer told him to stand against a wall post and hold the lamb tight, with its back against his chest, arms wrapped around it, each hand gripping two legs. The shepherd took delicate hold of the lamb's empty scrotum and with his sharpened knife sliced it off. Then he leaned towards the lamb and grasped one testicle in his teeth and pulled until the cord broke. This ball he spat into the bucket of water, then pulled the second likewise. The lamb squirmed in Leo's grip, pushing its head up against his chin. The boy held him tight. Vance Brewer spat some of the tobacco juice from his mouth into one testicle cavity, then again into the other.

'Put im down, boy,' the shepherd said.

The boy glanced up. The old man's unshaven face was stained with brown tobacco and the blood of the tup lamb. Leo held the lamb upon the ground and with the same knife Vance cut off its tail. Leo carried the lamb away, bleating furiously, and lifted it over the hurdle to seek its mother amongst all the ewes.

Vance told Leo that they would give the stones and the tails to Juliana to cook. He licked his lips. 'She'll make us a lamb's tail stew with chopped onion, and a pie-crust on top, summat lovely.'

That night Leo told Wilf that he was right. This farm was an infernal place. He would be leaving in the morning. The stockboy told Leo that he would depart penniless. Leo said that he intended to ask for the wages owed him and that if Wilf left too they could present their demands together and so make a stronger case.

In the morning the boy checked the sheep with Vance Brewer as on any other day. They studied the lambs to see that their wounds were healing. All of them were subdued in their behaviour compared to the playful young of two days before. Wilf brought the cows in for Juliana to milk, and took them out again after.

At breakfast, when they had eaten their customary sop, the gaffer said they should get to work.

'Not me,' Leo said. 'I'm leavin today, Mister Pepperell.'

The farmer and his wife and their shepherd stared at the boy as if he had spoken in some strange language they could not understand.

Then the stockboy said, 'Me, too, gaffer,' and all turned to gape at him likewise.

'You cannot,' said Cyrus Pepperell eventually.

'We can,' Leo said. 'I must ask you for my wages. I been here over six month. Call it twenty-four weeks. Half a crown a week. It come to three pound, gaffer.'

Cyrus Pepperell laughed, and said, 'Your horse fodder cost me more'n that, boy. You owes me. You want to leave, you'll ave to give me a good five shillin.'

He turned to Wilf and said, 'I sin you. I minds how you bin lazin about, ever since the boy show up. And now you wish to up sticks and quit on us after all my missis and me done for you? You'll leave on the day I kick you out, lad.'

The farmer might have finished what he had to say then or he might have had much more. Leo could not be certain. Whichever it was he spoke no more, for Wilf rose to his feet and as he planted them upon the floor so he leaned back and then came forward, swinging his fist, and caught Cyrus upon the jaw. The farmer fell back in his chair. He cracked his head upon the flagstones and lay inert, though he may have been unconscious already when he hit the floor.

Juliana Pepperell began to whimper and shrink back from the blow she imagined might be coming her way, but Wilf ignored her. He went instead directly to the bureau in the corner, pulled out a drawer and began to rummage amongst what he found there. Vance Brewer watched through wide, frightened eyes. He did not move, or say a word. Leo rose to his feet.

'Grab us some food,' Wilf told him. 'And some a that best cider of is.'

Leo found a loaf of bread, a jar of jam, potatoes, turnips, and put them along with a flagon of cider in a basket.

'Here's your three quid,' Wilf said, handing him the coins. 'I've took five. No more.' He nodded towards Cyrus. 'Had you best not see to yon gaffer, Juliana?'

The farmer's wife rose, quivering, and took a step towards the prone form of her husband. Leo saw blood on the stone beside Cyrus's head. He turned and went out of the house and directly to the stable. There he bridled the white horse and brought him out. Wilf came from the house carrying the shotgun and a canvas sack containing his best suit. They mounted the horse as on one of their Sunday expeditions, Leo holding the reins, Wilf behind him, carrying the gun, and rode away from the farm.

11

When they gathered firewood in the trees around their chosen site Wilf searched upon the ground but Leo looked up as the gypsies had shown him and found dry kindling in the branches overhead. Wilf was neither impressed nor distracted.

'We're still too close,' he said.

Leo wished to tell him that his moaning made for a sorry song, but did not.

'We should a gone further,' Wilf said.

'The horse wouldn't stand it,' Leo told him. 'We rode him all day. All the way up over the moor and beyond.'

'Should a rid him down.'

'Don't we need him tomorrow?'

They lit a fire and began to drink the cider. Wilf rolled himself a cigarette and lit it with a burning stick.

'I tell you what, though,' Wilf said. 'My days as a stockman is over, boy. I've had enough a beasts a burden. I know you likes your horses but me, I don't like any of em, not really.'

Leo asked Wilf what he intended to do instead. He said he would seek work as a navvy. Or in a factory some place. 'Must be plenty a jobs up country,' he said. 'Or maybe I've had enough a workin. Might help myself to what I wants for a while.'

Darkness fell. The fire crackled. When they had a bed of red hot embers Leo used two sticks to place four potatoes amongst them.

'Spose us better have a bite a bread,' Wilf said, 'to soak up some a this cider.'

In time they grew tired waiting for the potatoes to bake. Leo retrieved one with the sticks and passed it over. Wilf took it but it was too hot and he passed it from one hand to the other for a while before dropping it on the ground and cutting it open with his knife. He dug out a piece and raised it to his lips, blew upon it, then ate it. Leo watched him chew, his mouth open and inhaling air to cool the food further as he did so. He tried to speak while eating but could not and shook his head. When finally Wilf swallowed he exhaled loudly and said, 'It will do. Leave t'other one in a while.'

They ate in silence. When they had each finished their first potato Wilf said, 'It isn't much, bread and spuds, and it's about all we got, apart from this fine cider, and there won't be none a that left in the mornin.'

Leo said they should have brought a pan to cook in. 'Could a mashed the spuds up with herbs. Garlic. I smelled some back there.'

As the night cooled, the horse came closer to

the fire and stood, the forward part of his white form illuminated, looming like the spirit of a horse. A spirit visitor brought forth as if the lads were not cooking their supper but conducting a seance such as Wilf said he had heard of. He asked Leo if he believed in ghosts. He himself did not believe that everyone who died passed directly to the other side. Up top or down below. 'Some folk ud lose their way, I reckon,' he said. 'Some ud get left behind. Or wander off, just like in life.'

Leo said he thought that perhaps Wilf never went to Sunday School. Or he'd attended but was not listening. For he seemed to have forgotten that there was a place where those destined but not yet ready for heaven were obliged to dwell, a place by the name of purgatory, and if we saw ghosts that was who they were. 'They are waitin to be let in,' he said. 'We should give em a wave, that's what my mother always said us should do.'

They drank. Leo went away from the fire to piss. He looked back and saw the orange flames in the trees, the lad his friend, the horse. All aglow in the darkness.

Wilf asked Leo if he planned to accompany him in search of work. Leo told him that he was headed for Penzance. 'You could come too,' he said. 'We might even find us another horse on the way. Ride together.'

Wilf said he had enough of an idea of the shape

of the West Country to know that Penzance lay at its western tip and there was more chance of escape by going east. The land opened out that way. It closed up the other. 'You realise they'll be lookin for us,' he said. 'The last place I want to go's back to Bodmin Clink.'

They remembered the second potatoes and ate them, though the skins were charred. The flesh was much softer than the first time. They drank the cider. Wilf rolled a cigarette and passed it to Leo. Then, though his fingers fumbled, he built himself one the very same. After he had smoked that one Leo gave him the first. Wilf thanked him and said he was a generous lad to give away his last fag and he proposed a toast to friendship. He raised the flagon to his lips and drank. Then he placed it on the ground and stared at the fire.

'We should a brought blankets,' he said.

Leo agreed and said so, though he heard the sound come out of his mouth more like a gurgle or a burp than in words. He staggered away from the fire through the trees to piss again and came back. He sat clumsily and gazed at the fire that he might see how it functioned. Where was its engine? What made this twig flame, that branch smoke? What caused those sparks to fly up into the night sky? He tried to see the pattern or logic but was unable to. It made no sense. He told Wilf that he was going to lie down now, though again he doubted whether he had said the words aloud. Wilf grunted.

The boy laid his head upon the unsteady earth. He closed his eyes, and a rolling sleep absorbed him.

Leo woke, shivering, in the early-morning light. The fire had gone out, though the smell of woodsmoke was strong on his clothes. His head throbbed and his eyes ached. Blinking, he rose stiffly to his feet and looked around. Wilf was not there sleeping by the fire. Perhaps he had just woken and gone for a piss or a shit and a wash. There was a stream nearby that had made them choose this spot. Leo looked around for the horse. It was not there either. He found their tracks and followed them through the wood. A low pale sun flickered between the trees. After fifty yards or so Wilf's footprints disappeared where he'd mounted the horse and ridden on, eastward.

Leo looked up at the pallid sky and closed his eyes, then dropped to his knees and leaned forward, until the earth took the weight of his head, and wept. Whether for the betrayal by his friend or the loss of the horse or just his loneliness he did not know. All, probably. After a while he rose and wiped his muddy face. Leo retraced his steps back to the fire and gathered what morsels of food Wilf had left, then he turned west, and walked on.

PART SEVEN
THE GARDEN PARTY

1

Lottie, May–June 1914

Lottie Prideaux discovered that she was invisible by degrees, during the fifteenth year of her life. It was not a sudden revelation. She was already accustomed to passing through the rooms and along the corridors of the manor house unnoticed by the maids, or riding her horse Blaze unseen by the stable lads or farm workers, for all were busy with their chores.

When Ingrid Goettner requested a word with her employer, one day in April, the subject of their conversation stood behind the curtain in her father's library. 'Her studies she is neglecting, Lord Prideaux,' Ingrid told him. 'She is cutting up dead animals instead, and shooting birds with your under keeper, and so on and so on.'

Lord Prideaux murmured to himself, then said that he would have a word with his daughter. No doubt his cousin in Weimar would organise a more rigorous education but he assured Ingrid that he had every confidence in her in the meantime.

Neither father nor governess seemed able to see Lottie, though her feet could surely be spotted easily enough by anyone who wasn't blind.

'Also, she is growing prettier by the day, your lordship,' Ingrid said. 'Yes, it is hard to believe but she is becoming like her mother in this portrait. Lottie might have been *eine hässliches entlein*, but not any more. And one must not blame swans for getting up to mischief.'

When William Carew came to visit later the same month, Lottie remembered him well enough from the shooting party the year before last. He was a brilliant shot, but so shy that he had not said a word to anyone. Now, he told them stories of his travels in the United States of America. In the state of Montana he had shot a huge bull elk with antlers like a leafless tree. He had shot an alligator in a South Carolina swamp. The sole remnant of his old reserve was that he did not look them in the eye as he spoke but gazed elsewhere, as if he had spotted some blemish upon the ceiling, or found the stitching of the tablecloth more agreeable than their faces. He also spoke quietly, so that both Lottie and her father had to lean towards him.

'I stood on a cliff top in California,' he said. 'Looking down to where a whale had been beached. Dozens of grizzly bears had come to feast. They went inside the great whale to eat. When they were replete they slept on the beach, until their hunger returned.'

Perhaps Mr Carew had acquired the art not

merely of conversation but of exaggeration, too. Lottie wondered why he was visiting. After lunch she changed her clothes and stalked the men as they walked through the garden, listening to her father explain how many farms there were upon the estate, what arable or grazing land each farm possessed, how many sheep or cattle. Perhaps they caught a glimpse of someone in the vicinity but, absorbed in their tedious conversation, merely took her for the gardener's boy.

The girl knew that she possessed a talent for stealth. But it was on Sunday the third of May in the year 1914 that she believed herself to be entirely invisible, through no agency of her own, while seated in the drawing-room taking tea with her father and Alice Grenvil. Her father said that he had never been happier in his entire life. Alice said neither had she but she did not believe it out of the question that further happiness yet lay in wait.

'In fact, dear Arthur,' she said, 'I believe it likely.'

'Our wedding, my darling,' he said, 'shall be attended by our friends and relations, of course, but I should like to throw a party to mark our engagement for all the people of the estate, to share with them this propitious event. In a certain sense the news is as good for them and their future as it is for myself.'

Alice said she thought this was about the most thoughtful gesture she had ever heard of. She would be glad should this be the first of many parties, in this beautiful house, of which she would be the proud hostess.

Lottie crunched ginger biscuits, apparently making no noise, and listened in disbelief as her father said how much he enjoyed attending the theatre and that he looked forward to many such visits with Alice on jaunts to the capital. How could he have uttered this brazen lie unless he was unaware of the presence of his daughter, who might reveal it for what it was?

'Would anyone like a refill?' Lottie asked, lifting the teapot. Both of the others said that they would, waving vaguely at their cups and saucers as they might to a maid.

'And I,' said Alice, 'look forward to getting to know all your horses, Arthur. Your noble steeds.'

2

All the farms on the estate spread the precious manure from their animals upon the fields, but a number of cartloads had to be delivered to the big house, as the gardener demanded. Then he and his under gardener and the gardener's boy dug the muck into the vegetable and the flower beds.

The gardener Mister Satterley was much envied for his independence by the other workers on the estate, for the Manor's garden was unaltered since the death of Lady Prideaux. His Lordship did not interfere. Mister Satterley had been liberated from oversight. The garden was immaculate. Terraced lawns led from the back of the house into shrubberies and woodland. The flower beds were shaped into crescents and stars and featured plants of different colours blooming all at once. Small tight clumps of blue lobelia, pale yellow calceolaria, scarlet verbena. Pink geraniums flourished in stone urns. The steps down to the second terrace were festooned with aubrietia and alyssum cascading down each side. The lawns were mown constantly, or so it seemed to Lottie, for any time she looked out of a window one of the gardeners was clipping an edge or pulling the roller or riding the Ransomes' New Automaton like some parody of a carter cutting the hay.

The garden looked just as it must have done in 1899. 'This be how your mother liked it,' Mister Satterley told Lottie. 'And this be how it is.' Alf Satterley was a dour bachelor of less than medium height but so straight a back as to make up an inch or two. He wore an old grey suit and tie. From a distance he might be mistaken for a gentleman amusing himself, but the closer one came to him the more ragged one saw his clothes to be. Yet he was always clean-shaven, his neat moustache freshly clipped. On his head was a scruffy cloth cap the girl could not remember him ever removing, not even while conversing with her father.

Since Mister Satterley allowed no innovation in his domain, so his under gardener and the boy had become accustomed to the yearly calendar of tasks. There was little need for communication beyond terse orders at the beginning of each day, so that Lottie thought of them as monk-like, silent members of some closed order of gardeners, their days spent in prayer. What could be more conducive to contemplation of the Lord's creation than wheeling barrowloads of seedlings from the greenhouses or mowing the lawns, endlessly, to and fro?

Alf Satterley had no friendships to speak of at the Manor, yet he had a soft spot for the girl. Her earliest memories were of being pushed in his wheelbarrow on a bed of pungent grass clippings. When her cousins came at Christmas he patrolled his garden and shooed them off into the woods, yet once they had gone Lottie returned, and to the incredulity of the members of the household she would chase her hoop deep into the flower beds with no reprimand. Flowers were sent to the house each morning in flat baskets. Two china vases, each with a fresh bouquet, were taken upstairs. One for the mantelpiece in the girl's bedroom, the other for that of her great-grandmama, lying motionless the day long in her bed.

3

'You looks like you stepped out of a bandbox, Miss Charlotte.'

Lottie looked at her reflection in the mirror, seeing a girl with but a passing resemblance to herself. She was dressed in a long white gown, with a huge hat upon her head and a feather boa wrapped around her neck.

'Then I should prefer to step right back in,' she said.

The maid Gladys approached her with a hatpin, but Lottie said that was quite enough for now and divested herself of this uncomfortable attire. Gladys laid the dress upon the bed and marvelled aloud at its beauty.

'It's easy for you to harbour such an opinion,' Lottie said. 'You don't have to wear it. I shall have it filthy within minutes.'

Gladys shook her head. 'You must not, Miss Charlotte,' she said.

'I shall.'

She had gone with Alice to London for each of them to be fitted with dresses for both engagement party and wedding, at which the girl was to be a bridesmaid. She believed herself as much corrupted by the role as honoured. Gladys said that she would love to visit London again, as she had when they went to the Derby last year. Once was not enough. Lottie said that she herself wished never to go again.

'For two days the city was shrouded in a thick yellow fog,' she said. 'If I held my arm out in front of me, I could not see my fingers. The Grenvils closed all their windows but still the curtains and furniture were covered in greasy dirt. All the silver and brass was tarnished.' Lottie pointed to the ceiling. 'If you looked up you could see a black film had settled on the mouldings. And when you thought about it, you realised that we had to breathe these foul vapours into our lungs, Gladys. Along with the smell of gas. Their entire house is lit by gas, which I hope we shall never have here.'

The maid took other items of attire out of the wardrobes and chests of drawers. Each one was held up and Lottie shook her head to indicate that it should not be thrown away or else nodded to confirm that it was something she had grown out of.

'I fear Alice will try to move Papa up to London,' she said. 'Especially once I'm sent to Germany and am no longer here to protect him. Oh, don't look so rattled, Gladys, he'd never give up the estate. But I can see her parading in the park every Sunday after tea, with Papa on her arm.'

'And little ones in a pram soon enough, with a bit of luck.'

'Stop it!' Lottie cried. 'Oh, you should see those awful parks, Gladys. The Londoners make so much of them but they're pathetic imitations of our countryside, only they have metal railings instead of wooden fences or hedges. The bark of the poor trees is black and the sheep are weighed down by grimy, sooty fleeces.' She stopped, and frowned. 'The only good thing is the damp pleasant smell after water-carts have sprayed the dusty paths.'

When they had finished sorting through Lottie's clothes the neatly folded stack of discards stood waist-high. 'To whom will you give those?' she asked. 'Shall we take them to the poor of the parish?' She shuddered and said, 'That was another thing I noticed in London— beggars everywhere. Much worse than last year. In doorways. Outside shops, theatres. We went to the restaurant in Debenham and Freebody's, Gladys. One beggar accosted us on the way in, another on the way out.'

Gladys explained that such clothes formed part of the junior staff's salary. They would pass them on to their families. Their mothers would make them up for themselves and the children.

Lottie asked whether there were other such hand-me-downs. Gladys said that there were.

'Such as what?'

'Tea leaves, Miss Charlotte.'

Lottie asked what she meant and Gladys said, 'Tea is made for the drawing-room, miss, then after that tis watered down for the kitchen. Cook likes a brew and so does Mister Score.'

'Well, and why shouldn't they?' Lottie said. 'They both work very hard, they deserve an occasional restitution. I see nothing wrong with it.'

'Then the leaves is dried and given to Missis Budgell, the gamekeeper's wife, for Mister Budgell likes his tea and all. Bones is another thing.'

Lottie asked what a person would want with bones.

Gladys gathered the clothes in a pile. 'When Cook's made soup,' she said, 'her'll wrap up what's left in the stockpot and give em to one of us if we're goin home to visit. The same with hambones or beefbones.'

The maid lifted the clothes in one great armful, and bore them away.

4

'Lottie, darling,' Alice Grenvil said, 'would you introduce me to the gardener?'

Alice wore white gloves and a wide hat tied with a chiffon veil under her chin. They walked out of the French windows and across the stone-flagged terrace onto the upper lawn. The gardener's boy was digging out moss from between the steps down to the lower lawn. Lottie asked him where Mister Satterley was. The boy said that he believed the gaffer was in the greenhouse. Lottie turned to go in the direction of the walled garden at the southern side of the house but Alice put a hand upon her arm and said to the boy, 'Fetch him for us, would you?'

The boy put down his trowel and stiff brush and walked away. Lottie sat down on a step and Alice said, 'Yes, there are no seats here.'

Lottie looked around. 'Where?' she asked.

'It is remarkably bare, isn't it? A garden is a place where visitors should be able to find a pleasant spot in which to read or draw or simply enjoy the view.'

'Papa and I don't have many visitors,' Lottie told her.

'Or a quiet sheltered place for conversation, in greater privacy than in the house.'

Lottie pointed across the lower lawn to the shrubbery and wood. 'We've got the jungle,' she said. 'I must have made a hundred dens in there.'

'Dens are indeed for children,' Alice said. 'Places of repose are something rather different.'

Alf Satterley came walking out of the door in the wall. He did not cut diagonally across the lawn towards them, but took the path and thus the two sides of the triangle, his boots crunching on the gravel.

Lottie rose. 'Hello, Mister Satterley,' she said when he reached them.

'Miss Charlotte,' he said.

'This is Miss Alice Grenvil,' she told him. 'To whom my papa is to be married.'

The gardener did not doff his cap nor bend forward an inch in deference as he said, 'Honoured, miss.'

Alice untied the chiffon and pulled it from her hat and looked at the gardener. Lottie judged that his eyes were at the same level as Alice's.

'I was just saying to dear Lottie,' she said, 'what a wonderful job you have done here, Mister Satterley.'

'Thank you, miss,' he said.

Alice turned and gestured with a sweep of her arm to indicate the lawns and beds all around them. 'It is in such gloriously regimented order.

297

Which gives it something of the nature of a blank canvas, do you not think?'

Mister Satterley frowned and said he did not quite follow Miss Grenvil's tack.

'You have done all the donkey work, Mister Satterley, have you not?' Alice said. 'What Herculean labours must have gone into creating this.' She shook her head, as if it were not possible fully to articulate her admiration. 'No,' she said, 'one could really do something with this garden.'

The gardener said nothing nor did his expression change. He stared back at the young woman addressing him, though she was no longer looking at him but rather gazing around the garden.

'A lily pond, for example, rimmed with rushes,' Alice suggested. 'In the middle of this lower lawn. A low brick wall around it, with all sorts of spiky plants, and goldfish swimming in the water.' Alice furrowed her brow, indicating the profound intellectual effort being made behind it. 'Break it up, you see, Mister Satterley. Remove a few of those trees over there, place a seat beneath a pergola with a view to the countryside beyond. Or over here,' she said, pointing along the path so that the gardener had to turn to appreciate her vision, 'create an alley of wooden arches with roses climbing all over them.'

Alice paused, to let the loveliness of what she proposed sink in. Lottie said nothing. She watched Mister Satterley. He turned slowly back to face Alice Grenvil. Lottie could not tell what he would say, or do, and waited. But before he might respond, Alice said, 'Of course, such things are for the future, no doubt. Ignore them, Mister Satterley. Disregard my fanciful proposals. No, I am merely a messenger. Lord Prideaux wished to have your opinion on where to place the marquee. On the lower lawn, of course, but on this side, up against the hornbeam hedge, or on that side towards the stables?'

The gardener surveyed this section of his domain with narrowed eyes. He turned back to Alice. 'I should say, miss, that his lordship may have the marquee whichever side you prefer. Please excuse me. I'd best be back to work.'

Mister Satterley turned and walked away along the same route by which he'd come. Lottie watched him go, leaning forward a little as if into a faint wind. When she turned back she saw that Alice had left her, and was walking across the upper lawn towards the house.

5

On the morning of the day before the party the timber and ropes and canvas of a white marquee were delivered by waggon, and four men armed with mallets began to erect it. A convoy of waggons arrived, some bringing trestle tables and folding chairs, others food. Lottie gazed at the list pinned to the kitchen wall. *150 lbs of beef. 90 lbs of ham. 8lbs of poultry.*

'Someone must be free,' said Cook.

2 cwt of potatoes. 50 lbs of apples. 70 lbs of cherries. 80 lbs of mixed fruit.

'Is there no one?' Cook yelled.

What she called a field kitchen had been set up in the scullery, with free-standing ovens and burners upon which pans bubbled.

Lottie had never seen so many people labouring in the kitchens. All the house maids had become kitchen maids. There was a squawk from the doorway to the scullery and all looked in that direction. Gladys stood and held an egg up for all to see. 'I was drawin a chicken,' she said, 'and this come out.'

The male servants too carried cheeses or bottles or boxes from one room to another. Even Lord

Prideaux's valet wore an apron and stirred a pot of seething meat.

'Surely, Mister Score, someone can be sent?' the flustered cook was saying.

'What do you need?' Lottie asked her.

'Oh, we are short of treacle, child. Missis Prowse will have some at the stores.'

'I shall go,' Lottie said.

'I cannot send you, Miss Charlotte,' Cook told her.

'No one will know,' Lottie said. 'Please. I want to help.'

Cook wiped her brow with a cloth and handed the girl an earthenware jar. 'Tell Missis Prowse to put it on my slate.'

The girl carried the jar to the stables and put it on the bench in the tack room. She went to Herb Shattock's bothy and asked him where Blaze was grazing. He said that she was in the pasture beyond the training paddock and that he would send a lad to fetch her. Lottie said no, thank you, she would prefer to fetch the mare herself.

'I had a look at her this mornin. Her's in fine fettle,' he said. 'Takin her to the gallops again, Miss Charlotte?'

The girl frowned. 'I fear I cannot tell you where we are going, Mister Shattock. It is a secret mission. If I told you, I'd be putting you in as much danger as myself.'

Herb Shattock smiled. 'In that case,' he said, 'you had best go.'

'You have not seen me,' she said.

The groom looked around his room and shrugged. 'I could a swore I eard a voice,' he said to himself. 'But no one's there.'

The girl rode her pony past the white ducks on the pond, past Hangman's Wood, past Manor Farm, and out of the estate and on to the village.

The store was owned by the Prowse family. It smelled of bread but otherwise only an indeterminate aroma derived from all the foods they sold. Mrs Prowse was serving an elderly man. At the end of the counter a boy about Lottie's own age chopped a loaf of hard white sugar into fragments. His mother said, 'Gilbert. Not too big.'

Lottie walked to the end of the shop and looked through the door to the bakery. There Mister Prowse reached his peel or paddle into the great brick oven and withdrew two quartern loaves upon it. Crisp, crusty bread. Beside the door were shelves of ironmongery: benzoline and paraffin, lamps and candles.

A woman was served before Lottie. She requested a taste of the cheese. Mrs Prowse inserted a small, tapered implement into the truckle or wheel of cheese. She withdrew the taper and a length of cheese with it. The customer broke a piece off the end and chewed it. Mrs Prowse eased the twig of cheese back into its slot. The woman said that she would take a half-pound.

On the highest shelf above and behind the proprietress stood large tin canisters. The woman asked for a quarter of one and two ounces of another, in combination. She watched as Mrs Prowse mixed the tea leaves in the exact proportions.

When her turn came, Lottie held up the earthenware jar and asked for dark treacle for the Manor kitchen. Mrs Prowse told Gilbert to weigh the jar for Miss Charlotte. The boy put down the chopping tool beside the sugar and came along the front of the counter. He took the jar from Lottie and removed the cork lid and placed it on the pan of the weighing scales. He added weights to the other side until the jar rose. He told his mother what the jar weighed then placed it on the counter beneath the tap of a large green urn. He turned the handle of the tap and they watched the dark syrup flow into the jar. Gilbert leaned over and looked inside and put his hand back on the tap and after a short while turned it off. As the stream of treacle slowed the boy passed his finger through to catch the last of it and raised his finger to his mouth.

'I told you before,' his mother said.

Gilbert returned the jar to the scales and

weighed it and told his mother. She wrote the figure with a pencil on a pad, above the figure for the weight of the empty jar, then carried out a subtraction. Lottie read the numbers upside down and did the calculation in her head. She worked out the answer. A moment later Mrs Prowse wrote the number down. Meanwhile Gilbert pressed the cork lid into the neck of the jar and slid it along the counter. Lottie took it, thanked him and Mrs Prowse, and went outside. She carried the jar to where her pony was tied to the rail, wrapped the container in cloth, and placed it securely in the pannier. Then she unhitched Blaze and mounted up and rode on home.

6

Alice Grenvil burst into the dining-room as Lottie and her father took their breakfast. She said that she was sorry to be so early but she had woken at dawn and could not get back to sleep. Her poor maid was forced to help her pack and her father's chauffeur to crank-start the car and drive her over at hair-raising speed but there was no help for it. She was too excited. This was going to be the most wonderful day of her life.

Arthur Prideaux asked his fiancée if she was hungry.

Alice looked surprised. 'Yes, I am,' she said. 'Why, I had no idea.'

Lottie rang the bell and the maid came and laid another place at the table.

On the stairs Lottie met her great-grandmama's maid coming down. She said that her lady-ship was calm. Lottie said she would visit her anyway. Nellie said that she would look in upon the old lady intermittently through the busy day.

'No,' Lottie told her. 'Once the party starts

you're off duty, all of you. I'll see to her. If I need help, I'll find it.' The maid nodded and thanked her and carried on.

The girl climbed the stairs and walked along the corridor, past her father's bedroom and her own and the empty guest bedrooms to the end. She opened the door and walked over to the bed. Her great-grandmother had lain here for many months upon her back. She had shrunk. On warm days all that could be seen was the faint outline of her bony form beneath the sheet, rising at the end to her toes. In recent weeks she had turned upon her side and begun to curl up. It was a fascinating process. Lottie knew that babies grew curled in their mother's womb and believed her great-grandmama was reverting to this state. Her head was sunk into her shoulders. A few wisps of thin white hair straggled from her cap. In order to take her hand Lottie had to ease her fingers apart, for they were clawed in upon themselves, fists of knuckle and bone. Then she withdrew, as the old lady slept once more.

All the people on the estate were invited to the master's engagement party on the sixth of June 1914. In the late morning they set off, some in carts, most on foot. Lottie saw them from a window of the attic nursery. From this height they did not look as if they were possessed of any autonomy but rather, like the members of an audience in a London show Alice had described, mesmerised by a hypnotist. Being pulled all in their Sunday best, on a hot but overcast summer's day, towards the big house. She ran downstairs.

When she reached the landing Lottie stopped stock still. Alerted by a sound, she stood and listened. A far-off gurgling in the pipes? No. A bird trapped in a distant chimney? No. A floorboard groaning at someone's tread? She followed the sound towards its source, and entered her great-grandmother's room. As she approached the bed Lottie saw that the old woman's eyes were open wide and her mouth too. The strange noise was produced when she breathed in. She breathed out silently. Then she inhaled once again with a rasping, fluttering, wheezing sound, incredible from such a tiny frame. Lottie took hold of her hand, and put her other hand on her great-grandmama's forehead, and the noise ceased, just like that, for the old lady all of a sudden stopped breathing.

Lottie stood beside the bed. Nothing had changed except that her frail great-grandmother was utterly still. The girl did not know what to do. But then she realised there was nothing she could do, and nothing to be done, and so only one course of action open to her. She let go of her great-grandmama's hand, kissed her forehead then left the room.

· · ·

The farmers and their carters, stockmen, shepherds, and all the members of their families. The sawyers. Over two hundred people. The grooms at the stud farm, and Herb Shattock at the stables and his lads. The gamekeeper Aaron Budgell and his wife and the under keeper Sidney Sercombe. All those who worked at the Manor itself, indoors and out. Only Cook and her scullery maids had to work this day long, and the master promised they would have a holiday after he and Miss Grenvil married in August and took their honeymoon. Cook was assisted by women from the village, whose daughters also became waitresses for the day.

As the guests arrived they were ushered around the side of the house to the back terrace where they were met by Lord Prideaux and his fiancée and his daughter Miss Charlotte. They shuffled past, murmuring congratulations to His Lordship. Some said the same to Alice but either not knowing her name or in the confusion of the moment addressed her as 'My Ladyship'. Alice accepted the premature ennoblement, whether out of social grace or presumption Lottie could not tell. Some even congratulated Lottie herself. She tried to stop herself from scowling, and said nothing.

The guests passed on, to be offered glasses of sherry or lemonade and invited to spread out across the lawns. The idea was that they would carry their glasses with them. But it was not thought to suggest this and as no one was accustomed to such behaviour most raised their glasses and knocked back the contents in one, and returned the empty glasses forthwith to the trays upon which they'd been proffered, the sudden shot of alcohol causing one or two elderly cottagers to sway as they stepped off the terrace.

During a lull, the hosts surveyed the scene. Those who had arrived stood or walked stiffly, the men sweating in their heavy suits. The estate workers regarded the house servants as flunkeys; servants thought of the farm workers as dim, slow-witted beings, one step up from the beasts they tended. Various groups kept to themselves or nodded awkwardly to neighbours, even though many were related, exchanging the minimum of stilted conversation. Alice Grenvil sighed. It was her hope that an informal start to the party would relax the estate families. Instead all looked as if they would rather be elsewhere, even at their customary labours. Arthur Prideaux reassured her. It was always like this, he said. Their reserve was a sign of their respect and loyalty, and would ease as the day wore on.

At twelve-thirty a gong was brought out by Mister Score and banged loudly, its reverberating clang not merely silencing but stopping the guests stock still as if it were the prompt for a game, some variant of Musical Statues. Lunch was served. People sat where they wished at trestle tables set up down one side of the upper lawn. The waitresses brought plates with pressed beef and silverside of beef, ham, tongue, galantines, new potatoes with mint, peas, asparagus in butter, carrots. The men drank ale. When they needed to relieve themselves they went down into the shrubbery beyond sheets of canvas erected as a shield. The women went inside, to the lavatory behind the scullery, where they soon formed a queue.

The master and his intended sat at a table on the terrace looking down upon the scene. To Alice's left sat her father Duncan Grenvil, then Lady Grenvil, then some Scotch relations who were staying for the summer. To Lord Prideaux's right sat his daughter. The girl imagined they must look to the guests below like those celebrants of The Last Supper, reproduced in a book of the world's greatest paintings that her father had recently given her for her fifteenth birthday. Beside her was William Carew, then her German governess.

William told Lottie in his quiet voice that she had no idea how fortunate she was to grow up in such a paradise. He himself had the misfortune to be reared in the smoky metropolis. Eton was little relief. He had also visited many beautiful places in the Empire and beyond and thus knew what he was talking about.

Lottie thanked him but said she had a good idea, and that was why she had no wish to leave it.

'Perhaps it is best that you go—not only for your own education,' William told her, 'but also to give the new Lady Prideaux a chance to establish herself without the encumbrance of a stepdaughter.'

Lottie said she did not wish to pursue this line of conversation. She asked if it was true that he was to be employed by her father to manage the estate. He said it was. Lottie said that she herself would be able to do the job if her father would only let her. She was fifteen years old now. Then she asked why a gentleman should wish to take on such employment.

William Carew laughed. 'It's very simple,' he said. 'My own father squandered our inheritance.'

'That sounds dramatic,' Lottie replied. 'How did he do it?'

William shook his head. 'I'm afraid it's merely tawdry. He gambled.'

Lottie nodded. 'On horses,' she said.

'On horses,' William agreed. 'On cards. On financial markets. He shot himself. With one of my guns, would you believe? Not a very fatherly thing to do. He left my mother and sisters and me penniless.' William smiled, as if what his father had done had been somewhat amusing. A good-humoured jape. 'And who knows?' he said. 'Perhaps it will be the making of us. One of my sisters is training to be a teacher. The other, a nurse. I am here.' He raised his mug of beer. 'And there is nowhere I would rather be, Charlotte.'

Over to one side of the lawn the members of a band who had come out from Taunton set up their music stands and instruments. The plates were cleared away and desserts brought out. Jam and fruit tarts, stewed fruit, blancmange, custard and jellies. Ingrid admonished Lottie for the gravy stains on her white dress. Lottie said that perhaps she was not fit company for her cousins in Weimar.

Ingrid shook her head slowly. 'We Prussians, I am afraid,' she said, 'are not for our table manners renowned.'

Lottie's father beside her stood up and tapped one of his glasses with a fork. Indoors perhaps the sound would have been of sufficient volume to hush the assembled company, but outside it was lost amongst the clanking of utensils and the hubbub of conversation, which with the consumption of ale had gradually increased in volume.

Adam Score, though nominally a guest like any other, saw the master's predicament and took it upon himself to retrieve the gong, which he bashed again and so silenced the gathering.

'My dear friends,' Lord Prideaux began. 'I am in a most privileged position. For I have not one but two families. The first, of course,' he said, gesturing to his daughter beside him, 'given to me by blood. The second . . .' and now he opened out his arms to indicate and so include all those whom he addressed '. . . the second by inherited right and responsibility. You are my children just as surely as is my dear Lottie here. Just as you serve me with your sweat and toil, so I serve you and always shall. Which is why I wish to share with you, dear friends, the most unexpected happiness that this beautiful young lady'—Lord Prideaux turned to his right and indicated Alice— 'has brought me in my middle age.'

He took a deep breath and sighed. 'I hope, and I'm sure you too will join me in this, that as well as happiness my future wife will bring us more: flesh and blood, with whom and through whom this estate will continue to flourish and thrive, unto further generations.'

Here Lord Prideaux was forced to pause, for a general cheering rose from the lawn below him.

'I ask you, dear friends,' he resumed, 'to raise your glasses in a toast to Miss Alice Grenvil, and hope that you will all welcome her to our home, and that she will come to cherish it as we do.'

The guests rose from their seats, holding their glasses and mugs, and drank and cheered his lordship and his fiancée. At a signal from her father, the band began to play, a tune Lottie recognised, though she could not name it. When she looked down at the guests she saw one nodding her head, another tapping his foot, and could feel the music do the same to her—making her want to move in time to it.

Her father and Alice Grenvil rose from their seats and walked around behind their companions and down from the terrace to the lawn. There they moved among the trestle tables to speak with the estate workers and their families.

Lottie watched a group of lads and maidens sitting together at a table. Some, she knew, were cousins. The under keeper Sidney Sercombe. The maid Gladys. Herbert Sercombe, once under carter on Leo's farm, had somehow persuaded the tall red-headed maid Elsie to sit on his knee. Lottie rose. It occurred to her that her invisibility might be a fleeting phenomenon. Adults did not see her for she was not one of them. Children likewise. She was in between. She turned and walked into the house, up the stairs. She went to her great-grandmother's room. All was as it had been before. The smell of roses predominated, but with something else behind it, which could have been the coming putrefaction of the flowers themselves but was not. The girl looked upon the face of her great-grandmama. The powdered yellow flesh was sinking onto the bones of her skull.

Lottie climbed further, to the nursery, and changed into shirt, breeches and boots. She descended the enclosed circular staircase to the cellars then climbed the steps that led back up into the west side of the house. She crept along silently, past her father's office—soon to be occupied, presumably, by William Carew—past the flower room, to the gun room. She took out one of the light Churchills Alice had given her from its case and put some shells in her pocket and went back down to the cellars and through their dank corridors to the greenhouses and out through the walled garden to the woods.

The sound of the band playing drifted from the lawn. It felt less like man-made music than something rising from the trees and the undergrowth. Lottie walked on and soon the music faded out of earshot. She walked fast, tripping over roots, and came out of the wood into fields. Sheep grazed in one. The next was empty. The girl walked along the hedge. She broke open the breech and fumbled with the shells, inserting one then the other. Then she closed the gun, and walked on. She knew she should walk slowly, warily, but could not. Something moved in the hedge. Lottie raised the shotgun to her shoulder and took aim. The gun trembled in her hands. She lowered it and walked on, sobbing. She did not know why, exactly. There were many reasons. Her great-grandmama's death. Her father's marriage. Exile to Weimar. Thoughts of all that she was losing combined to make her miserable and she could see no end to it.

Lottie walked on to the meadows by the river. They were filled with buttercups among the grass, as if the fields had been planted with heavenly fodder for some ethereal beasts. Horses in the Elysian fields or some such. The girl laid the gun down then let herself fall into the grass and lay there, amongst the sweet-scented plants. The clouds lifted. There had been no need for the marquee after all. The sun beat down. Insects buzzed around her head. She closed her eyes.

'Miss Charlotte?' The voice reached her from afar. 'Miss Charlotte?' It was familiar. The girl raised herself to her elbows and looked up. The under keeper Sidney Sercombe came over and stood above her. 'Are you all right, miss?' he asked. He held the gun. It was broken open and the shells were gone.

Lottie rose and walked to the river. She sat on the bank. It was mid afternoon. The lad came on after her and laid the gun down and sat on the riverbank some yards away. Lottie wondered how Sidney came to be there. Had he heard the gun go off? No. She had not shot it.

'Mister Shattock saw you,' Sid told her. 'He asked me to keep an eye on you, miss, make sure you was safe.'

The girl looked across at him. The lad rolled himself a cigarette. It was strange to see him in his Sunday suit. He and the head keeper Mister Budgell wore fine attire for the annual shoots but otherwise dressed in everyday working clothes of frayed corduroy, aged whipcord. Sid licked his cigarette paper and rolled it tight.

'I should like one,' Lottie said.

Sid looked over, frowning. 'I don't know as I should, miss,' he said, but she held him with an unflinching gaze and he relented. 'Shall I roll im for you?' he offered.

Lottie nodded. Sid placed the one he had made behind his right ear. He pulled a cigarette paper from the packet and rested it open and grooved between thumb and forefinger of his right hand. He teased a twist of tobacco from the pouch and pinched it out along the paper. Then it seemed he had a fresh thought or recalculation. He reached up across his face with his left hand and took the cigarette from behind his right ear. Holding the paper and tobacco in its place in his right hand, Sid rose and stepped across and gave the girl the cigarette and his box of matches. Then he returned to where he'd been sitting and finished rolling the one he'd interrupted.

When Sid had licked the new paper Lottie lit her cigarette and tossed the matchbox over. She inhaled smoke into her mouth then removed the cigarette from her lips and blew the smoke out.

'Beg pardon, miss,' Sid said. 'But what made you go shootin? On yer own? What was you after?'

The smoke was foul and acrid and Lottie feared that it would make her cough or even vomit, yet she felt soothed. Whether by the smoke or the action of smoking she was not sure.

'I planned to ride,' she said. 'I was going to go to the stables. But I was in a vexed state, Sidney. I did not wish to impose my condition on poor Blaze. Why should she suffer it? So I came shooting instead. I cannot remember why.'

This inconclusive response appeared to satisfy Sid. He smoked and watched the seagulls who came dipping and swooping along the river in the cooling afternoon. Lottie watched them too. They would go upriver and out of sight then reappear and come back down. Out of sight again then back the other way. The same birds or perhaps always new ones, she could not be sure. She knew they must be taking insects in their beaks but she could not see it. They seemed more as if they wished to dive into the water or become like ducks and float upon it but did not quite have the courage to do so. On occasion one came so close to the water that its claws brushed the surface like a raptor's talons after fish.

The girl asked the lad if he had heard from his brother or knew aught of him. Sid said he had received a postcard a while back, which surprised him. He'd not been sure that Leo could even write, yet his script was fine.

'What he wrote,' he said, 'didn't make much sense, I suppose . . .'

Suddenly Sid stopped talking and sat gaping at the girl. He looked away then back at her, realisation dawning. 'I is so stupid, Miss Charlotte,' he said. 'I'm sorry. His message said: *I shall return, and see you both again.* Bin tryin a work out ever since who the both of us is. I ad a wrinkle twas me and Mother, and Leo was gone soft in the head. Now I realise this was a message for you, miss. He will return.'

Lottie nodded. 'I know he will,' she said. 'I do not doubt it.' She thanked Sid. The cigarette she held had long since gone out. She flicked it into the water and rose and said that she should get back. She let Sid carry the gun without objection. He followed close behind her. They walked up out of the buttercup meadows and along the hedges of the pasture fields and over the fence into the wood.

Sid said her name: 'Miss Charlotte.' She stopped and turned to face him. He stood stock still, watching something in amongst the trees. She followed his gaze. 'I sin it before,' he whispered. 'Only once. Never sin it so early in the year.'

In this portion of the wood among a stand of conifers stood anthills. Upon one, a jay spread its wings. It shifted position and shuffled about. It took ants in its beak and pressed them into its feathers. Reached in between its feathers and took other ants out. Lottie could not see whether the bird then ate the insects but she thought it must.

'What on earth is it doing?' she whispered.

Sid did not look at her but kept his gaze fixed upon the jay. 'I don't rightly know, miss,' he said. 'I don't think no one does.'

'Won't the ants bite?' Lottie asked.

'That's one a the strange things about it,' Sid said. 'Mister Budgell reckons the bird seems to know to use the sort that don't bite.' He nodded, as if to some proposition of his own. 'I hopes to find out the reason for this strange behaviour one a these days. There must be someone on this earth has an answer.'

They stood watching. The bird seemed in no hurry, but eventually it hopped and took off. Lottie watched the blue flash among its feathers disappear in the speckled shadows of the wood.

'I need to tell my father something,' she said. 'We had best get back.'

She turned and headed on towards the house. The young under keeper followed.

PART EIGHT
IN THE WOOD

1

Leo, May–July 1914

There was a faint wind. It seemed to come and go. In, and out. In, and out. As if some unseen presence was breathing. The boy could feel God, breathing. The sky was a mottled grey. The moon broke through high up, above the grey. During the morning more and more blue came through, mottling white clouds, turning them wispy. By mid-morning the eastern side of the sky was clear blue. It was still murky in the west.

He slept in a wooden lean-to shed in an empty field. It was already early May but the night was cold. He woke trembling uncontrollably. He could not stop his teeth chattering, the top row and the bottom row knocking against each other. He thought he was sick but forced himself up from the ground and walked and realised that he was simply bone cold. As he warmed up, the trembling lessened. After a mile or two it had ceased.

In a wet, green wood there were still odd daffodils in flower, childish splodges of yellow. From a house he passed below came the sound of someone playing solo some kind of flute or horn. Smooth breezy melodies. He recognised neither the music nor the instrument. Towers of brick rose from the earth and through the trees and above them. No longer functional, they were like monuments to the men who'd built the mines beneath them.

He saw things that he had never seen before.

He watched a thrush fly directly along the horizon, from the south to the north, precisely, mathematically parallel to the land, its distance from him unchanging.

He passed a field of swans. Leo could not believe it. They looked like livestock there but could surely fly away. They were wild swans that had congregated in this field, perhaps summoned by some call inaudible to the human ear. Most sat upon the ground, their legs beneath them like women surrounded by their white skirts, and stretching their long necks they grubbed with their orange beaks at something in the wet grass.

Another night he slept in a railway tunnel. When he woke, water dripped and splashed around him, seeping through the roof. The ground was damp and so was he. He wished that humans could sleep standing up, like horses. He rose and walked out of the tunnel and walked on along the railway line. The moist air smelled fresh from the rain. He counted out the paces from one telegraph pole to the next. The wire strung between them sang in the wind. It buzzed and swung. The track ran flat and straight across the crooked land but if he raised his eyes and looked ahead he could see that it always curved away, and dipped or climbed around the contours of the earth. If he paused and turned and looked behind he saw the track had deviated conversely.

In places the railway was built upon a ridge and the boy looked out across rolling pasture. In others it was dug into the ground so that all he could see were high banks covered in scrub rising on either side. When trains approached, he stepped back and stood and watched the people inside framed like pictures, stationary, motionless, hurtling past him.

The stations announced themselves with large nameplates. Lostwithiel. Par. At each, Leo climbed onto the platform and studied the time-table printed there to reassure himself that he was one station nearer to Penzance. He also found a drinking fountain or tap and slaked his thirst. In St Austell he walked into the station café and bought a ham sandwich and an iced bun. Wilf had taken most of his money but left a few coins in the bottom of Leo's pocket. He took the items and carried them until he was out of the town once more and sat on a bank and ate them. Around him the ground was dusted with specks of white powder, like a fine snow that had fallen briefly yet not melted.

At Burngullow station a branch line curved north amongst tall brick chimneys or towers.

Leo looked towards white hills, which seemed in the soft warm light of evening to be of perfect conical design.

He thought that he would seek a hidden place to sleep, but the smell of meat cooking made him salivate. His footsteps led him in search of it. No, he had no choice in the matter. Half a dozen men sat around a pit of blazing logs. Leo watched from a distance. His stomach grumbled. The men's faces, their clothes and hats, were white. Perhaps they were bakers, covered in flour. One of their number ladled stew into each man's tin or enamel bowl. They ate in silence save for a kind of murmuring or low groaning of satisfaction. Then one looked up and gave a yelp of surprise, and said, 'Dazed if I an't seen a ghost.'

Others raised their heads. The one who had served the food said, 'You'm be an idiot, Tozer, give me more'n a fright than any ghost. Come here, boy.'

Leo stepped closer to the fire, into the sphere of its orange illumination.

'When one a these gannets is done you can ave is bowl, son,' the leader said. 'Sit yourself down.'

Leo did as he was told. 'Beg pardon, sir,' he said. 'Tis I who thought you was all spirits.'

The leader told him they were working in the china clay pits. There was work for men like them—itinerants, tramps. They could stomach some days of it. Tozer there was hosing the clay off the walls of the quarries. Others wheeled barrow-loads up the ever-growing pyramids of waste. He himself had been loading ships at the docks down at Charlestown, carrying sacks of the white stuff up a gangplank all day.

A man finished his stew and belched loudly and spun his empty bowl in the air towards the man who spoke. He caught it and filled it and passed it to Leo along with a wooden-handled spoon.

'Thank you, sir,' the boy said, and ate. He could not tell what animal the gristly meat came from but he judged it one of the finest dishes of his life. There were potatoes and carrots with it, and other vegetables less easy to identify.

One or two of the men rolled cigarettes. Another filled his pipe. One man asked if anyone knew the gingernut maid amongst the women who scraped the blocks of china clay.

'Never give up, do you, Frizzell?' another replied, and others joined in with ribald observations. Leo could not understand everything that was said for each man seemed to speak with a different accent and most of these he had never heard before.

The leader turned from the fire, and called behind him, 'Fancy another bowl, Rufus?'

There came no reply. Leo peered into the darkness. After a while his eyes began to make out indistinct shapes. He came to understand that he was looking at a donkey. When he had scraped his tin bowl he gave it and the wooden-handled spoon back to the cook and asked him quietly if the Rufus he had addressed was a beast.

The cook explained that the donkey had no name. It belonged to Rufus, who preferred to dine alone. He was one of their number but apart from them.

The man on the other side of Leo overheard and said, 'He in't never bin right since the Zulu War.'

'Neither have you, Tozer,' said the cook, 'and you never even went.'

Their laughter had a bitter tang to it. The men passed round a flagon of rough cider. The boy sat amongst them. The cook gave him a blanket. He pulled it tight around himself and slept.

In the morning the men rose and walked north towards the tall chimneys and white hills. The one they called Rufus loaded bags on his donkey and set off west. Leo followed him. They walked along the highway. The occasional coach or farm vehicle passed them. Rufus did not acknowledge the boy dogging his footsteps. Neither did Leo close the gap of twenty yards or so between them. An odd, rancid aroma was in the air. He realised that it came from one of them, the man or the beast, he was not sure which. Perhaps both.

After an hour or so the man turned off the road and walked down a tree-lined avenue towards a large house. In front of the house was a semi-circular drive or turning area of shingle. Rufus followed a path around the side of the house. He left the donkey standing and approached the back door and knocked upon it. Leo stood beside the donkey, stroking its neck. It was not the animal that stank. A woman opened the door.

'Any jobs want doin, missis?' the tramp asked her.

The woman studied him for a moment. 'You again?' she said. 'Either the seasons is slowin down or you's speedin up yer rounds.'

'I was just passin.'

The woman looked past him and said, 'You got a lad with you now? Learnin the trade, is he?'

The tramp did not turn round but said, 'He ain't with me. I don't know who he is.'

The woman returned her gaze to Rufus and screwed up her face. 'You stink of old badger fat,' she said. 'I thought you washed it off come spring.'

Leo saw the man shrug his shoulders. 'Still a mite cold at night,' he said.

The woman led him into the kitchen garden and showed him a bed she wished dug over, and a pile of manure to be applied. She went to a shed and came back with a spade held upright in each hand like a queen bearing her sword and sceptre. She gave the larger one to Rufus and held the smaller spade towards Leo, beckoning him forward. He left the donkey where the animal stood and came and took the spade. The woman turned without a word and went back indoors. Rufus began to dig a trench at the side of the plot. Leo went to the other end and did likewise.

They walked side by side. The tramp allowed Leo to lead his donkey by the halter rope. Rufus walked at a slow pace. Leo glanced at him occasionally. He was a man of middle height. He wore no hat or cap. He had wild grey hair and a beard much the same. His skin was tanned and lined. His blue eyes were wide and staring and made him look startled by what he saw. Leo followed the direction of the tramp's gaze, in case there were something notable, but could see naught save unremarkable hedges, and fields.

The tramp asked Leo where he came from. The boy told him a little of his childhood among horses, and Rufus said that he was a horseman of sorts himself in his youth. An illegitimate one. He had run away from home, for what reason he could no longer remember, and first worked, he said, as a strummer, one of a string of thieves who passed stolen horses from the West Country up to London. He was not proud of it but he was young at the time. After that, three years in a row he spent the spring as a stallion walker, taking a sire from farm to farm, to impregnate the female carthorses.

When he spoke to Leo, the old tramp did so

with lucidity and ease, in a West Country accent little different from Leo's own. Yet at other times as they tramped along the road Leo noticed that he muttered, as if in conversation with an invisible other, walking with them. Perhaps he addressed the donkey. At any moment, like Balaam's ass, the beast would acquire from an unseen angel of the Lord the power of speech. Or was it God Himself whom Rufus addressed? The tramp walked slowly along the rough highway, mumbling to God.

In the middle of the day they stopped and ate the remains of the bread and cheese and ham the woman with the garden had given them. The donkey grazed the verge. Rufus said that he should have gone to America, really, as a clear-thinking acquaintance of his had done. This fellow had received a land grant in the Middle West of the United States.

Instead, Rufus said, he had made the mistake of going into the army. He went with the mules. 'Now it's just me and this deaf old donkey,' he said. 'And my friend that I live with, my old pal, when I've had enough a the road. I'll introduce you, if you like.'

Leo asked if this abode of his would be on the way to Penzance, for that was where he was headed. Rufus said that it was.

'You'll like my old pal,' he said. 'He's a good old boy.'

They walked on in the afternoon. They proceeded along a low ridge and when the boy looked up he saw something ahead of them that made him stop. He could not make sense of what lay before him. Rufus too stopped a yard ahead and they each stood and watched whatever it was growing larger, approaching them through the air. Bearing down upon them, flying low and fast along the ridge, straight as arrows. Leo felt his knees weaken. Then understanding rose from his legs to his brain, along with the increasingly loud sound of wings beating. Just as he and Rufus began to duck, the two mute swans rose and flew over them, a yard or two above their heads.

2

They came to a wood. Rufus told Leo that the boy would soon meet his pal. He walked towards a wall of closely growing ash trees and parted branches to let the donkey through. Leo had thought her tired but, revived by her homecoming, she set a brisk pace upon a path that veered between the trees. Rufus followed, Leo behind him. After some minutes they came to a clearing. At its centre was a fire pit. Nearby a log bench, a rustic table. Cooking pans and flagons hung from branches. The encampment was a room whose rustling walls were made of leaves and branches, its ceiling the sky. The trees were of different species. One was of a sort new to Leo. Not its leaves, which he recognised as those of purple beech, but the way its branches grew not approximately perpendicular to the trunk but sweeping out and down to the ground like some grand woman's dark purple dress.

'I shall introduce you to my chum,' the old tramp said. He parted two of the hanging branches. Leo followed him into a dim space around the trunk, to which his eyes soon became accustomed. A mattress lay upon a wooden scaffold two or three feet above the ground. Rufus put his hand upon the smooth trunk of the tree and turning back to the boy said, 'This here is my pal. He has no name. He gives me shelter and friendship. Never asks nothin in return. He's always here when I come back from my wanders.' He stroked the tree and shook his head. Leo could make out letters carved into the bark. 'Listens to my twattle, never says naught back. Not yet at least.' Rufus then turned and addressed the tree, peering up into its higher regions. 'This here young lad's a goin to rest with us.' He turned back to Leo. 'Let's get us a fire goin,' he said, and walked back out into the clearing.

Just as a kitchen is furnished with cupboards and shelves stocked with implements or produce, so was Rufus's camp. Glass jars hung by twine made from bramble stems, stripped of their skin and plaited. These jars were filled with walnuts, hazelnuts, wild shallots pickled in spiced vinegar, blackberry jam. Leo tried to identify the contents of each jar but usually failed. Dried mushrooms. Pickled damsons. Dandelion leaves. Plums, greengages. Ledges and niches were cut into parts of trees for storage. The ham of a badger which Rufus had smoked over the fire and cured like that of a pig hung in the canopy of a birch, and he cut slices from it and made a stew. Leo wondered if insects did not help themselves to the hanging meat. Rufus said they probably did but had done him no harm, there were none hereabouts like the mosquitoes of Africa.

Water came from a spring. A brick enclosure had been built around it, with a wooden lid. Rufus lifted the lid and placed a bucket upon a slab of rock, and the bucket slowly filled with cold, clean water.

The boy said he thought that tramps lived upon the road all year. Rufus said that most did, no doubt, but some had an abode of sorts to which they retreated and where they kipped for as long as they could stand it. At such times he was more of a hermit or recluse. Until the urge to light out rose once more. At least so it was for him.

Rufus cut a number of willow sticks and planted them in a circle. He had Leo help him pull the tops of the sticks towards each other and tie them. Then the hermit sat down, clutching his stomach. He told Leo in gasping breaths to continue threading those other, slender lengths around the curved uprights to create a latticework. By the time that Leo had done so, Rufus had recovered from whatever pained him. Over the frame they stretched pieces of canvas and hide. The hermit told Leo this was his guest room, for the boy's exclusive use.

3

The next morning, after they had eaten reheated stew and drunk camomile tea, Rufus gathered a set of clothes, as old as those he wore day and night but washed, which constituted what he called his summer attire. He hung these from branches. With a stick Rufus mixed the hot ashes in the fire with the thick sediment of cold ashes beneath, then removed his clothes. He was a solid man, with a great barrel chest and belly, heavy thighs, a thick stub of a knob. He kneeled beside the fire and with a long-handled spoon ladled warm ash from the pit and rubbed it into his skin. The ash stuck fast. When he was done he was covered from neck to ankles in grey dust and his face too for good measure, ash adhering to the badger fat. He rose and stood, a ghostly figure.

'Come,' the old man said. He pulled on his boots. 'I shall wash off this fat and these ashes.' He walked out of the clearing. Leo followed him. The donkey followed after. They walked through the trees then out of the wood and across three fields. The sun shone upon them. The boy was sure they would be seen. What would a witness make of such a sight? Rufus was like a man who has seen the Lord, and repents in dust and ashes. Pursued by his one young acolyte.

Or perhaps those who lived nearby knew the old hermit and accepted his eccentricity.

They came to a pond. It was home to lilies and ferns and, though greenish from a distance, up close Leo could see through the water for it was fed by an audible spring and a similar amount must drain away. There were no beasts grazing, to raise the mud with their hooves. Leo tested the temperature with his finger. The water was icy. Rufus walked slowly into the pond. He appeared impervious to the cold. He neither gasped nor shivered but proceeded with the dead calm of a sleepwalker. By the time he reached the middle, the water was up to his waist. There he promptly sat down, closing his mouth, for the water came up to his nose. Then he shut his eyes and leaned forward, and it was as if some sly invisible hand ducked Rufus's head underwater.

The old man rubbed and worked the ash first from his hair and face and beard then, standing up, the rest of his body. At some point he began making odd noises, grunts and hoots. The donkey watched, impassive, like one who has seen all this before. Soon Rufus came up out of the pond, his hairy skin pink and clean, and set off back to the wood at a fast pace, shivering. Leo trotted to keep up with him.

'Us'll c-c-catch c-c-carp in there,' Rufus said, teeth chattering.

Back in the clearing Leo got the fire blazing and the old man, once the water was dried off his skin, pulled the garments from where they hung and put them on. His trembling subsided. Leo made more tea. He handed Rufus his mug, and it struck him, now that it was absent, how strong, and unpleasant, the rancid stink of the badger fat had been.

4

Sugar, Rufus obtained from sycamore trees. He showed Leo how. 'The tree needs to be the right age,' he said. There were some at the edge of the wood. 'Forty or fifty year old.' He chose one and made an incision in the bark, and placed a jar below the cut which he tied in place with twine around the trunk and to a higher branch. Leo watched a colourless sap squeeze its way out of the tree. They attached half a dozen jars to other trees likewise. Then they sat and waited for the jars to fill. Leo asked if the trees did not suffer from the injuries that Rufus inflicted. Either these sycamores or indeed those in his camp that he cut for shelves and so forth.

The hermit said that he did not believe that trees feel pain as men do. It was a good question, he said, and he was glad Leo had asked it, for it showed that he and the boy shared a kinship of the mind. He himself had contemplated the nature of both. Men and trees. He said no more but gazed out from the wood and out across the quiet field before them. Occasionally he muttered something, but only to himself.

Leo waited for Rufus to expand upon the

subject but he did not. So eventually the boy asked whether Rufus had reached conclusions of any kind.

The old man gazed out a little longer, then he turned to the boy, his eyes wide and piercing. 'I believe,' he said, 'there is bits missin from the Bible. Whether to keep them hidden from the likes of us or because they were not found by those who compiled it, I cannot say.' He nodded as for emphasis, or as a sign to the boy to pay attention. 'In the beginnin God created the heavens and the earth, as I expect you knows.'

Leo nodded.

'The spirit of God moved over the face a the waters. A mist rose up from the earth and watered the whole face of the ground. Plants growed and I believe trees was the most important of them. To keep watch, you see, on those to come.'

'Sentinels,' said the boy. 'I believe horses was given the same role.'

'Is that right?' Rufus asked.

'I have heard it,' Leo told him.

Rufus murmured his interest, then continued as before. 'The Lord God formed man of dust, and breathed into his nostrils the breath of life.' The old hermit shook his head, as if in regret. Perhaps that God had created man too soon.

'When Adam and Eve ate the fruit of the Tree of Knowledge, and lost their innocence, and knew good and evil, what did God say?' Rufus looked again at the boy with his startled, startling eyes. 'Do you remember?'

Leo thought that he should recall from church or school what God had said, but he could not. The hermit's piercing gaze did not help.

'God said, "Behold, the man has become like one of us."' Rufus shook his head again but this time he was smiling through his curly, ragged beard. 'We became like gods, you see,' he said. 'But do us live like gods? No. We live like trees. Come, boy, let us see if them jars is fillin.'

The sycamore sap they poured into a pan back at the camp and boiled on the fire until the bulk of it evaporated, leaving a sweet residue of syrup. 'Birch is less sweet and might be better for you,' Rufus said. 'They say it's good for the bladder. But I prefers sycamore myself.'

5

It took Rufus little time each day to take care of his fundamental needs. He lived off what he had hanging from the branches of his outdoor abode. He assured Leo that there were many days in the year, most of them in autumn, when he was obliged to slog, foraging and conserving food for the following seasons. Rufus said that if Leo were still here then he would show the boy the site of every apple and damson tree, wild plum or bullace, greengage, walnut, hazel. But still, the boy wondered why his father and brothers and all he knew in his childhood laboured so intensively. The old hermit preferred to while away the hours wandering in the vicinity of his wood, pausing, watching. Talking to himself. He gave the impression of a man waiting for something, of whose imminent arrival only he was aware.

Rufus smoked a pipe into whose bowl he pressed not tobacco but a concoction of his own made from dried herbs and weeds. Coltsfoot, sage, marshmallow leaf, moistened with diluted sycamore syrup. He added other herbs as he came across them, mint or lavender or suchlike. Leo considered the smell of the smoke more pleasant than that of tobacco. Rufus agreed with this opinion and offered the boy his pipe. Leo took in a lungful of smoke and coughed it out. He thought that he would puke.

'Oh, aye,' Rufus said. 'It do take some gettin used to. Good for the lungs, though.'

Leo told the hermit that he would like to learn how to live off the land, how to glean the hidden harvest, but that he would have to leave soon. He had business to attend to in Penzance, seeking his mother's family. Rufus said that, of course, the boy was free to leave at any time. Leo nodded. 'I do not know what I will find there,' he said. 'There may be naught.' Rufus told him he could stay for as long as he wanted. He should consider the bender his own.

One afternoon they observed a falcon gliding high above a field. It disappeared into the white sky then reappeared. It might have been putting on a display just for the two of them. Then they saw it come sliding out of the clouds, falling, all the way to the ground. It took off again with something in its claws. A twitching, quivering ribbon or coil of something. 'Is that a viper?' Rufus asked. 'My eyesight ain't so good as once twas.' They watched the falcon rise, the snake thrashing in the air, till both vanished far above them.

6

When they went back to the pond with rudimentary fishing tackle, they spent a day waiting for the carp to bite, contemplating the surface of the water. In the afternoon Rufus said abruptly that he would sleep and the boy should not bother him. He curled up and lay on his side. Leo could see that Rufus was not sleeping, for though his eyes were closed his face was contorted with pain. He held his gut as he had before. The boy said nothing. After a while the hermit sat up and said how well he felt, a good kip, that was all he needed, and took up his rod. They caught one carp each, and back at the camp grilled them and ate them with blackberry jam.

Rufus had a catapult and taught the boy to use it. It was little different, the hermit said, from the slingshot with which David smote the giant Goliath. Leo proved adept and hit the triangular targets Rufus constructed from twigs and set on branches. He soon came to know the feel—the weight and shape and heft—of pebbles suitable for the purpose, and collected them like large coins in his pocket. He noticed that when the old man pulled the string back from the forked stick and held it taut, his big hands trembled.

After dark they walked across the pale cloudy land to a different wood. Rufus said that pheasants roosted there, on low branches. They crept through the undergrowth. Rufus touched Leo's arm. The boy looked up. He could see the birds, their formless shape against the grey sky. The old man took aim at one and sent the pebble swishing through the air. It missed the bird by so wide a margin as not even to disturb it. Rufus passed the catapult to Leo. With his first shot the boy struck the bird. It tottered, and fell slowly from the branch, then plummeted to the ground. He carried the floppy carcass by its claws back to their clearing. The old man hung it up and on the day following showed the boy how to paunch and pluck it. They made a stew and ate it. Leo said that he had eaten chicken and this tasted similar. Rufus said this was because they were hungry and had only hung the young bird overnight. An older pheasant hung for longer would taste much stronger, but the boy said that as far as he was concerned it tasted vitty just the way it was.

Rufus explained that the taste of an animal depended in part upon what it in its turn had eaten. A gamekeeper had kindly if unknowingly fattened the pheasant for them. The best rabbits came from a coombe where wild thyme grew, he would take the boy there. Leo asked what badgers ate. Rufus said that their diet was as varied as any animal he knew of. He himself had seen them consume grass, blackberries, wasps, snails, earthworms, mice and fallen apples. He thought a brock a fine animal and snared but one a year, for its meat and its fat. For which crime he believed it possible that his illness was punishment.

The old hermit seemed to have little adherence to a pattern of wakefulness in the hours of daylight, and slumber in those of night. There seemed to him little difference between the two. He wandered off at night muttering, though without a word of explanation to his guest, and made up the sleep he needed the following day.

One night Leo was woken by loud desperate yells. Some angry. Others terrified. Wide awake he crawled from his bender and stood outside the weeping beech.

Rufus shouted, 'Leave it! Run! Run!'

There was a pause, then another man pleaded, 'No, please don't. Mercy. Mercy.'

Leo stood in the dark, listening. He understood there was no other man, only Rufus, now whining.

In the morning Rufus told Leo that he had suffered one of his nightmares. 'I would not believe you could sleep through it but ye did,' he said. 'Noisy as it was.'

'Aye,' Leo said. 'I heard naught, Rufus.'

7

Some days Rufus did not emerge from his quarters beneath the weeping beech. Leo called to him. Rufus called weakly back that he needed no food, only a little more sleep, and would get up in a while. Leo pottered about with the donkey, went for short wanders, came back to see how Rufus was. It was time for him to go but he could not leave the old man.

One morning Rufus was up before Leo. He declared that as it must be about the middle of July it was time to pay his rent. Leo was taken aback for he had assumed the tramp when in residence did so incognito. The idea of a formal agreement was intriguing. He followed Rufus through the wood and up out of the valley until after a mile or so they came to a large farmhouse. Behind the house was a yard where Rufus accosted a man and demanded ladders, rope, shovel, bucket, brushes, the usual. Once these were gathered the old hermit hoisted the heavy wooden extension ladder over his shoulder and bore it away. Leo managed awkwardly to pick up all the other implements and followed. He watched Rufus carrying the ladder, and it occurred to him that when the Lord bore the Cross towards Golgotha, perhaps there was a lad like himself who carried the hammer and nails and suchlike utensils.

They walked further from the big house. Rufus said that water had been piped to it since 1894. They came to a group of six cottages, arranged in attached pairs on three sides of a square. The fourth, open side had three strips of allotment or vegetable garden. The well was in the middle of the yard shared by all the houses. Equidistant from each back door and kitchen, for the use of home and garden both. It was very beautiful in its simplicity.

The well was perhaps four feet in diameter. The summer had been dry and the surface of the water was a long way down. Rufus drew some water in the bucket that was there already and invited the boy to drink some. The morning was warm but the water was deliciously cool.

They removed this bucket and rope and lowered the ladders into the well, extending them as they did so. When it came to rest the uppermost rung was just below the top of the well. 'A perfect fit,' said Leo.

Rufus said that he would start but Leo should watch him so they could take turns. Holding a stiff brush, he climbed over the edge and onto the ladder, and down a few rungs. Leaning against it, he began to scrub the brick walls, which were covered in some kind of dark moss or other matter.

The old hermit worked the brush with remarkable vigour. Soon, though, he slowed down, and after a while longer he climbed out and Leo took his place. Periodically they threw a bucket of water at the wall to wash off the loosened dirt. The work was slow and tedious, but they made gradual progress, shifting the ladder so as to be able to reach right around the wall before descending further.

When they reached as far as they could without stepping into the water below they withdrew the heavy ladders and set to removing the water. Rufus reckoned the well to be about a third full. He showed the boy his recommended technique. Holding the rope tight, he dropped the bucket upside down. The idea, he said, was to knock the air out of the bucket, so that it would sink, and turn, and fill with water.

Leo copied the old hermit's method, then quietly adopted his own style, lowering the bucket to the surface then flicking his wrist to turn the bucket into the water. They emptied the buckets by throwing the contents behind them. That part of the yard became a wet mess.

At some point late in the morning a girl appeared with food and drink. Rufus thanked her and asked her to leave the provisions on the bench nearby, saying they could not stop for they were working against time. Against the inflow of water from whatever underground spring fed the well.

The removal of the water revealed a thick sediment of silt or muddy sludge. This Leo was sent down on a rope to shovel into a bucket that Rufus pulled up. Each bucket was heavy. Leo was at the mercy of the rope and of Rufus's strength and concentration and grip upon the rope. He hoped that they would hold.

Up at the surface the old man emptied each bucketful in a pile on the ground. 'They can chuck this on their gardens,' he yelled down, his voice echoing in the brick chamber. 'Beautiful soil, I reckon.'

By the time he had shovelled up as much of the silt as he could, leaving little on bare rock, Leo's muscles moaned with complaint. He called up to announce that this bucket was the last one and watched it rise. He wondered whether the ladder or at least a rope would be sent down again. What if Rufus suffered some palpitation of the heart or was otherwise spirited away, leaving Leo abandoned at the bottom of the shaft? Water would trickle in and eventually he would drown. They would find him floating. He had too lurid an imagination. The ladder came down.

At the top, Leo stretched his arms and shoulders, grimacing. Rufus laughed and said, 'Who's the one what was liftin them buckets full a mud?'

They sat and ate the cheese and beef sandwiches the girl had brought for them, and a bottle
of tepid tea.

'This is how you pay the rent on your small
portion of a backwoods no one had a use for?'
Leo said. 'I reckon your landlord's drove a hard
bargain.'

In the afternoon they scrubbed the walls below
what had been the waterline when they started,
then extracted a few buckets of scummy water.
They withdrew the ladders for the last time. Leo
asked if Rufus customarily did this all on his
own.

'Normally they gives me two lads to do as
much as you done, boy,' the old man told him.
'Sometimes three.'

Finally Rufus drew Leo's attention to the
bucket that was used by the residents. It was full
of water. Rufus asked him to look closer and he
saw that there were two or three shapes in it like
short thick worms. 'Leeches,' Rufus told him. 'To
keep the water clean.' They lowered the bucket
until it stood upon the damp rock, and tied the
end of the rope to a hook on the outer wall above
ground.

'The spring water'll feed in and come up over
the top a the bucket in due course,' Rufus said.
They carried the implements they'd been given
back to the farmyard and left them leaning
against a wall. Then Leo returned to collect the

plates and bottle the girl had brought them. These they took to the back door of the farmhouse. The same girl answered the old man's knock. She thanked him. He told her the sandwiches were much appreciated, and turned to Leo, who nodded in agreement. The girl told Rufus that Mister Devereaux was in his garden and should like to see him.

The garden was a lawn, surrounded by flower beds. As Leo and the old man entered it, they disturbed some black birds, which flew up from the grass. A man of middle age was sitting upon a bench. He rose and beckoned them. He was tall and had white hair, though his face was not that of an elderly man. They sat, Rufus in the middle of the bench, Leo beside him.

'I heard you have an apprentice, Rufus,' the man said. 'I suppose this means that my wood will have its tenant for another generation, does it?'

The old hermit said that he could not answer for the boy, but neither man invited Leo to do so for himself so he remained silent. Instead the farmer asked Rufus if birds could smell.

Rufus pondered the question for a while but clearly could not answer, for he merely repeated it. 'Can birds smell?'

'They do not have noses that I can see, only beaks, so I cannot believe that they are able to. But sit quietly and watch.'

The two men and the boy sat on the bench looking out upon the garden. They remained like this for some time. Leo studied the flowers. There seemed to him to be many herbs mixed up amongst them. Rosemary. Sage. Upon the lawn first one then another of the crows they had disturbed returned. These birds walked very slowly across the grass. Periodically each paused and inserted its beak into the ground.

'You see?' the farmer said. 'You see, Rufus? They are surely eating insects' eggs or larvae. How do they know they are there unless they're sniffing them out?'

The hermit nodded. 'I never heard a such a thing. It don't make no sense to me. I should say they be listenin.'

'Listening?'

'Aye. They hears the beetles feedin on stems and roots a grass, and then they peck em out. Either them or their larvae as you say.'

Mister Devereaux scratched his head. 'Well,' he said, 'I never thought of that.'

8

They walked back in silence. Then Rufus said, 'Why is us here, Leo?'

The boy was unsure what the old man meant. Why were they taking this route back to the camp? Or why was it the two of them were here, together, at this moment? Or why were they here, in this landscape, this county, this kingdom?

'I do not know,' he said. 'Why is we here, Rufus?'

The old man stopped. He turned to Leo and shrugged his shoulders. He looked at him with those startled blue eyes and the boy wondered what they had seen. 'I know not either,' Rufus said. 'Unless it be to look down deep into the heart a things.'

'What things?' Leo asked.

'It don't matter,' Rufus said. 'There at the heart of anything you'll find it.'

'Find what?'

When he saw the boy's serious expression the old man grinned. 'Whatever you choose to call it,' he said. 'Any man can call it what he likes.'

The old man turned and resumed his journey. Just as Leo caught him up he stopped again. This time he laid a hand on the boy's shoulder. Leo felt his old friend's weight, that Rufus was using him for balance. 'Just bear this in mind,' he said. 'The deeper you goes, the further you be from the surface. That's the danger.' They stood like this for some time, as if Rufus judged the boy needed to ponder the matter. Then he lifted his hand from Leo's shoulder, and they walked on.

9

They sat at the fire. Leo cooked stew but Rufus said he was not hungry, despite the work they had done. He drank blackberry wine. It probably made him sicker, he said, it was terrible bad stuff, but it helped, too. 'I don't know what I got,' he said, 'but it's a killer. I seen it happen to others. Grow sick and weak and thin, lose all their muscle and fat, what's the use a that?'

'We'll get you to a hospital,' Leo suggested.

'You know where there's a hospital hereabouts?' Rufus asked.

'Mister Devereaux will know. He will help us.'

Rufus shook his head. 'No,' he said. 'I do not want no hospital.'

The donkey stood close by. It seemed to Leo that like his lost white colt, the beast derived some ruminative pleasure from watching the flames, just as men do. With this notion Rufus agreed.

'I went to Africa with the mules,' he said. He gazed at the fire. After a while he spoke again. 'We trained them mules so that if our ship couldn't get to port they could swim ashore. The best pack animal there be.'

Leo said he knew nothing of mules, and

wondered whether they possessed a temperament and intelligence similar to horses.

Rufus said that he could not see why not, since they were a cross between a mare and a donkey, with big ears like a donkey and a mare's tail. So one might expect them to have much in common with the breeds of their parentage.

He discoursed upon the subject of genetics. 'See, boy, a hinny is a cross between a stallion and a she-ass. It will have a horse's small ears and a donkey's short tail. The forequarters of a cross resemble those of its father, the hind quarters those of its mother.'

Rufus said that mules possess remarkable powers of endurance, can withstand long periods of thirst, cope with dramatic changes of climate, and are not fastidious as regards food but will scoff whatever is available.

'Their hide is tough,' he said. 'Which helps protect it from galling.'

Leo asked what it was like in the army. In the war.

Rufus said that mules are generally cheerful and clever beasts. They appreciate proper handling. If treated badly they will rebel. They have a fearsome kick, as everyone knows. But if treated well, they are easy to groom and keep in condition.

'Did you see much fighting?' Leo asked.

Rufus sat a while in silence. 'There were

some,' he said, 'who reckon mules is no good on account of their tendency to stampede under fire. But our company trained the habit out of em and they only let us down when it was real bad.'

Rufus stared at the flames with his wide open eyes, trembling a little as if the warm evening were cold, the flames cool, then shook himself loose from whatever reverie possessed him.

'How did you train the mules not to give you away?' Leo asked. 'If you was creepin close to the enemy and one a they animals suddenly neighed?'

'No,' Rufus said. 'That would a been no good. They can make a hell of a racket once they get started. No, they had to be devoiced, a course they did. The animals was brought in, one by one. There'd be four of us, with a short rope each, which we tied to the hooves. On the shout a three we turned em over. They was so surprised they made no fuss.'

Leo remembered his father single-handedly casting the mean hunter for Herb Shattock, in the master's stables.

'Then the veterinary surgeon come with a chloroform rag,' Rufus said, 'put it over the mule's mouth. One of us soldiers had to sit on the mule's head, but we had to take that job in turns or the chloroform would knock us out too. As soon as it went to sleep the surgeon cut into the mule's throat and took out the voice box.'

Leo asked what a voice box looked like.

'Like a tiny piece a jelly,' Rufus told him. 'The vet put on a dressin. We undid our ropes and waited for the water man. When he come with his buckets, he threw water over the animal and it looked up, all glass-eyed, and struggled to its feet. It tried to make a noise but no sound come out. The whole thing took no more an ten minutes.'

After some while considering this account, Leo asked the question that troubled him. 'Was horses cut the same way?'

The old man nodded. 'Horses, ponies, mules, the lot.'

10

It was morning. Rufus was still abed. Leo groomed the donkey. The old man said she was not used to such treatment and might not appreciate it, but she seemed to.

The boy did not hear the intruder but Rufus did. He came out from beneath the weeping beech. With a finger to his lips he motioned Leo to keep quiet, and with eyes downcast Rufus tilted his head the better to listen in a particular direction. Then Leo too heard the footsteps approaching. Rufus nodded, suggesting that he recognised them. He looked at Leo, still nodding, as if he assumed that Leo did likewise, or was confirming some conjecture he had made earlier.

Mister Devereaux walked into the clearing. He carried a long leather case.

'Good morning, Rufus,' he said. 'And you, boy.'

'How goes it?' the hermit asked him. He sat upon their bench. 'Will you join us?'

'I should like to, Rufus, but I can't today. Perhaps when you bring the gun back I shall have more leisure at my disposal.'

'You have a job for me?'

Mister Devereaux gave the case to Rufus, who laid it across his thighs.

'I do. There's a fallow buck on his own. Lives in that wood on the far side of the pond. At night he comes and helps himself to Sarah's roses.'

'I'll take care of it,' Rufus told him.

'I realise it's entirely the wrong time of year, but keep as much venison as you can smoke. There's a dozen bullets in there. It's my W. J. Jeffery. The four-oh-four.'

Rufus nodded. 'Should do,' he said.

'Good hunting,' said Mister Devereaux, and took his leave.

The old man sharpened two knives. One was much the older of the two and had been sharpened countless times before. Its blade was half the depth it remained at the hilt. Its wooden handle, though rubbed and scarred, Leo reckoned not to be its first. The other knife was younger. Rufus sharpened them one after the other on a whetstone, testing the blade on sticks until he was satisfied.

Then he took the rifle from the case and studied it. He told Leo that it was not much more than ten years old and had been made for Mister Devereaux by the famous gunmaker. He asked Leo if he was much of a deer hunter. Leo told him of his brother Sid, who for his own amusement liked to creep up on a roe deer, to see how close he could get without it knowing he was there. If he got close enough, when he frightened the deer it would bark in alarm before running away. Rufus asked if he could do likewise. The boy confessed that he himself lacked this capability.

Rufus said that he had clearly acquired the wrong brother. He could also do with a dog or two at such times. As a boy he had hunted otters. His father's otterhounds were rough-coated animals, of Welsh extraction. Their cry or howl came out of their chests. It was the most beautiful, in his opinion, of all hounds' cries. As he spoke he handled the rifle to feel the heft and balance of it, and stroked the walnut stock, murmuring with satisfaction.

A hundred feet or more away from where Rufus took up position stood a tree whose trunk separated into two not far from the ground. Rufus lay on the ground and aimed with his shallow V rear sight just below the V in the tree. After each shot he hauled himself to his feet and walked all the way over to study where the bullet had entered, then made minute adjustments to the sights. After the fourth shot he said that would do and they set off, Leo leading the donkey.

They sat upon the warm ground in the middle of the wood beyond the pond, each leaning against the trunk of the same tree. Rufus said that they should wait, that patience was a better course of action in a case like this than running around in search of one solitary fallow deer. This buck would come to them.

And so they waited. Leo was alert. Any sound might be their prey and he looked about him. But no deer came and in time his attention wandered. Insects buzzed in the summer sun. Birds warbled from the canopy of leaves above him. Breezes shifted the leaves and the sunlight rippled as it filtered through them. He watched the changing patterns in the undergrowth around him as he would the flames of a fire. He recalled waiting for Lottie on the morning of their fateful picnic, and wondered whether when he returned she would remember him. Of course she would. How much altered could he be?

The boy sat with the old hermit and waited for this deer to show itself. Perhaps it was all a ruse, cooked up by Rufus and the farmer. There was no errant buck. They wished to teach him some lesson. He closed his eyes and slept and saw a bird. *'But they that wait upon the Lord shall renew their strength, they shall mount up with wings as eagles, they shall run and not be weary, they shall walk and not faint.'* He saw the bird but the bird was himself. Half boy, half bird. Then he saw another, a heron, which rose from a rock beside a pool and flew away in the slow, regal manner of its species.

The sound of the shot woke him. A boom,

resounding among the trees. Leo scrambled to his feet and over to Rufus, who knelt on one knee. The rifle rested in the V of a stick he must have cut for the purpose, whose other end he'd inserted in the soil.

'Help me up, boy,' he said. The old man staggered. Leo held him upright. 'It's only my stiff knee,' Rufus said. 'I can't hardly unlock it when I been kneelin any length a time, see?'

They walked over to where the deer lay. 'Shot him through the shoulder,' Rufus said. 'At the base a the neck there.' He showed Leo the exit wound, a small hole barely larger than the bullet itself, above the right shoulder. He asked whether the boy had ever dressed a deer. Leo said that he had not.

Rufus kneeled and slit the dead deer's throat. He explained that the carcass must be bled. Dark red blood spilled liberally onto the ground and soaked into the dry soil. Next, he said, they should remove the glands inside the buck's rear legs, which secrete a powerful-smelling musk during the rut and if left will contaminate the meat. Rufus removed these using the same knife that he had used to bleed the animal. When he had done so he tossed the tiny glands into the undergrowth and inserted the blade of the knife into the ground. Then he asked Leo to fetch the donkey. When the boy returned Rufus was standing up, some yards from the dead buck.

He asked Leo to uncork one of the water bottles they'd brought in the pannier and to pour water over his hands. Leo now saw that Rufus's hands were covered in mud. He washed them, rinsing off the mud he'd used to absorb any scent he might have picked up from the glands.

They laid the deer upon its back. Using the second knife Rufus cut the skin around the deer's anus. Then he leaned forward and took hold of the penis and lifted the scrotum and cut around its base and kept cutting towards himself, towards the anus, until he could pull the creature's genitalia away. He threw it off to one side and stood and looked up to the sky, with his eyes closed and mouth open, and gasped. He rubbed his back with his left hand and with his right hand, though it held the knife, his stomach.

Leo feared the old man would lose his balance and fall. He held out his arms in readiness. 'Is you all right, Rufus?' he said.

The old man breathed heavily, his eyes still squeezed shut, sweating. He swallowed and opened his startled eyes wide. 'I'm fine,' he said, and lowered himself upon the ground beside the deer. He spread the deer's hind legs and made a small incision in the muscle wall around the middle of the pelvis. He inserted two fingers and lifted the tissue away from organs and entrails beneath, and in the V thus made inserted the knife and cut up through the middle of the deer, following his fingers. Rufus paused periodically to get his breath back, as if this were the most arduous labour, though the boy could see that it was not. Rufus shifted position, shuffling on his knees along the side of the carcass. When he reached the bottom of the ribcage he stopped and showed Leo the sternum or breastbone. Leo leaned over to get a closer view. Rufus said that in truth he could now do with a bigger knife, but that this one would suffice.

'Move away,' he told the boy. 'You's too close there.'

Leo stepped back. Rufus grasped the handle of the knife with both hands, placed it under the breastbone, then thrust it forward and up and through the bone, his hands on the knife shooting into the air. This he repeated, right up through the ribcage and on up the animal's throat. He remained there, breathing heavily, for some time. Leo waited.

'I'll cut loose the trachea now,' Rufus said, 'and the gullet.' He then opened out the ribcage and showed Leo the deer's vital organs. Its heart and lungs. He showed the boy the diaphragm and cut it loose on either side.

'What I intends to do,' Rufus said, 'is to take hold of the trachea and gullet and pull them and all the innards of the deer down and out in one fell swoop. But first I'll split the pelvic bone.' He shuffled back to the lower end of the carcass.

'Mind you avoids the bladder here,' he said.

Rufus used the knife as a saw upon the bone. He admitted that a saw with teeth would do the job better. He held the bladder and perhaps other organs out of the way with his left hand as he cut the bone with his right. In time it gave and he opened the two sides of pelvic bone apart.

'Help me up, boy.' The old man rose awkwardly and stepped along the side of the animal to its forelegs, and reached in and took hold of the trachea and oesophagus. When he pulled them up all the other entrails followed suit. Once or twice he paused to cut the diaphragm loose where it was sticking. An entire amalgamation of the animal's innards came loose and out through the channel he'd cut through the pelvic bone and, earlier, the anus. All this he hurled into the undergrowth.

Leo helped the old hermit roll the deer onto its front so that any blood remaining in the chest cavity might drain away. Then they lifted it together and threw it over the back of the donkey. Leo retrieved the rifle and they made their way back to their own wood.

The carcass smelled of blood and meat and the smell was growing sweeter.

'The day's too hot,' Rufus said. 'A course it is. You should always butcher cold meat. Tis madness to cull a deer in summer.' It was a hot day but the temperature could not account for how heavily the old man was sweating. 'But Mister Devereaux might have his reasons. I do not question them. And it'll be easier to pull off his hide while it's warm.'

They hung the carcass by its rear legs. Rufus made a cut in the hide on those legs, a neat line on each side from the thigh up as far as the tarsal glands around the knees. He told Leo that he must cut upwards through the hide from underneath, not down, for if he did so he would find hairs in the meat.

Rufus then bent down and made the same cuts in the forelegs, except that it seemed that his vision was shot, or the co-ordination of his brain to his fingers, for his knife wandered in zigzag slices from the knee joints up through the armpit to the open chest.

The old man cursed. He returned to the top legs and began to peel the hide off where he'd made the first incisions. When the hide did not lift easily he cut the tissue that held it to the flesh beneath. Then he stepped back and put his hands on his knees, and stared at the carcass, on his face a furious expression, as if the deer in death were in some way defying him. He lowered his gaze to the ground and he held the knife out to Leo. 'You do it,' he said. 'Cut around the knees.'

Leo cut the skin around both hind and forelegs as best he could.

Rufus had retreated and sat upon a log. 'Give

me the knife,' he gasped. 'Go behind him and grasp hold a the hide with both hands and pull it down.'

Leo did as he was asked. He gripped the hide and pulled it. It did not come at first, but he summoned all his strength. He discovered that he had more than he'd ever had before. The skin came down and off the carcass.

'Beautiful,' Rufus said. 'You looks like some gentleman taking the coat off the back of a lady there, boy.'

When he had the hide free Leo laid it on the ground. Rufus rose and without a word set to butchering the carcass. This time he did not ask the boy to help. He seemed indeed to have forgotten he was there. Leo watched him in disbelief. The old man attacked the carcass like a butcher suddenly blinded, cutting chunks of flesh and dropping them to the ground, muttering to himself that he must get the meat to the farm and the Devereauxs' cool larder or pantry as soon as he could. The boy knew enough from seeing pigs butchered that the old man was not working in accord with the skeleton or frame of the animal but extracting crude chunks of flesh. The hermit was covered in blood and gore. The hanging carcass was a gruesome spectacle. Eventually Leo could watch no longer and said, 'Rufus, please, stop. What are you doing?'

The old man paused, and looked up as if he had

heard a voice, not from the boy behind but from the crowns of the trees above. Then he turned. He grinned. 'There you are, boy. Where you been? Pick up a piece a this meat. Us'll have ourselves a good venison stew this evenin.'

11

The hermit had willed himself to full strength to shoot the deer. Then he relapsed. He sighed and stared at the fire. The stew was delicious but Rufus hardly touched his. Instead he swigged his blackberry wine.

Leo said nothing.

The old man sighed. Then he took a deep breath. 'Don't let me give you the idea that transport's a good choice, boy,' Rufus told him. From the grimace on his face it seemed to hurt the old man to talk. 'It is not. I hope you got that. Choose somethin else.'

Leo did not know of which choices Rufus spoke. He was unaware of having any.

'Bein somewhat of a horseman, you might be thinkin on joinin the cavalry. Keep out a that too, boy, whatever you do.'

'I have no plans, Rufus.'

The old hermit drank the wine and talked more easily. He told Leo that the number of horses killed in the war in which he'd served was unprecedented, and in the next would only be worse. When General French relieved Kimberley, he said, the cavalry rode five hundred horses to their death that day.

'At Ladysmith,' he said, 'we was ordered to slaughter our horses for food. After the meat, we boiled down the bones and the bits to a kind a jelly. Hot water was added and we drunk it like beef tea.'

'Wait up there,' Leo said. 'Ladysmith? I thought you was in the First Boer War, not the Second.'

Rufus stared at him with his wide eyes. 'How old do you reckon I am, boy?'

Leo looked at the hermit's leathery wrinkled features, his wild grey hair.

'Seventy?' he said. 'Eighty?'

Rufus laughed. The laughter turned to coughing, which in turn became what sounded like sobbing. Eventually he recovered, and took another swig from his bottle. 'Think I've had my three score year and ten already, do you?' He shook his head. 'I'm not quite fifty yet, boy.' He asked Leo if he was any good with boats.

Leo thought of the ferry on which he and the white colt had crossed the Tamar. Was that a boat? If so, it was the only one he'd ever sailed in or floated on.

'I'd go on the boats if I was signin up now,' Rufus told him. 'One a them battleships. That *Dreadnought*. They say tis like a floatin hotel. They got to look after you, see? You ain't goin nowhere, and neither is they.'

Leo said he had not looked beyond seeking brethren in Penzance. An uncle. Cousins, perhaps.

He had no particular wish to travel the high seas.

'I spoke with a man,' Rufus said, 'had work loadin in the Plymouth dockyards. He told me the Germans have been buildin the big ships, and we have too. Bigger and bigger battle fleets. Us to protect our Empire, them to create one. But I been considerin the matter. And I can't see but one end to it.'

Leo asked what this end will be.

'Them ships is built for war,' Rufus said. 'And war is what they'll bring.'

Leo took their bowls to the bucket and washed them. When he came back to the fire Rufus asked him, 'What do you look like?'

Leo pondered the question. It was more like a riddle. 'How do I know what I look like?' he said.

'I shall tell you,' Rufus said. 'Like a damned baggabone who's stole some younger boy's clothes.'

Leo rose and, standing, bent forward the better to see himself. The hems of his trousers were up around his ankles. The sleeves of his jacket above his wrists. He was like a parody of Dunstone, the old boy back on the estate. Now that he considered the matter, he realised that the jacket was tight across his shoulders. The trousers pinched his belly.

Rufus rose with a grimace and stepped around the boy and pressed his own back against Leo's. 'Stand up straight.'

Leo stood and felt Rufus's rough palm flat atop his scalp. Rufus stepped away and came back around and stood before the boy. He still held his hand on top of his own head.

'Be as tall as me, boy. How'd you do that?'

Leo frowned. 'You must a shrunk.'

Rufus turned and struggled over to one of the oak trees at the edge of the clearing and reached into one of the small niches he had cut into its trunk. He withdrew his hand and showed Leo a pair of gold coins. 'I been savin these for somethin, I never knew what,' he said. 'Now I do. You must buy yourself a new suit.'

On the day following Rufus got up though he could barely move without wincing in pain. He gave the boy some strips of dried badger ham wrapped in dock leaves for the journey. He said he would have liked to come too and help but hoped that Leo would understand, he would not be able to cope with the crowds in the town. Leo said that he did.

'Find a tailor first, mind,' the hermit said. 'Let him get the measure of you. He can't cut a suit on the spot.'

'I shall.'

'There might be a tailors who can, but I never eard a one.'

'That will be the first thing I do, Rufus.'

Leo told the donkey that he was honoured to have made her acquaintance.

There was one more thing, Rufus said. He told Leo that he had something to ask him. He did not know how to, but he must. It was a request.

Leo interrupted and said that he probably should leave now. Not a moment later. He'd been here long enough, too long, already.

Rufus agreed. It was time for Leo to leave. But before he did, there was this one thing he could help the hermit with. 'It seems a shame not to use the gun as we got it, see?'

'I do not see,' Leo said.

'Will you help me, boy?'

'How?'

'How? Shoot me, a course.'

Leo turned and walked around the clearing. He said that he could not.

'I can try it on my own,' Rufus said. 'But it would be cleaner if another did it.'

Leo walked in a circle around the hermit, unable to look at him. Then he stopped and stood before Rufus. He looked at the ground. He said that he would not do it, he was sorry, he could not. Rufus told him to dry his tears, it did not matter. It was too much to ask.

'I cannot shoot you, Rufus,' the boy sobbed. 'I cannot.'

'You go and tell Mister Devereaux, boy. Go and fetch him. You'll do that for me, won't you?'

Leo left the wood and walked to the big house. The same girl as before answered the door. Leo asked for Mister Devereaux. The girl fetched him. Leo requested that he come to the wood. Rufus had for him.

Mister Devereaux walked straight to the clearing, Leo walking behind. The landowner said nothing but parted branches of the weeping beech and entered. Leo remained outside. After a short while Mister Devereaux came out carrying the gun and said that it was done. Rufus had made as good a job of it as could be hoped for. He asked whether Leo had seen a dead body before. Leo said that he had but one, that of Isaac Wooland, the stockman on the farm his father worked on, who was kicked by a cow.

Mister Devereaux nodded. 'You do not need to see this one,' he said. He turned and looked around, and said, 'You could do with your own tack, boy. You can have his if there's anythin you want. Indeed, you can rest here if you wish.'

Leo explained that he had to go to Penzance, he had only stayed this long as Rufus declined. Mister Devereaux shook the boy's hand and said that he was going home. He wished Leo a good journey.

Leo said, 'Is us not goin to bury him?'

'Why?'

The question did not make sense. 'Tis Christian, in't it?' Leo asked.

Mister Devereaux shrugged. 'Rufus would never forgive me if I gave him a church burial. Wherever he is now, he's gone from here. What's left there's nothing but meat and bone. Carrion. We can bury it and feed it to the centipedes and worms, or we can leave it where it is for the birds and the flies. Seems to me to be about the same difference.'

'I do not mean to be rude, sir,' Leo said. He bit his lip.

'You may speak your mind,' said Mister Devereaux. 'You think I am callous, is that it?'

'You do not seem sad,' Leo told him.

The farmer nodded. 'I am sad,' he said. 'I am very sad. Believe me.'

The donkey stood some yards away. Whether or not she was aware at all of what had happened Leo could not say. He recalled what the Orchards had done to Belcher's horse. He gestured towards the beast. 'What about the donkey?' he asked.

Mister Devereaux nodded. 'We'll look after my brother's donkey.' He turned to Leo, and after a moment said, 'You look surprised. It is no great burden. She can see out her days in a corner of a field.'

'I did not know you was brothers,' Leo said.

The landowner shrugged. 'All our lives,' he said.

12

The late-summer day was warm and the sky clear. Leo walked through waist-high grass. There were purple corncockles and yellow buttercups. The seeds at the top of the grasses had turned brown on the green stalks. Thistles grew, taller than the boy, their purple flowers like blobs of paint. Poppies were crimson smudges and there were blue cornflowers too in pale ripe corn.

In a pasture shorn close by sheep a section of the field was covered with the brown cones of molehills. To the smallest insect, he thought, they must be like a range of mountains. Into his head came the word, *Himalayas*.

There were black butterflies he'd never seen before. Perhaps all over the world different kinds of butterfly inhabited their own patch. Or some did so, while others spread far and wide, according to their temperament.

In a wood he walked through, all was quiet. There were purple foxgloves. A breeze soughed through the trees, stirring the leaves. Then the breeze died and the leaves were still and the silence returned. He stopped walking. Stillness and silence. The wood was holding its breath, the trees aware of him. Waiting for him to walk on. He did so.

All about him Leo could sense the energy of plant life that burst forth out of the earth, of creatures, from the smallest specks in motion. In the grass adorned with daisy and buttercup, the black crows on yellow flowers, gulls drifting inland from the sea. Black flies of some kind flew around him, less like autonomous insects of the air than black scintillae dancing at the edge of his vision. He felt a strange new energy inside him and understood that he was not separate from what he saw but part of it.

Leo slept in a hay barn and walked into Penzance in the morning. The air tasted briny and the light was dazzling. There was a great amplitude about the vistas before and around him and the sky overall. The harbour was dry save for puddles. Askew across the mud, boats leaned over as if ailing, waiting for the tide to bring a cure.

At the first tailor's he came to on the steeply sloping main street Leo entered and said that he needed a new suit. The man looked him up and down and said he could see that for himself. He called Leo 'Sir' and apologised but said that he would need proof of Sir's ability to pay before proceeding further. Leo showed him the gold coins. The tailor laid out for the boy a selection of swatches of material. Leo chose a grey serge of medium thickness. The man asked him to stand straight and measured him with his tape. He licked his pencil and wrote the figures in a book. When all the necessary dimensions had been recorded, the tailor scrutinised the figures and did some sums and informed Leo that the suit would cost him nineteen shillings and sixpence, half the payment in advance or in other words now. The rest upon collection, which could be as early as this time tomorrow if the young gentleman should wish to proceed. Leo said that he did. He gave the tailor a gold sovereign. The tailor went to his till and came back and gave the boy his change.

He walked up to the top of the street and turned to his left and walked on and down towards the sea. He could have closed his eyes and reached it, for he could smell salt and fish and seaweed all drawing him towards them. He walked along the Esplanade of which his mother had spoken. Women in black skirts and white blouses, wearing straw hats and carrying closed parasols, strolled along. Some pushed prams, or chastised older children who strayed too close to the steep drop to the beach, though iron railings ran right the way along. Dogs that seemed to belong to no one trotted jauntily along the Esplanade. Old men sat on the benches gazing out to sea. Behind them, a building announced its function with a large sign: *Mount's Bay Hotel*. Next door, the

Queen's Hotel was more discreet. A flagpole rose from some kind of tower or balcony upon its roof, though on this day no banner flew. Horse-drawn carriages rolled along a metalled road in front of the hotels.

Leo leaned forward against the railings. Below, children played on the sand and shingle beach. Parents or others lounged. They looked to the boy indescribably bored. He could not understand why they did nothing. When a woman all in white rose from a bench behind him and moved away, Leo took her place. From there he watched boats of different sizes move lazily across the great wide bay, and out on to the ocean. He thought of what the hermit had said. The ships looked like they were skating slowly across the surface of the sea, but he knew this to be an illusion. They were huge, heavy vessels, half-submerged in the water. And the ocean was deep and vast.

He did not know how long he sat there. Perhaps he dozed. He considered returning to the safety of the wood. To live as Rufus had lived, the tenant of Mister Devereaux. How easy it would be to live in the clearing, to sleep in the shelter of the beech tree. No one to hurt or bother him. He could be alone there.

When he realised he was shivering he looked about him and saw that many of the sightseers had gone from the seafront. He rose and followed the smells of cooking and bought fish and chips, served in newspaper, and a lemonade, which he consumed sitting on a wall.

As it grew dark Leo walked back into the town and saw through a gate a large house surrounded by gardens. Those nearest to the house were formal, those closer to the wall around the outside were relatively untended. He climbed over the gate and found a shed full of mowers and tools and other gardening implements. The shed still held warmth from the sun. In a corner he found canvas sacking and lay down and was soon asleep.

In the morning the boy walked back to Market Jew Street and to the tailor. The suit he had ordered was ready. He tried it on and the tailor told him it was a good fit, there was a little room for growth which was just what a lad of his age required. Leo did not know enough to do other than agree. The new serge was a little scratchy on his skin. He bought a shirt, socks, and underwear and put them on in the changing cubicle. When he emerged the tailor told him all he needed now was a tie. Leo thanked him, but said that he would rather do without. His cap and his boots would also last him longer. This, the man said, was a shame, for they spoiled the effect of the new clothes. Leo shrugged. He paid the tailor what he owed him and left.

A little further up the street Leo found a cafe,

and bought a pasty and a mug of tea. He asked the woman who served him where the post office was and she sent him in the right direction. There he made enquiries and was passed from one person to another until he stood before a man of middle age who reckoned to know most of the adult population of the town, if not personally then at least by their address. Leo told him his mother's name, Ruth Penhaligon, and age, which he judged to be thirty-seven years. The postman wondered whether she was a daughter of Captain Richard Penhaligon of Leskinnick Terrace, who died not three or four years back. No, Leo said, that was not possible. Both her parents had died years ago.

'Of course,' the postman said. 'Did she have a brother name of Thomas?' When Leo nodded to indicate that it was so, the postman said, 'I'll show you where she lived. It be just down from where the Royal Mail coach is sat. There be no Penhaligons there now, mind. Nor been none for some while.'

They walked up past the Market House which the postman pointed out and past the Public Buildings and St John's Hall and out of the centre of the town into Alverton Street. A pair of Royal Mail coaches stood outside the First and Last Inn. The postman said their horses were fed and watered in the stables at the back, and their drivers inside the inn likewise. They walked on a hundred yards and stopped in front of a terraced house of two storeys and dormer windows in the roof.

The postman left him and Leo stood before the house. The front door had a decorated stone lintel and surround. Large sash windows were on either side. A three-sided oriel window jutted out above the front door, with sash windows on either side as below, so that the facade of the house had a pleasant symmetry. It must belong, Leo reckoned, to people of some standing. He understood all at once his mother's airs, her desire for her children's education and betterment, her frustration at their failures. Why she had left Penzance in the first place, how she had made her way across two counties, to settle with an ill-educated horseman, became no clearer than it had ever been.

Leo knocked on the blue door of the house next door. There was no response so he rapped hard once more. After some time an elderly lady answered and demanded to know who was making this racket. She wore a black lace cap upon her head, and a black dress. When Leo began to tell her who he was and the purpose of his intrusion she yelled at him to speak up, and so he began again.

'I know my mother had a brother,' he finished. 'I wonder if you know where he went, missis?'

The woman squinted as she studied the boy's face. 'You look nothing like a Penhaligon,' she said. 'Nor speak like one. Yes, I know where Thomas went. Up there.' She pointed a bony finger towards the sky. 'He was a good man who respected his parents and his neighbours and loved God, who took him to His bosom.'

Leo stared at the old woman. He asked her when and how Thomas had died.

'Pleurisy,' she said. 'Tuberculosis. Pneumonia. The poor fellow.'

'Did he have children?' Leo asked.

The woman shook her head. 'He was frail,' she said. 'No wife. No children. You'll find no more of your Penhaligons hereabouts. Now leave me. You should be ashamed of yourself disturbing a lady in her rest time.'

'Where shall I go?' Leo heard himself ask, though he thought he meant only to ask it of himself. It came unbidden from his mouth.

The old woman pointed down the street, west, away from the town centre. 'Follow that road you'll come to Land's End,' she said. 'From there it's a short swim to America.' Apparently pleased with herself at this witticism, the woman grinned, showing an almost full set of yellow teeth, then closed the door.

Leo turned east and followed the road back to the centre, down Market Jew Street and out of the town and away, and on, to walk back across Cornwall, towards the port city and the boatyards of Plymouth in the County of Devon.

PART NINE
DUCK BREEDING

Lottie, Summer 1915

The girl walked to the cottage in the early morning. Birds greeted her from the trees and though she could identify few she whistled their songs back at them as best she could. When she reached the cottage she let herself in through the front gate and walked around the side to the garden behind.

Even before her arrival the ducks were quacking loudly to demand their release. When they heard her, the volume increased. She did not oblige them but lifted the flaps at the back of the shed to see how many eggs had been laid. One after another she counted them. Six. Two more still to come.

Lottie went instead to the hatching shed. There, on clutches of duck eggs, sat hens. She was not yet accustomed to this surrogacy. Chickens incubating ducks. It tickled her. Each hen could manage a dozen eggs. Lottie took their tin hoppers to the feed shed and refilled them with corn. Then she took the waterers to the well.

Florence Wombwell opened the back door of her cottage and came hobbling out on her sticks. She asked Miss Charlotte as she did every morning if she would like a cup a nettle tea. Lottie declined. The girl renewed the waterers and took them back to the hatching shed. None of the hens moved but remained where they were, peering silently at her from their gloomy nests inside orange boxes, one hen in each of three partitioned sections. Each hen would sit upon her clutch for four weeks.

Lottie closed the door of the hatching shed and returned to count again the duck eggs laid that morning. The clamour of the ducks to be let out had risen. She counted seven eggs. Still one more.

From one of the three duckling sheds came a fainter quacking than the full-grown ducks'. From another a twittering sound. Each shed housed ducklings of a different age. The fourth was still empty, for the breeding season was only three-quarters through. Lottie lifted the portals and the ducklings came out into their runs. These were shallow pens made of thin boards eighteen inches high, fixed tightly in place with stakes. From the run with the oldest ducklings, Lottie selected the one she reckoned the largest. It would be ten weeks old. She lifted it with one hand around its neck then put her other arm under its body to take its weight and carried it to the plucking shed. She returned to the pen and selected three more likewise.

Lottie checked the eggs again. The last one

had been laid. She went around to the front and opened the door, and the white ducks shoved and tumbled out of their captivity. Within moments, however, the drake assumed his place in front and the eight female ducks settled into a line behind and they set off at as fast a pace as they could, waddling comically like rollicking sailors just stepped upon dry land.

Florence Wombwell was in her kitchen seated upon the stool, her sticks laid against the wall. She had two pans of water on the stove, one with chickens' eggs boiling, the other with rice.

'We shall soon need more boards from the sawmill, Miss Charlotte,' she said.

'Yes, Mrs Wombwell.'

'And we shall need more sittin hens. I used a get em from Ruth Sercombe over Manor Farm. Lovely heavy crossbreeds they was, with nice feathers on the legs.'

Florence Wombwell's elder son had gone as soon as he could. Her younger son was the only provider for his crippled mother and did not have to go, but Lord Kitchener's campaign had persuaded him and he soon followed likewise.

'The little chicks all there?' Florence Wombwell asked. Lottie assured her that they were, she had counted them. Mrs Wombwell said the trouble was a chick was vulnerable to almost any animal. 'I once saw a wood pigeon take one,' she told the girl. 'Twenty year or more ago, so pigeons might a become more peaceable creatures since then, but I shouldn't bet on it.'

They shelled the eggs and chopped them up with the rice and added a little fine meal. Lottie carried this mixture to the duckling runs, along with scalded greaves. These were residue from the tallow-chandler, dried skin and glutinous shreds of animal matter from which the fat had been squeezed or rendered to make tallow for candles and soap. The greaves were mixed with a pollard of wheat bran and a little barley meal. Lottie shovelled this into bins in the runs and the ducklings waddled over and gorged themselves upon it. They put on weight almost as she watched them.

The four full-grown ducklings she had selected were quacking in the plucking shed. Lottie herself called it the killing shed, though not out loud. When she'd first helped Mrs Wombwell some weeks earlier she could hardly bear to watch her kill them, with her arthritic, clumsy fingers. Yet she had soon grown used to it and when she volunteered herself it was clear her young hands were better suited to the task. More efficient. Perhaps what afflicted Mrs Wombwell's legs had spread to her upper limbs. Now Lottie preferred to perform all the daily slaughter herself so as to minimise the poultry's suffering.

She picked up the first duck and took it back outside. With her left arm she held the duck tight against her body, her left hand around its neck. With the other hand she gripped its head behind the skull, with her thumb under its beak. The girl stretched the neck of the bird and pressed her knuckles into its vertebrae and pulled its head back. Then she swiftly yanked the head, dislocating the duck's neck, in as confident and abrupt a manner as she could.

When all four ducks had been slain Lottie laid them on the bench in the plucking shed and went to the cottage and told Mrs Wombwell the birds were ready. It was as if it was now the cottager who had become squeamish. Florence Wombwell said that she would go and dress them now. Lottie said that she would be back later. She went out of the door and walked around the side of the cottage and back to the big house.

Breakfast awaited, and then lessons. Lottie had not gone to Weimar. Instead her governess, Ingrid, had with great reluctance returned to Prussia. Lessons now were intermittent. William Carew had been teaching Lottie Latin and Greek until he'd left for France some months ago. Once a week the vet Patrick Jago tested her knowledge of anatomy and gave her instruction in veterinary medicine. Her father read history with her until one or the other of them nodded off. Gibbon, Carlyle. Her stepmother Alice tutored Lottie in playing the piano and sketching, though it was clear the girl had little aptitude for either.

• • •

At midday Lottie returned to the cottage. She changed the straw in the ducks' shed and filled their feeders with corn then asked Florence Wombwell if this was a good day to take the half-grown ducklings to the pond. Mrs Wombwell said it was.

Lottie raised one of the wooden boards. Those ducklings nearest spilled out of the pen and others swiftly followed. The girl guided them to the lane and she followed behind. They were not hard to control for all wished to keep close together. Those on the outside of the phalanx did not allow themselves to be separated from the main body and pushed their way back into it, condemning others briefly in their turn. The girl copied the sound the little birds made, breathing in through her teeth as she did so, while the gang bustled along.

The pond was at a midpoint between three of the six farms upon the estate and a number of the cottagers or farm workers bred ducks who spent their days there. As soon as they saw the water Lottie's ducklings quickened their waddling pace. Those breeding ducks and drakes who were already on the pond saw them and made towards the water's edge in welcome. The ducklings rushed into the water. They swam and dived and flapped their wings with the appearance of familiarity or custom, as if this visit to the pond were their regular indulgence, yet it was their first visit and last. It would supposedly help them to feather properly.

Later the girl herded the ducklings home again. When she had secured the wooden board she heard the sound of trundling wheels and went inside the cottage. Florence Wombwell sat in the chair beside the stove.

'He's here,' Lottie told her. 'You stay there. I'll fetch them.' She went to the cool chamber or larder where Mrs Wombwell, having cut off their heads and feet and plucked them, had placed the carcasses of the four dressed birds in a hamper. The duck man came to the door. He took the hamper from the girl and gave her an empty one, and an envelope. Lottie went back inside and gave the envelope to Florence Wombwell and took the new hamper to the larder. When she came back out Mrs Wombwell requested that the girl allow her to give her something at least of the money for her trouble, but Lottie refused. She told Mrs Wombwell that her sons were heroes. And that if she were a boy she would like to have joined the cavalry, and be now in northern France as they were. She said she would be back later to shut up the drake and ducks after they had made their return journey, and the ducklings likewise.

In the afternoon the girl saddled her horse. A warm rain fell, as it had not done for many days. Everything that grew—each flower, tree, weed, vegetable, shrub, cereal, grass—grew from the soil. The rain fell lightly on the thirsty land and the roots of all the plants absorbed its life-giving moisture. The smell that rose into the air held all this information, somehow. Lottie rode her pony Blaze out to the gallops. Closing her eyes, she raised her face to the rain and relished it upon her skin. No one else was there, but in her mind the boy Leo Sercombe rode beside her.

Patrick Jago had told her that thousands of horses and mules were shipped out to the South African war and died there: some from bullets and bombs but most from sickness, starvation, ill treatment. He told her that in this present war they were of no use in battle, not against machine guns. She did not believe him. When she reached the gallops she reined Blaze in and leaned forward and told her she was the finest and the bravest horse in all the Allied lines. The German trenches were a hundred yards distant. Lottie told the pony she must not be afraid of the explosions or the smoke. Then Lottie drew her sword. It was a wooden copy of her great-grandfather's sabre made for her by the estate carpenter. She would have liked to use the iron original but it was too heavy. Leo, and many others too behind them now, awaited her order. They drew their swords. She spurred her mount and as Blaze cantered towards the enemy lines, Lottie raised the wooden sword and pointed it forward, yelling for the world to hear the one word: *'Chaaaaarge!'*

ACKNOWLEDGEMENTS

Thanks to The Museum of English Rural Life, University of Reading.

Thanks to India Vaughan-Wilson at the Morrab Library and Katie Herbert at Penlee House, in Penzance, for attempting to clarify what the town's seafront was called in 1914.

Romany Routes periodical was vital, as was *Tales of the Old Gypsies* by Jennifer Davies.

Trevor Beer's *Naturewatch* series of books were inspiring, and provided wonderful material, from a true observer of nature.

The Edwardian Lady by Susan Tweedsmuir, *Good Neighbours* by Walter Rose and *Wild Flowers* by Sarah Raven were also useful.

The grizzly bears are borrowed from *Beartooth* by Pascal Wick.

Many thanks to Bloomsbury people, Madeleine Feeny, Philippa Cotton, Angelique Tran Van Sang, Francesca Sturiale, Lynn Curtis and Katherine Ailes.

ABOUT THE AUTHOR

TIM PEARS is the author of nine novels, including *In the Place of Fallen Leaves* (winner of the Hawthornden Prize and the Ruth Hadden Memorial Award), *In a Land of Plenty* (made into a ten part BBC series), *Landed* (shortlisted for the IMPAC Dublin Literary Award 2012 and the Royal Society of Literature Ondaatje Prize 2011, winner of the MJA Open Book Awards 2011) and, most recently, *The Horseman*, the first book in The West Country Trilogy. He has been Writer in Residence at Cheltenham Festival of Literature and Royal Literary Fund Fellow at Oxford Brookes University. He lives in Oxford with his wife and children.

timpears.com

Center Point Large Print
600 Brooks Road / PO Box 1
Thorndike, ME 04986-0001 USA

(207) 568-3717

US & Canada:
1 800 929-9108
www.centerpointlargeprint.com